THE EDIT

THE
EDIT

A Novel

J. Sydney Jones

MYSTERIOUSPRESS.COM

OPEN ROAD

INTEGRATED MEDIA

NEW YORK

Copyright © 2016 by J. Sydney Jones

Cover design by Mauricio Díaz

978-1-5040-3873-7

Published in 2016 by MysteriousPress.com/Open Road Integrated Media, Inc.
180 Maiden Lane
New York, NY 10038
www.mysteriouspress.com
wwww.openroadmedia.com

For Tess, first born—bibliophile and *mensch*

THE EDIT

PROLOGUE

I was down at the sea this morning. The water was sluggish on our bay, washing against the shore with boring regularity: white noise punctuated only by the hiss and pop of foam bubbles in the ebb.

Some of the village fishermen, up since four, were already returning to the harbor, their outboard motors slowly and lazily idling. The faint scent of diesel reached me from their engines.

Sitting on a large rock, I looked across the horseshoe of the bay at the farmers' carts at the esplanade and only then remembered that it was Wednesday: market day in our tiny village. A radio was playing, perhaps from the café on the waterfront. Snippets of a song, sung by a female, drifted across the water. The singer's voice was poorly trained; it had a raspy urgency that the uneducated ear mistakes for passion.

Watching the water, being lulled by its rhythms, I decided that today, I am meant to begin my memoirs.

Long planned, these memoirs have, in the past, been kept on hold. Hardly surprising, given that the statute of limitations on war crimes has no expiration date—except in my native Vienna. So why should the smells and sounds of the ocean on our small bay suddenly act as an impetus to this writing when nothing else in my fifty years of forced exile has?

Why, indeed, begin memoirs with such commonplace observations? We have all been taught by that old charlatan Freud to look below the surface.

Do I intend, by such an oblique opening, to imply my own sluggish state: the boring regularity of my life, its eternal placidity, the dissipation of my vital forces like the sucking out of so much flotsam in the ebbing tide? If so, why not baldly state it thus: *I am a man of a certain age, somewhat paunchy. My arches have long ago fallen and my breath is as acrid as a copper penny. I find myself falling asleep in a straight-backed chair. I feel as tame as the sluggish ocean outside my door.*

Some such opening would do: a simple statement of fact. Yet I circumvent the direct approach. And why begin here on this quiet morning in 1995 on the western coast of the Americas at all? Why not start with my childhood in central Europe instead? Why not employ straight chronology instead of metaphor?

I have no answers for these questions. I frankly do not know what I mean by starting with the ocean rather than with the state of my feet, or my soul. I pun—is that also a form of prevarication?

A conundrum, then, one's life story. Perhaps that is the proper introduction to this memoir: my life as a jigsaw puzzle with no frame, no corner pieces with which to safely begin.

PART 1

I was born in the difficult year of 1916. The year of my birth saw not only the coming defeat of Austria, but also witnessed the death of the old emperor Franz Joseph. The collapse of everything anyone living had known, that is what was presented to us in 1916, yet we had to endure the lingering denouement for two more terrible years of war. Life is a bad playwright.

I first saw the light of day in the pauper's ward at the Lainzer Hospital in Vienna's Fourteenth District. Of course, at that time, it was hardly a crime to use the services of such a ward. Weren't we all near starving then?

I have very few memories of the first five years of my life. Perhaps they are stored somewhere deep in what is known as the subconscious, but I—now an old, if not an elderly, man—have much time for reflection. Every instant of my life I eagerly pore over, sorting through the exhilarating and boring alike as through a box of yellowing and curling photographs. If such early memories were there to be found, I fully believe that my mental Dominicans—my very own hounds of God—would have sniffed them out by now. Either I had no experiences until five years of age, or at about that age, my perceptive and receptive faculties became fine-tuned enough to begin the lifelong task of recording and storing experience.

My first remembrance came on a snowy evening in Vienna. Some places associate themselves in one's mind with certain weather. Snow and Vienna are indelibly matched in my mind. Snow is to Vienna as sun to Hawaii, the monsoons to India. Growing up, there was a water-filled glass bubble enclosing a miniature Steffl—the south tower of St. Stephan's Cathedral that stands at the very center of Vienna's old city—on my bedside table (I have it here with me now, as well, on the mantel). One turns the bubble upside down and a flurry of confetti snow swirls around the steeple. The same storybook recollection of Vienna in the snow forms the backdrop for this very first memory.

It had been snowing heavily all day. I lay awake in my bed in the single-room apartment and listened, for a time, to the scraping shovels of neighbors clearing the sidewalks outside. This was followed by the crunch and huff of plows coming muffled through the closed shutters. The pillow was partly over my head to shield my eyes from the light. Frau Wotruba from across the hall was sitting with me while my parents were out for their monthly fling: a show at the Volksoper opera house—Lehár, as I later discovered—and a hot chocolate at the Café Museum afterward. This must have been the beginning of our "affluent" period, for even so little as a night out per month was a great splurge in those miserably poor days.

Frau Wotruba lit another cigarette. I remember looking over to where she sat in my father's armchair. It was the one decent chair in the flat, and she lounged in it like a marionette whose strings had been cut, her heavy winter stockings rolled down beneath her knees and one hand busily scratching at a bite or some minor skin irritation on her lower thigh. A weekly illustrated magazine rested in her lap. With her other hand she guided the oval cigarette to heavily rouged lips, puckered, and drew in a tremendous amount of smoke, which she proceeded to jet out of her nostrils. Sitting under the only light in the room, she was wreathed in a blue halo of smoke. Her lips went back to forming silent words as she read, then a smile as something in the article pleased her.

Her right hand continued to scratch, and she lifted the hem of her dress higher to get at the itch. I liked Frau Wotruba—she would sneak me an occasional bit of sugar, though the entire ration in our home went into my father's morning coffee—and I felt vaguely that it was wrong to spy on her thusly, but I could not bring myself to break off watching. Quietly and cautiously, I peered on, afraid even to breathe lest I remind her of my presence, for her hand continued to wander up her thigh, searching out the itch.

I must have moved or somehow caught her attention, for she looked up suddenly from her magazine and caught me staring at the full expanse of her milk-white thigh. (Later calculations put Frau Wotruba at thirty-one at the time at which I write. She had survived two husbands, one lost in the war and another a tram driver who died a grisly death, run over by his own tram as he descended to throw gravel on icy tracks.)

"You're awake, are you, *Schatz*?"

I didn't reply, hoping my silence would fool her. My eyes closed now, I heard the squeak of springs as she got up from my father's chair. Footsteps approached my bed.

"Hello, possum." Her hand brushed my cheek.

I opened my eyes as if awakened from a sound sleep.

"Frau Wotruba . . . Is it morning already?"

She chuckled merrily at this. She had—and it was one of her finest traits—a very full laugh. But now it was only a pleasant snicker, an ironic recognition of my deception.

"Soon, *Schatz*, soon. Are the plows keeping you awake?"

I nodded. How to tell her it was the reading light and her oval cigarette, the glimpse of her dimpled thigh?

She sat on the bed next to me and a strong, warm, womanly scent enveloped me as snugly as the eiderdown comforter covering me.

"Why don't I rock you?"

I did not need to be asked twice, but quickly positioned my torso in her lap, my legs still tucked under the comforter. The soft curve of her left breast pressed against my cheek. She rumpled my hair and laughed again, then hugged me to her, rocking back and forth on the creaking bed, humming a folk lullaby that haunts me to this very day. For years, I will lose the melody. There are no words, you see. Nothing to fix it mnemonically. Then one day some other melody intrudes—I have music around me constantly (at this very moment, I am listening to Richter playing Brahms's Second Piano Concerto)—and the music will remind me of the lullaby in some inexplicable way that occurs before knowledge, before perception. Then Frau Wotruba's song rushes back to me all in a blur like a fast-moving train.

"Better, *Schatz*?"

Her breath, heavy with the aroma of nicotine, was hot in my ear. It tickled. I remember the sensation still! Such a tickle as to reach my very soul. I pressed my cheek more closely to her, and she brushed my face with her soft hand. I felt a sharp object scrape against my cheek. It was the garnet ring that her second husband had given her shortly before his death. It was Frau Wotruba's one bit of "opulence," one that she now, in hard and evil days of hunger and soup lines, wore stone inward to avoid potential thieves on the streets. Yet it was not a particularly noble ring, nor was the stone all that large. I believe it had been in the husband's family for a time, but that does not establish worth other than sentimental. Perhaps it was Frau Wotruba's vanity that made her turn the stone inward—the finest ladies in Vienna were doing so with their diamonds at the time; neither was there a single fur wrap to be seen on the Kaerntnerstrasse.

I winced at the touch of the garnet and she pulled her hand away, frightened. There was a small scratch on my cheek from the setting, and she was solicitous, patting it with kisses transmitted from her rouged lips to the fingers of her right hand. I wanted desperately to feel her bright red lips on my burning cheek. Nestling closer, I felt a hardness through her dress. It was a mystery to me, this erect hardness amid the softness of her bosom, and I was drawn to it. I soothed the scratched cheek by rubbing it against the muslin front of her dress, caressing her breast inadvertently as I did so.

Frau Wotruba was very silent; only the crunch of the plows from outside and the slightest creaking of the bed-springs could be heard in the room. After what seemed a long time, I heard another sound: the deep, trembling breath of Frau Wotruba. I was startled, for I thought I had done something to make her cry. Looking up, I saw her mouth barely open, her tongue pink on drawn lips. Her eyes were closed, and there was an expression something like pain on her face. The pain seemed to intensify when I stopped brushing my cheek against her front. She pulled my head to her bosom again and I continued brushing against her. Then a sound like a whimper escaped her mouth; she leaned down and kissed my cheek. Her lips were warm, soft, moist. They felt like angel wings caressing me.

When I awoke, it was morning. Father was putting a celluloid collar on his shirt; a cup of coffee was steaming on the table. Mother was carefully measuring out the grains of sugar from a tiny silver spoon. Frau Wotruba was no longer there.

———

So! I can hear you muttering. *That explains the man. Sexually abused as a child. Son of a strict authoritarian who would not even share the sugar ration. Such are his determining influences.*

There is self-satisfaction in such a summation. I know that only too well from personal experience. One likes to have one's preconceptions confirmed. It is pleasing to be able to encapsulate the world in the cause and effect, bump and grind, of psychology. Yet, unfortunately, it is not all that simple or clear-cut.

Frau Wotruba may have been my initiator into the world of sex; she did not, however, determine my behavior or ruin the experience for me. Granted, I did learn from her that a woman's breasts are magical butter gourds: hard and soft at the same time. For some women they are buttons of pleasure to be turned on and off at will. For others, they are unseemly and these women do not want them noticed, let alone touched—not even by the softest cheeks.

I did learn from the strange pleasure of pleasing someone else sexually: the mixture of sensuality and power it evokes. Yet, I hardly think that ruined me either.

There is one evil thing our sex games may have done, however, and that was to give me false expectations about men and women. The synchronism of men and women is almost nonexistent in reality. Few women are so uninhibited as Frau Wotruba; most achieve their satisfaction only after the most arduous of efforts on the part of the man. They hold on and on after a man has reached his moment, squeezing the last drop out of him. And sex is only the most obvious example of this disharmony between the sexes. Romantic love is yet another: By the time a man finally wins a woman's heart, he no longer yearns for it. We give ourselves up at such vastly different rates and frequencies that we are forever out of step with one another, we men and women. A man wants a woman's heart at the outset of a relationship, not halfway through! For a woman, however, love is like achieving orgasm: a long, uphill struggle.

But if a false impression about the ease of men and women together is the worst that could be said of Frau Wotruba's gift, then it was a fine thing, indeed. What Frau Wotruba and I had that snowy night, and what we continued to share once a month for the next four years, was a warmth and a softness. A giving in to each other that defies understanding or explanation, just as does the capture of her lullaby in my memory.

I shall have more to say of Frau Wotruba in these pages.

Our apartment, as I said, was on the ground floor of a building on Hubertusgasse. The tall windows began just above street level, so looking out, one had a view of hats and glistening umbrellas on rainy days; of bonnets and derbies on fine ones. Men and women did not go about hatless as is the custom today. Most even wore some form of headgear to bed.

These windows took up one side of the flat. Against the

opposite wall was my bed, partially shielded from the rest of the room by a faded Chinese screen that my mother had found at the flea market. Mother was a frequenter of such bazaars; they were, in fact, a mania with her even later in life, when she could well afford to buy new. It became a challenge for her to see what bit of another person's detritus could become something essential for us. The screen was such a purchase, though it was found only after the scene with Frau Wotruba that I have just related.

Next to my bed there was a wardrobe of elephantine proportions. Lord knows it had to be large, and this is not simply an aberration of a child's memory, for it contained the clothing for all three of us—four with the arrival of my sister, Maria. Surmounting this wardrobe was an elaborately carved finial, all flowing scrolls and bird wings, done in cherrywood. This bit of artistry was dwarfed by precariously stacked wooden boxes full of off-seasonal clothing: winter coats safely mothballed in the summer; shorts and sandals likewise stored during the winter. Here also was the logical hiding spot for any present that it might have been my great good fortune to receive.

Mother and Father slept in a bed near the windows, which, by the clever addition of large throw pillows covered in Turkish cloth, was transformed into a sofa in the daytime. Above this bed hung photos and etchings of relatives long deceased: the "family album," Father derisively called it, for these pictures depicted none of his blood relatives. Immediately between the photos and the pillows was a strip of paisley cloth, giving their corner something of the feel of the opulent late nineteenth century. For those readers who have no idea of that period, the closest parallel might be the classic photo of Freud's couch.

In the center of the room, under a chandelier made of

wrought iron and frosted glass, was the table, circular, with four matching chairs. It was a solid bit of furniture, able to withstand not only spilled dishes of hot broth, but also my unsteady feet when Mother had me climb atop it to make tailoring adjustments on father's hand-me-down pants, or on other "sharp purchases"—her words—she found in the Jewish bazaars in the Second District or the mean cobbled streets near Ruprechtskirche in the First District. This table and its chairs were a deeply stained oak, the thick legs ending in roughly carved lion paws. The massive stature of this furniture derived from what is called the Alt Deutsch style of the late nineteenth century.

Between the wardrobe and my parents' bed, against the west wall, was a coal stove, and near it stood Father's arm-chair. This was as massive as the table, an enormous coquillage that engulfed the sitter, covered in a floral print that looked more cottage style than something that belonged in an urban flat, but of which no one complained. It had been a wedding present from my mother's parents, intended most likely for her pregnancies, but appropriated by Father.

(Lest I give the wrong impression about Father—that is, that he was the ultimate tyrant in our home—let me say now that Mother and he had their separate spheres of power. What Father appropriated in the home—the sugar, the armchair—was what Mother allowed him to appropriate. More of this presently.)

One tiny cubicle, reached via a door between my bed and the wardrobe, a room much too small to be anything but practical, held the wood-burning range upon which Mother created her less-than-appetizing meals. Any raised eyebrow from Father at one of her concoctions would bring an instant storm of abuse, prefaced always with: "You want fancy French cuisine, you bring home a fancy wage."

These were the physical borders of our life. The temporal borders were equally well defined, and they revolved around my father's getting up, going to work, and returning from work. It seemed all the household was planned directly around these contingencies: the weekend could not even begin until he returned from his Saturday half day. It was our custom on these days to have a large midday meal, which meant that Father, who liked to tipple now and again, was not free to stop with his friends at the local inn for a *viertel* of wine, but that he must return home immediately from work to the steaming plates of whatever it was Mother had solemnized the day with. On Saturdays, there might be meat—a bit of overdone bacon or wurst. Later, I learned that her Saturday mealtime caveat was Mother's way of controlling the wage packet, for Saturday was payday, and she was not about to have Father squander a *Groschen* of it on wine.

On Saturdays, Father never raised an eyebrow at the food, for we were to spend the rest of the day ensemble; to begin it with a transgression that would irritate Mother would make the hours before us unbearably long and tedious.

After "dinner," as Mother called this heavy lunch, we would sometimes take a walk to a nearby park; but if the weather was inclement, or if Father felt weary—which was as often the case as not—then we three would simply lean up against one of the windows and partake of the passing scene in the street below, commenting to one another on the peculiarities of the pedestrians we would see. These windows were double, the space in between the two frames being plugged up for air leaks by tiny bolsters. Our bolsters, as was typical on that block, were covered in damask of surprisingly fine quality. But of course they had to be, for they were all that passersby could see of our life, and Mother always insisted that we put our best foot forward for the outside world. It was the only way to get ahead, she would say.

Well, we would open the inner panes and lean our elbows against these bolsters and discover a new connection between one another as we surveyed the Saturday streets. There was a private sort of publicness to these afternoons. We grew closer as a family unit from such activity. The roles between us, normally so strictly defined, broke down imperceptibly as we stood at the window commenting on Frau Frank's new coat. Mother would make some catty remark to which Father and I would wink at each other. Or I would notice Herr Wachman, the butcher, closing his shop later than usual—the 12:30 closing hour on Saturday was a legal statute—and Father would joke that he was going to have a fine joint of meat off the man to keep this little infraction quiet.

This was our practice, at any rate, until Mother started showing—Maria would come along shortly and make our happy threesome a foursome. I remember being amazed at seeing Mother have to stand farther and farther back from the window as her stomach swelled with the growth of the baby.

Our favorite spectacle was Herr Braunstein, who ran a frame shop in the inner city and thought himself very fine. He was an immaculate man for a Jew, always wearing smart tweeds and a fine starched shirt. He had a dachshund that was his only friend. He and the little dog were inseparable, and, like clockwork on Saturday afternoons at 1:30, they would go out for a constitutional. The dog, of course, was meant to do his business on such occasions, likely as not directly below our window. What a recalcitrant animal it was. I am a dog lover, but this little vermin was really insufferable. It strutted along on its clothespin legs as if it was the most beautiful thing in the world, and when it decided to do its business, it simply did so straightaway in the middle of the sidewalk, to the constant mortification of the tidy Herr Braunstein. The dog would not be curbed. Led there, it simply looked up aggressively at its purported master and waited to continue the walk, whereupon it would leave its filth smack in the middle of the sidewalk.

Inevitably, Herr Braunstein would have to soil his fresh spats scooting the pile off the sidewalk into the gutter. This we three found unbearably funny. What a show Herr Braunstein in his fancy suit and carrying an ivory-handled cane provided us, hastily scraping at the leavings, looking around nervously that nobody should witness this degradation. While all the time, directly above him, we watched and sniggered to ourselves.

Imagine my surprise when, almost twenty years later and after the Anschluss, I recognized the natty form of Herr Braunstein—thicker by some pounds but no less expensively dressed—stooped over a wooden washing bucket with a slew of other Jews, cleaning the cobbles of Annagasse near his frame shop with a jeering crowd surrounding him! Such are the ironies of this world we live in. It was as if his fate had been foretold on those Saturdays on the Hubertusgasse, scooting his dog's leavings into the gutter.

What became of his dog, I do not know.

I dearly loved those hours spent together at our window. When such Saturdays coincided with my parents' monthly night out, then my happiness would be complete, for that meant that Frau Wotruba would come to me.

———

Well, I have made a good start on my memoirs, for a novice. From the books I have read on writing books, I know that this is a typical phenomenon: The first pages come fever hot and alive onto the page, then comes the plodding hard work. Then comes the structure. Then comes the guts of the book. And at last one arrives at that saddest of salutations: "The End." My green metal wastebasket under the trestle writing table attests to the false starts I have made in the last couple of days. Perhaps my problem is that I am trying too hard. It is said that Mark Twain wrote in bed; he swore that words that needed to be sweated over were no good. I am no great fan of that North American humorist, but it sounds as if there might be something in this idea. Perhaps it is worth trying.

————

Writing in bed is a messy business, I must admit, especially when one uses such an old-fashioned writing instrument as a fountain pen. I now have a set of badly stained damask sheets—dear enough material in this part of the world, I can assure you—for the entire bottle of black ink tipped over in bed as I was filling my Montblanc pen. And another wastebasket full of false starts.

————

I think I know what is troubling me, why I cannot push ahead from this excellent start I have on my memoirs. I am limited. I limit myself. My "rough draft of history" has floundered because I strive for too much organization. Actually, writing one's life is less like picking from neat alphabetical and chronological file cards in a pine file box than it is like dipping one's hand into the frothing sea and not knowing whether one will come up with kelp or cod.

But there is a larger reason for this writer's block: namely, my long-kept secret. It holds me back, making me prevaricate here, tell a half-truth there, and all in all drop absurd hints of some dreaded past from which I am escaping.

I had intended to work up to this point rather more gradually, to show rather than tell. I had intended to let the reader discover things for himself, but this one thing, this primary thing in these memoirs, is keeping me from telling the whole story, inhibiting me at the outset. And the whole purpose of writing these remembrances is to free me from that past, to exorcise that inhibiting influence on my life, for it is strangling me after so many decades of prevarication.

It is the world of the victors that judged me guilty; in my conscience, I am guiltless.

See! It is just such dubious remarks and foreshadowings that I wish to avoid. Surely any intelligent reader has by now done the mathematics requisite to place me, as any other man of my generation, squarely in the eligible warrior category for the Second World War. I describe a childhood growing up in Vienna; unless there was later a major resettlement for my family, I presumably was on the side of the Reich during that conflict. Any intelligent reader has therefore most likely already asked himself this question: What did our protagonist do during said war?

My number was 323498. It is still tattooed under my left arm. I was not an especially early member of the elite Schutzstaffel, what others like to call the SS. However, only foreigners and historians call it the SS; I shall from here on refer to the corps as the Staffel or the Black Corps, or even sometimes, as Himmler preferred, the Clan.

Though my number was not low, I was fervent until the end. Those ignoramuses at Nuremberg called me a war criminal. Perhaps not in a league with Eichmann—under whom I served for a time—but high enough on their rosters for there to be no statute of limitations on my conviction in absentia. I was branded a war criminal in 1946; a war criminal I remain today and till the day I die. That is my admission, and these memoirs are being written in part to set the historical record straight about just what it was like to be a member of the Staffel.

I also prevaricate about the tiny bay upon which I live: somewhere "on the western coast of the Americas" I have written. This vagueness makes it sound as though I fear the searching eye of Herr Wiesenthal or the Israelis who might storm my residence, capture me, and return me to Jerusalem for more of their "justice" as they did with Eichmann. But such is not the case. I have lived so long with the threat of capture that it no longer fills me with fear. All this subterfuge on my part is merely habit. I wish to rid myself of such deathly custom!

So, baldly put:

I live in one of those Central American states derisively labeled a banana republic. The language spoken here is Spanish, the climate is warm, almost tropical. Palm trees and curiously named and scented foliage abound. I was made welcome with open hands here in part because I did not come empty-handed—though I have labored long and hard to make it appear to the locals that the charter fishing service I operate here is my sole means of support. Another reason for my welcome was the political proclivities of certain powerful men in this country. And I have proved helpful to these men: In fact, I make a bit of a side income (not that I need it) in arms and insurgency. When called upon,

I run guns and sometimes unmarked parcels wrapped in hemp that tend to leave powdery traces on my deck boards.

The irony is that this is hardly an occupation with which I had any experience before coming to this country. For my current "employers," my Staffel past is my cachet: any former member of that elite corps is assumed to be some sort of military superhuman—cold as ice, calculating as a computer, stealthy as a jungle cat, and ruthless as a Jerusalem greengrocer. I have not told them of my lowly bureaucratic past. I let them believe what they want, for it is a form of insurance for me.

So, that is the lay of the land, gentle reader: a Schutzstaffel man and Nuremberg war criminal hiding out in Central America, augmenting his income and position with a very specialized import-export trade.

———

A strange call and a strange woman interrupted my work today. I was just settling down with the next installment on Frau Wotruba when the ringing of the phone intervened. I answered it reluctantly and was greeted by a woman's voice speaking English and some very bad Spanish with a strange, lilting accent. She excused herself for calling on a Sunday; she had heard of my skill with boats—a reputation deservedly earned, I might add. Coming from landlocked central Europe, I am entranced by the sea. I have come to know this bay as well as any local skipper: every shoal and reef; where to go for bottom fish when the surface feeders are inactive; and where to go for the big ones when the warm currents bring them in to feed. I know by a sixth sense when a fish is going to strike the line.

It seemed that this woman had been talking with people

at the harbor and now she wanted to come by to speak with me about hiring my boat for an extended period of time. Her lilt over the phone inhibited my understanding at first. I tried to place the accent. My silence made her wonder if I were still there. When she said my name, I finally placed the singsong intonation as an Irish accent. She repeated the small speech and I told her to come at one in the afternoon.

"It won't disturb your siesta?" she asked, suddenly solicitous.

"No," I told her.

It would not disturb my siesta, for I have never gotten in the habit of sleeping away half of the best part of the day. Such practices are only for drunkards and sloths.

"So, come at one," I repeated.

I had my suspicions about this caller immediately: It is not often that a woman alone finds her way to our bay and then determines to set about a course of sportfishing. Suspicions and paranoia—they have grown boring in my long life of hiding. Yet they have also kept me safe and I could not shake mine now.

But to out and out refuse the fare would itself draw suspicion back on myself; turning down a prospective hire at this time of year, just as everything is dying down toward winter and one would naturally want to tuck something away for the slow months, would draw unwanted attention from the locals. I would have to be more inventive than that, so I invited her over to tell her face to face, thereby winning some time to conjure up a good reason to refuse her offer.

She arrived punctually at one by Cordoba's taxi. He has the monopoly in our village: the only car, apart from my Land Rover, that regularly runs. His is a 1956 Ford for which he could, by now, earn a vintage price. He has overhauled the engine so often that it is like an old lover to him. Cordoba sometimes joins me for a drink and an evening of cards at my home. A sentimentalist like myself, he is generally a welcome guest.

I could hear his car approach from a great distance, for my house sits on the edge of a mango grove abutting a ravine at the end of a half-mile drive. The jarring of a car in the ruts of my simple drive always alerts me to the arrival of visitors. Cordoba finally pulled to a stop, and we saluted each other as I came out to greet the lady. I wanted Cordoba to stay, to be there to drive the woman back to the village after I had politely refused her offer. For I now had an excuse at hand: a busted drive shaft on the propeller for which our poor village had neither a welder nor parts.

But the woman paid Cordoba off immediately, sending him on his way before I could invite him in for a drink. He is a polite man: for him, business is business. He had brought a fare to the house and it would be wrong for him to turn it into a social call once he had received remuneration for his services. She seemed to intuit such things. It aroused my interest, if not curiosity, in her.

I spoke of Frau Wotruba earlier. Well, this Irish had something in her manner, a way of cocking her head questioningly at one with amusement in her eyes that immediately reminded me of my old friend. Physically, she was nothing like Frau Wotruba but for the light brown hair worn up in a bun as my occasional chaperone was also wont to do. On the cusp of her forties, she was tall and angular. Rather more like a robust Virginia Woolf, the mad Englishwoman, than the buxom, full-bodied Austrian woman who initiated me into the ways of physical love. Yet it was the curious cocking of her head and her defiant, playful eyes that captivated me.

Introductions were made as Cordoba sped off in his taxi. Miss O'Brien, her name was. Miss Kate O'Brien. I realized that the only polite thing to do was invite her in for a cup of tea while I explained the impossibility of accepting her offer. She responded to this invitation with a rather startling comment: She would give her second virginity for a cup of tea.

I believe I pulled up physically and abruptly at this statement. I am isolated here with only the weekly paper to inform me of events in the great outside world, plus my shortwave radio on which I listen to broadcasts of news and culture from Berlin once a week. I disallow myself more than a once-weekly dose of such programs; any more and I should grow homesick and maudlin. Our village is a place out of time where the Internet has not yet intruded. Thus, somewhat cut off from current trends, I have little experience with so-called modern women. Hers was a humorous comment, apparently; one hardly meant to be bawdy. Still, the remark shocked me.

"I'll see what I can brew up for you," I said in my best English. "If successful, I will not extract the reward, however."

She laughed at this, and again I was reminded of Frau Wotruba. As we entered the front door of my home, I found myself surreptitiously examining the woman's breasts, neatly rounded appendages under the blue chambray blouse she wore. Old habits in an old man. A dangerous combination.

At this point, I should explain one particular of these memoirs. There will be sections—and the following is one of them—that will be the faithful transcription of recordings of actual conversations, and of the silences intervening. Indeed, while transcribing my tapes, I am always amazed at the amount of time given over to silence. When I am actually with the person in question, I hardly notice such cumbersome halts in conversation. But in the tapes, there are long patches of time when all there is to be heard is the ticking of the mantel clock, the clink of ice cubes in glasses as I mix drinks, the rustle of magazine pages, or the squeak and groan of springs as someone sits down or rises. Sometimes a cough, a clearing of a throat, a sneeze. Then my polite "*Gesundheit*"—I have created the fiction of Swiss extraction to explain my occasional lapses into German.

Yet these sounds and nuances will be largely missing from my transcriptions. What I will present instead is simply the dialogue as it was spoken. Some geographical names, as well as my own, have, understandably, been deleted altogether from these transcripts. I shall not try to make interpretations upon these spoken parts of the memoirs, or attempt in any way to describe them, the people in question while speaking, or the settings.

These sections are taped mainly in my home, or perhaps even aboard my boat, the *Clan*. This habit of mine is a matter of personal security, of insurance, rather than a sign of paranoia. I often go over phone conversations and personal visits afterward to assure myself of their true meaning. In the middle of a conversation, I can hardly be expected to evaluate every statement made for hidden meanings or subtle blending of intent. A wanted man, with a price on his head as I have, cannot be too careful, even after all these years.

"My God! It looks like a wee cottage from the outside."

"It's built over a ravine. There are three stories."

"Hardly a bachelor pad. Those windows!"

"I'm happy you approve."

"Like having a Rousseau painting come alive."

"The builder thought I was insane, I can tell you. 'Floor-to-ceiling windows. Whatever for?'"

"Marvelous. Open-beam ceiling, tile floors. You could play basketball in here, Señor ____."

"Well, I call it home."

"Yes. It's what one would expect."

"Expect, Miss O'Brien?"

"From a romantic. You are a romantic, aren't you, Señor ____?"

"I don't know about that. Won't you take a seat? A romantic? I pilot a boat. Many of your Irish countrymen do the same. If that is grounds for being romantic, I plead guilty."

"___"

"Black tea, I assume, Miss O'Brien?"

"Lovely. . . . Sorry if I put you off just then. About my second virginity and all. A way I have. Irritates the bejesus out of some of my friends."

"Not at all. Refreshing, really. Breaks the ice, so to speak."

"Very baronial, this fireplace."

"___"

"And a fine lot of small statuary. This one in particular. She's quite lovely. May I?"

"Go ahead. She's an indestructible old girl. I call her my Kreuzberg Venus."

"Like the Willendorf Venus. . . . This is real Stone Age, isn't it? Not a reproduction?"

"As a younger man, I had a certain fondness for archaeology. These little totems were being turned up quite often."

"Great-breasted with hips for birthing."

"—"

"And this. I loved these snowy globes when I was growing up in Donegal. Not much actual snow there, you know."

"That's from my youth."

"Vienna, isn't it? The main cathedral. What's it called?"

"St. Stephan's. The Steffl. You get around, Miss O'Brien."

"It's been a long time since Donegal, Señor ____. I live in New York now. My writing takes me to out-of-the-way places. . . . All the fluttery snow when you turn it over. Lovely."

"Those next to it are Mayan."

"I thought so, Señor ____. Museum quality. Naughty you. I didn't think private collectors could lay their hands on these anymore."

"I'll just put the water on for tea, Miss O'Brien."

"This jaguar is fine work. But frightening, don't you think? You don't have any real pets?"

"My life's too erratic. I'm at sea a good deal, you know."

"Which I suppose brings us to the purpose of my visit."

"Just a moment. I can't hear you very well from in here."

"Which I suppose brings us to the purpose of my visit!"

"Yes. That's good, then. Just let it steep for a moment. I quite understand your urge for good tea. It is one of the finer things in life. Not easy to come by here, either. I have a connection with a shop in ____. They send such extravagances as Darjeeling tea, marmalade, chutney, and wine at regular intervals."

"A cosmopolitan romantic."

"Just about ready. Lemon or milk?"

"Oh, white, please."

"It's from the goat."

"As it comes. About the sea—"

"Yes. I do hate to disappoint such a cordial potential customer as yourself."

"They say you're the best."

"Sufficient. But you see—"

"And I need the best. It's for my work. I'm a journalist."

"Here you are. It might remind you of home."

"*Mmm*. Good. Very. Smells like the bleeding heather in bloom."

"I do believe you're doing a stagy Irish accent for me, now. But as I was saying—"

"I know what you're about to say. A rough idea, anyway. I've visited your boat. It seems in fine fiddle. I heard the reluctance in your voice over the phone. Perhaps it's because I'm a woman. But I assure you, I'd be able to pull my own weight on board. My father and brothers are in the fisheries in Donegal. I grew up on boats smaller than yours in seas rougher than these."

"Exactly what is it we're talking about?"

"A story. Sportfishing in the region. Something very nitty-gritty for the big-fish crowd. It's really undiscovered country for such things. The Keys and Baja—those are well known. Even the Bahamas. But I think we may have something new here."

"Exactly. And I'd like to keep it that way."

"The secret is to warm the pot before steeping. I believe you know that, Señor ___. An excellent cup of tea."

"___"

"Yes. I quite understand your reluctance. Rather like cutting your own throat if you're a real fisherman—giving away all the best fishing spots. But you're in the charter trade, aren't you? You should be glad of the potential increase in business an article like mine could mean for you. And besides, if you do the leading, you can lead me away from your personal favorite places. But there's going to be an article, one way or another."

"___"

"You don't care much for the idea, Señor ____?"

"I must confess that I have very little use for journalists or journalism. The constant preoccupation with turning the world into tidy stories is just another step in the trivialization of life, of the encapsulation of experience into neat frameworks and packages."

"You sound as if you speak from experience. Your desk there looks as though it's used for something other than letter writing."

"I'm . . . assembling some thoughts, shall we say."

"Memoirs? At your tender age?"

"The flattery is appreciated, Miss O'Brien, but I really must decline your offer. My physical reactions are no longer as good as they once were. I am beginning to feel my age. In actual fact, I shall soon be retiring from the charter business."

"I can hardly believe that, Señor ____. Perhaps you'll let me read what you have sometime. I might be able to help. In an editorial way."

"Kind of you to suggest that. But they're really nothing more than the rantings of an old sea dog who has seen too many ports in his day."

"You're German, aren't you, Señor ____? I mean your accent. It comes from somewhere in central Europe."

"___"

"Sorry. It's the snoop in me. None of my business."

"No. Not at all. Swiss, as a matter of fact. More tea?"

(Conversation was interrupted by the tocking sound of liquid poured too quickly out of its container.)

"I am sorry, Miss O'Brien."

"Don't be. It's washable. You will, won't you? Hire out your boat, I mean. We get along so well. And I trust you somehow."

"Please do not tell me that I remind you of your father."

"In ways. But it's more than that. Your manner. It's so old world and solicitous. Gracious even. You don't find that very often these days."

"More flattery."

"No. A statement of fact. Please don't make me be insistent. I would hate you to think me stone-cold stubborn."

"I assure you, Miss O'Brien—"

"See what I mean? Delicious! Miss O'Brien. When most men would be using my Christian name by now, Kate-ing me up and down."

"It's hardly my prerogative."

"You're quaint. Cute, too. Let's do business. Come on, what do you say? It could be fun. You look as if you could use some fun."

———

She was right, of course. Fun is something as foreign to me as Swahili. Miss O'Brien is a good judge of people: She knows just where to press me. That I so readily agreed to her request for a charter—knowing full well that she could be a mortal threat—comes as a surprise to me.

Now, after she has left, I sit at the trestle table I have set up as a writing desk by the windows, and I look at my jungle ravine. My mind will not stop spinning and churning. *I must be going crazy*, I tell myself. *I am inviting disaster by allowing this Irish, this woman, this journalist aboard the* Clan. *Surely she is no more interested in big-game fishing than I am in needlepoint.* There can be only one thing to lure a journalist into this otherwise sleepy part of the world, and that is the unstable political situation in our neighboring country and the traffic in arms and certain undefined parcels that such instability encourages.

Surely Miss O'Brien is here to investigate charges of gunrunning from my neutral country. Surely it is that connection she is after. And just as surely, such searches will lead directly to my door. Does she already have such suspicions, or is her visit the purest coincidence? Never mind. These thoughts hold no particle of fear for me; rather it is a challenge. One I am happy to meet.

At any rate, we have agreed to make an initial excursion on Tuesday. Meanwhile, I have transcribed these notes. It is near sunset now and a drink is in order. A schnapps, perhaps. I will contact Cordoba about the Irish. His friends at the Interior Ministry may be able to tell me something about Miss O'Brien. At the very least, they will have her visa information, her place of origin.

Why do I bother with this; why not simply say no?

A schnapps now. Whenever I begin to ask myself impossible questions, a schnapps is indicated. And then, after dinner, I will continue with my memoirs. I feel an unexplainable urgency; I need to get my story down on paper.

After the birth of my sister, Maria, Father and I were thrown more and more together. Equally dispossessed of Mother's love (she now had eyes and breasts only for the hungry baby), Father and I formed an orphan's bond out of shared loneliness. As much as I hated losing Mother's undivided attention, I am grateful that it happened. I was not destined to be a coddled mama's boy as so many of my fellow Austrians are. It is the national curse. The Scots have bad spines, Parisians a tendency to consumption, Americans a sagging in the derriere—while we Austrians, most pitiable among the lot, are raised as pashas with our shirts boiled, our shoes shined, our lives planned by Mama. Which, outwardly, might seem a divine situation for the male: It appears that we have female slaves to tend to our every care. Yet, in reality, this is the grossest form of enslavement; in the end, man becomes the slave to woman, for we are made helpless by having always been taken care of. Any hope of independence from the cursed domination by women is thus kissed and soothed away from the very first instant Mama begins to hold her infant son. It is the same for all to women born.

Freud, of course, was the most notable among the rest of us Austrians to fall prey to this tyranny simply because he whimpered about it most loudly. Could Oedipus have reared his pink head in any other hothouse climate but Vienna? Even Hitler, a product of the same Vienna as Freud, fell into the early trap of maternal tyranny, a frame of mind that no doubt affected him to the very last day of his life in the bunker far below the streets of Berlin, his lonely death: returning to the very womb of the earth while the youth of the nation were laying down their lives aboveground.

But for helping me escape that fate, I am grateful to my sister, Maria, God rest her restless soul. She does not figure directly into my narrative at this point, else I would bring her stage center employing a full panoply of descriptive tools. No, Maria, *die Süsse*, comes later. Her arrival, and its saving grace, is what I speak of now.

Maria threw me—dislodged me, actually—out of Mother's lap and into the unwilling hands of Father, he who garnered the entire sugar ration for his own uses. But as I have implied earlier, his tyranny, his Franz Joseph paternalism, was on paper only. Mother saw through his bluster: Hadn't Father's own mother boiled his shirts for him? Wasn't he a product of the same castrating society of which I speak? And thrown together more with Father, I was relieved of a second childhood threat: awe of the father, of the male, the hairy, virile competitor for the mother—to dress it in full Freudian regalia.

It happened like this.

It was a Saturday afternoon one unseasonably warm autumn day. No longer did we three spend the afternoon leaning against the window and laughing behind our hands at Herr Braunstein's stained spats. It was now Father's and my time to be out of the house together. Mother's newest caveat: "I want one afternoon without the two of you moping about underfoot!"

Father and I had stolen a Pyrrhic victory, claiming the time as ours to be together, men out on the town enjoying ourselves. This particular Saturday of which I write was that of my seventh birthday. *Guglhupf* would be served at dinner; a gift had already been presented to me after lunch: a *Struwwelpeter* storybook with illustrations ghastly enough to keep me from picking my nose or telling lies. I had left it in the apartment when Father and I went out for our stroll.

He smoked a cigar on these walks. I do not recall him smoking at any other time, surely not in the flat anyway, for Mother was a positive demon about odors, throwing open the windows in the coldest of weather to air out the place after cooking. So much did Mother dislike Frau Wotruba smoking in our flat that I had to plead and cry and make a general nuisance of myself to stop her getting someone else—nonsmoking—to look after me when they went out.

I was filled with a secret admiration for Father as he strolled, thumbs stuck in his vest pockets, his derby tilted far back on his head, the black-brown cigar jutting out of a corner of his mouth. I fantasized we were an engineer and his train: the jets of smoke trailing behind us were proof of our progress.

Father stopped suddenly, gripping my arm as if he had just had a brilliant idea. "What about a glass of soda water, little friend?"

It was his feeble way of suggesting we stop in the little park café in the Volksgarten near the Hofburg, city palace, to have a *viertel* of wine or two. I usually had a raspberry soda on such occasions and was thus agreeable to the proposal. We chose a table set among the fine pebbles of the café yard, directly under a magnificent old chestnut tree. Wind filtered through its leaves, sounding them like brittle wind chimes, and I watched the resulting lozenges of sunlight dance underneath the sheltering branches. Dappled sunlight caressed us. Father was weaving gossamer threads of cigar smoke above our heads and draining large draughts of wine from a chilled glass.

The autumn day was still fine, and I wore the shiny gray lederhosen that were the Austrian national uniform for children in the summer. Father, ordering a second glass of wine, removed his heavy jacket and rolled up the sleeves on his white shirt (to which he had shed the constricting celluloid collar after he had come home for lunch). His forearms were massive. I remember them clearly—sinewy and thick as they rested against the tablecloth gaily embroidered with green bunches of grapes on the vine. His rough hands cupped the frosty glass of wine. His were the arms and hands of a laboring man, for that is what he had been for many years until working himself up to the position of foreman of his transport crew and began wearing ties to work. From track layer, he now directed other men in the laying and maintenance of track. Herr Wotruba and Father had been very good friends, both of them employed by the Municipal Transport Company. Hearing of Herr Wotruba's death, Father could only shake his head in wonderment. It was not the mystery of death that Father could not accept, but the stupidity of the man for not having set his brakes securely. Father was a meticulous man in his work habits. To be run down by one's own tram was not only a great tragedy, it was also bad form!

"This is the life, no, son?" Sweat glistened on his brow. One bead broke away from the rest, traced a rivulet down his brow to his eyelashes where it hung suspended like a crystal in a ray of the mottled sunlight, then dropped gracefully to his cheek and slithered down his stubbly cheek and neck, and thence into his shirt.

"Sitting here like proper kings on a Saturday, eh? What a life!"

We were miserable. We both wanted to be back in the flat, at the window, surveying the world at arm's length. Out in the midst of it as we were at this café, one was never quite secure enough of oneself to take stock of things.

Father ordered another wine. It was more than I had seen him drink before. He made a joke of it with the waitress, about how he had worked up a thirst walking. She had a mole next to her mouth with one hair sprouting from it. She did not smile but asked if the child wanted another raspberry soda. I declined.

After the wine arrived, we watched the passing scene in silence. The café was situated near a fountain that had partly clad maidens gripping enormous fish to their stone breasts, and out of the gaping mouths of the fish—carp, I believe—spouted heavy streams of water. This splashed and rippled into the fountain. Around these statues grew reeds as if in a marsh at Lake Neusiedl to the southeast of Vienna. In the spring, ramps were laid from the lip of the steep-sided fountain across the water to the base of the statues in the middle. Here baby ducks would practice their swimming under the tutelage of watchful hens. But the ramps were long gone now; soon, in fact, the water would be drained and wooden covers set in place over the entire fountain to protect the statues from the winter cold.

I listened to the splash of water in the fountain and smelled the sweetness of the air.

"There's a fine figure," Father said beneath his breath.

I turned to see what he was looking at and saw three fine figures: a man, his wife, and their black standard poodle. I was unsure which figure Father had referred to. One had from them the immediate impression of wealth. It was not, however, the kind of wealth Herr Braunstein paraded; the couple made him look a hayseed by comparison. The man was wearing a moss-colored linen suit; his finely woven straw hat was floppy but elegant, not in the least bohemian; and his mustache was full and seemingly proud of itself the way it curled up on each side of his nose. One knew instantly that this fellow was from the best society; that he belonged probably to the fancy gambling clubs on Kaerntnerstrasse; that he attended the trotting races at Freudenau; and that he most likely sent his male heir to the best *gymnasium* where he would learn from the best teachers and associate with only the best boys.

The woman wore a dress of silk that shimmered in the sunlight as she walked. It clung to her curves and was cut daringly short at the knee. Her slightly bobbed blond hair was topped by a saucy yet elegant brimmed hat of a shiny blue material reminiscent of a duck's back.

Even the poodle was well groomed, as if it had just come from a cutting at the most expensive of dog salons in the inner city. Suddenly and acutely, I felt the abyss separating me from them: This poodle, it seemed, had better opportunities in life than I, a son of a foreman with the Municipal Transport Company.

This realization was shocking enough for me, who had always viewed the world from the safety of our apartment window, who had always judged it from the benchmark of our tiny lives. More shocking still was what transpired next. A duck, low flying and out of season, buzzed over the back of the poodle and skidded in for a landing in the fountain. In a trice, the poodle had bounded away from its mistress and had plunged into the fountain after the duck. Of course the bird flew away, while the dog was left to flounder in the water. Swim the animal could, but it was unable to scramble up the scummy and steep-sided lip of the fountain to dry land. The man in his sharp-creased linens was loath to aid the dog; his wife quickly grew frantic. It was apparent, though neither wanted to create a scene, that the woman was going to do something desperate quite soon to save the struggling, whining animal.

Father threw down the rest of his third glass of wine and sauntered over to the pair. I remained at the table watching the tableau. Father tipped his hat to the woman and spoke some words at which the man nodded gratefully. Thereupon Father got down on his knees, leaned over the edge of the fountain, and grabbed the dog by its collar.

"Watch out! You're choking Henri!"

But Father was not to be daunted by the lady's yelps.

Tugging at the dog, he began extricating it from the water, but before Father was able to save the dog, he lost his balance and tumbled into the fountain himself.

I was not so certain of this: I had no idea if Father could swim and was sure that Mother would chastise me greatly if I came home without him. What sort of punishment would there be in *Struwwelpeter* for losing one's father? But Father quickly surfaced, spitting water and coughing, a lily pad on his head. He managed to get a hold on the side of the fountain. From that position, in the water and behind the dog, it was easier for him to boost Henri out.

The poodle, once out, churned itself from tail to snout, throwing a rainbow arc of water off its fur. Father put his hand up to the man for assistance, but the couple, Henri now in tow, hurried off in the direction of the Hofburg without a backward glance.

"Well, I'll be damned," was all that Father said, his voice echoing against the sides of the fountain. It was left for the waitress to give him a helping hand out of the fountain while I retrieved his derby from the water.

I still remember the squeaking sound his shoes made as we walked home that afternoon, his clothes steaming in the dying sunlight.

———

Monday.

I wrote quite well yesterday; my confessional has worked. Or is it the Irish? With something to look forward to, I begin to order my days once again. I do look forward to tomorrow when Miss O'Brien and I shall sail the main together. I am a foolish old man. I have been down to the harbor, getting things ready aboard *Clan* for an early departure tomorrow. The boat gleams in the sunlight: I have lovingly cared for its mahogany and brass throughout the tenure of my ownership of her.

I also took the Land Rover in to Cordoba to work on, as we had arranged last week. The Land Rover is leaking water from the radiator. In addition to owning the only taxi service in the village, Cordoba also maintains the only garage and is the only mechanic.

While there, I broached the subject of the Irish, and Cordoba said he would make some calls. There was a leering smile on his lips. Cordoba thinks that I am up to the same tricks his father got up to at my age. I did not disabuse him of this idea. He got on the phone to his friends at the Interior Ministry in the capital straightaway.

After calling, Cordoba said that he might be able to supply me with some information that very afternoon. I thus decided to wait in town. I sauntered over to the harbor, thinking that I might see Miss O'Brien on the way, but she was nowhere to be seen. Was that significant? I wondered. Then I remembered that she had arranged to take the early morning bus to San ____ to see the ruins today. Hence our boat trip was scheduled for tomorrow.

I sat at Hernando's Café on the esplanade and had a coffee, feeling vaguely downcast that Miss O'Brien was taken away for the day until Cordoba came along with his snippets of information from the Interior Ministry. Miss O'Brien is apparently what she purports to be: a journalist of Irish extraction living in New York. She arrived at the capital, ____, three days ago on a Pan American flight from New York.

I bought Cordoba a coffee with brandy in it and we watched the boats for a time, and then I took myself off home, enjoying the walk.

I must make an early night of it tonight, but meanwhile I shall continue with the excellent progress I made yesterday. Forward into the past.

I dip my hand into the froth of life's sea and come out with this scene.

No snow this time, but the evening wind is up in the trees: the *föhn*, a warm breeze off the Alps that puts most people's nerves on edge. The steady caress of it has always calmed mine.

I hang my head out the window of our flat as Frau Wotruba reads to little Maria.

Yes, several years have passed now from my first remembrance of Frau Wotruba. I am now twelve, large for my age, and still she sits for both me and Maria. And still I long for her touch. But time is running out. Mother has already indicated that I am getting old enough to take care of Maria on my own when she and Father go out. Her "big man" she calls me. I do not feel big so much as desperate. Tonight may be my last opportunity.

I watch the occasional passerby and feel the warmth of the breeze on my cheek. The air is pine-laden, as if the forests are invading the concrete of Vienna, reclaiming it for nature. It is Strauss that my parents are seeing this time. The *Gypsy Baron* in a revival at the Volksoper. I calculate the time Frau Wotruba and I have left: It is about intermission now and then comes the short final acts, followed by some hot chocolate, and they will be home. We have, at most, ninety minutes left. We: Frau Wotruba and I. Maria does not figure into this "we," as far as I am concerned.

Over the several years of our friendship, we have progressed painfully slowly with things physical. For months at a time, Frau Wotruba will act as if nothing has ever happened between us, as if the sighs she utters when I rub against her are merely stifled yawns. We never speak about this, you see. It is all forbidden territory as far as we are both concerned.

And then, out of the blue, she will cuddle me, and we will rock together until the exquisite frisson has been created for her and I am left breathless with a painful yearning. Then, for more months, she will again simply tousle my hair playfully if I attempt to put my head in her lap. She will read in Father's chair on these occasions, or worse, fall asleep there, her mouth agape, a sound between a purr and a snore emitting from her nose, while I toss in my bed, every muscle taut, the warmth in my belly turning into a searing heat.

From the window, I catch bits and pieces of the story the frau is reading to little Maria: "Such big eyes!" A streetcar jangles its bell angrily out in the main thoroughfare. I feel as impatient as that bell sounds. Time is wasting! Father and Mother will be home soon.

Turning from the window, I see Frau Wotruba kissing Maria's cheek. My sister has been drifting off to sleep, but the kiss awakens her. *So Frau Wotruba is consciously stalling tonight*, I think.

She sees me looking at her and lets Maria drift off to sleep now. I smile sheepishly and make preparations to get in my own bed. She seats herself in Father's armchair. I crawl under the comforter, and the cotton sheets are warm.

I watch Frau Wotruba settle into the chair. She knows my eager eyes are on her. She takes up a magazine and, licking her forefinger, begins plucking through the pages. Soon

Maria's sleep-heavy breathing can be plainly heard, but this seems to make Frau Wotruba even more frantically attack the pages of the magazine.

I whisper her name. She pretends not to hear me. I speak again, louder, and she looks up from the magazine to me, then glances at Maria.

"She's sleeping," I say in my normal speaking voice. "Nothing wakes her."

It is true. Baby Maria has the facility of such deep sleep that the first day home from the hospital, she would not wake to cooing sounds or to kisses from Mother, who thought the baby was dead. Whereupon Mother screamed loudly enough to wake the tenants of the Central Cemetery, which did the job that kisses and coos would not. In our household, where we all have to share the one large room, such a proclivity for deep sleep amid the toing and froing of the rest of the family is a definite plus.

"Will you say good night to me, too?" This from me, coyly. "Father and Mother may be home at any time."

The mention of my parents gets her going, for at our last meeting, I was already desperate enough to play a final card: I threatened to tell my parents about our little games if Frau Wotruba would not let me touch her flesh. She laughed at first, but then saw that I was serious and promised: "Next time, next time."

This is next time. This may be the last time. I am willing to risk all for one touch.

She gets reluctantly to her feet and pats absently at her hair as she moves across the room, attempting to assume an air of control and disdain. I know better: She is conquered. She is forced now to allow me to do things to her that I have always dreamed of but never dared ask of her. This delicious sense of power I have over her warms me throughout. My body shivers as I watch her approach the bed. A throbbing at my middle announces a painful erection: These have been happening more often of late. Feeling under the bedding and my pajamas, my hand grips it. How startling it is! That tiny, drooping worm, used up to now solely for micturition, has suddenly taken on a new size and shape. This transformation frightens me every time it happens, but I sense that it is part of the totality of the sexual experience. My hand tightens on the pulsing organ and the subsequent sensation is delightful, tinged not in the least with pain now.

"This is no longer right or proper." She stands over me, hugging her arms around herself.

I am silent as I watch a moistness forming in her eyes. One tear glistens down her cheek. My penis jerks.

"It was innocent to begin with. There was no thought. But now . . ." She spreads her hands, looking at the bulge under the eiderdown where my hand still grips. Her head shakes violently.

"Sit down, Frau Wotruba."

Her head continues to shake violently. I am afraid I have pushed her too far.

"I'm sorry," I say. "It was nicer before, wasn't it? I liked it then, too. Couldn't you just hold me one last time? Just to let us both remember the feeling?"

This is no approximation of my speech, for I had it memorized and can remember it verbatim even today.

Still she stands.

"Please." I pat the bed next to me.

She begins to sob as she crumples onto the bed. I do what I can to hold her, but she is still far larger than I; I cannot get my arms around her. My attempted comforting is clumsy, like trying to shake hands with someone who grips yours too quickly to allow you a firm hold. You are left wagging a part of the other person's hand almost effeminately. I feel ineffectual trying to console her thus. Besides, I am afraid if I scoot up any farther in bed she will see my erection.

Instead, after an attempted hug, I curl into her lap and burrow my head against her tummy. This is my inspired frontal approximation to a consoling pat on the back.

After what seems an age, her sobbing stops. I can barely hear her as she blubbers over me: "I just didn't want it to come to anything sordid. I feel so awful. You're just a boy. It's as though I've used you, hurt you somehow."

I assure her that what she has shared with me has been the grandest thing in my short life. Then I resume my furrowing against her belly, making an occasional sortie upward with my forehead to her left breast. At first, she stiffens at these touches, but soon I feel only that one part of her body stiffen, and that is what I have been waiting for. I leave the region of her stomach and begin actively caressing her breast and its taut nipple with my cheek. She wiggles against me, emitting the by now familiar, lazy sigh, and pushes her bosom harder toward my cheek.

I increase the tempo of caressing—first this cheek against that breast, now the other. Back and forth I go, around and around until I have her breathing fast and I feel my own erection will soon burst.

At this point, I do something I have never before attempted. I stop moving my face and place my hands instead over her ample breasts. I find the buttons at the front of her white blouse and begin opening them deliberately. She does not move; her breathing comes more rapidly now: a hiss in my ears. When my hand finally finds its

J. Sydney Jones

way to bare flesh, she makes a sharp intake of breath that startles me, stopping my hand against the heat of her skin.

After an instant, she begins to squirm insistently against my inert hand, her eyes closed tight. I renew the unbuttoning: It has been her decision.

Soon her blouse is open from top to bottom and a warm rush of scented air bathes my face. Having secretly watched my mother undress before, I am not surprised at the next layer of clothing that confronts me. Nevertheless, this I mistakenly attack from the front, though the stays are in the back. Soon, however, I have pulled one of the cups down far enough to expose a crescent of purple-brown areola and I fall to rubbing my cheek against it furiously. Frau Wotruba is electrified. My ministrations seem to drive her straight out of her mind. She begins muttering unintelligible phrases—little clucking sounds coming from deep in her throat.

Her arms, until now gripping me to her, suddenly loosen. She arches her back, fidgeting behind with her hands—her eyes still maddeningly closed—and suddenly the white, coarse brassiere drops from her, revealing the twin objects of my desire. Blue veins crisscross the top halves of each globe like rivers on a map. All tributaries seem to lead directly to the nipples: fat, deep red, and tasty looking like cherries. I cannot contain myself, and my mouth goes directly to these two little fellows, miniature replicas of my straining penis. I swirl them about with my tongue, sucking all the while, and Frau Wotruba begins a long, high moaning sound, pressing my head to her harder and harder. With her free hand, she is busy playing down my back to find the bottom of my nightshirt, which, once found, she proceeds to draw up above my waist. Her fingers now trace a course around to my front. As they pass over my abdomen, I twitch involuntarily as if an electric current has been applied to my body. Her hand then begins a slow, playful walking—finger by finger—down my belly, so arousing me that I no longer feel in control. I begin to squirm just as Frau Wotruba has been doing.

The breast in my mouth; her fingers inching ever closer to my erection—I am these two sensations only. And quite suddenly these two sensations fuse as her hand grips my twitching penis firmly—I feel her garnet ring bite into the base of my staff, the only piece of reality to ground me in the swirling water that I am entering.

Another moan, though this time it comes, surprisingly, from my own throat. She gently nudges me from her breast, then lays me out flat on my back as she reaches in back of her head, pulling hair pins out as slowly and deliberately as before I unbuttoned her blouse. As she reaches up, her breasts rise high and point out from her chest like marble obelisks, incredibly beautiful and at the same time terrifying. Her tresses tumble about her face, obscuring her features momentarily. She brushes hair out of her face and now her eyes are open, looking at my body, from my penis to my face.

"I guess you're old enough," she says with a laugh and then bends down over my body, her hair veiling me in a deep and exotic jungle. The hair bunches over my face and flows across my shoulders, soon to be replaced by the pink tips of her nipples dangling over my mouth.

At that moment, my extreme eroticism is replaced by another emotion, equally as strong: fear. I am suddenly terrified that she is going to smother me in her hair and breasts. I begin to hyperventilate; her hair continues its course down my chest to my belly. She makes little pecking kisses on my skin. When the horror and fear of suffocation is at its peak, I feel a great welling up in me and, as if in a scream, the lower part of me seems to explode. The fear and eroticism blend in the most vivid feeling I have ever experienced, a commingling of joy and despair, tension and utter relaxation. I continue to explode for what seems minutes. I feel my penis bobbing back and forth, my whole lower body gyrating madly. From a great distance I hear Frau Wotruba's voice: "Not in my hair!"

Her weekly bath day was only yesterday. She holds on to pragmatism in the midst of everything else. Like all women.

And then the apartment door opens and Father and Mother are standing in their shabby evening clothes gawking at me and Frau Wotruba as they might at a soprano and tenor who had sung off-key.

———

Disaster in the present. I shall record it all as it happened to me.

Tuesday was a peaceful morning. Bats were in the air just before sunrise: They hunt in the stand of bamboo just beyond my driveway. I walked to the harbor, for, as I mentioned, I had left the Land Rover in town on Monday for Cordoba to work on.

These minutes before sunrise are my favorite time of the morning, and it is no punishment for me to walk then. I had no need to carry anything, as I had already stored all we would need aboard the *Clan* yesterday. My hands were empty and the road stretched out before me magnificently as a purple ribbon in the crepuscular dawn light. A soft, warm breeze came off the land. As the sun rose over the hills in back of me, it illuminated cloud cover overhead.

There might be rain later in the day, I thought, but for now the sea would most likely be calm.

Bats continued darting about in the air, hunting before the rising of the sun. Unlike most people, I do not shrink from these tiny animals, not even from the vampire bat, which is indigenous to my locale. Such animal fear is reserved, in me, solely for snakes. Instead, I marvel at the agility of bats, at their extreme sensitivities. They construed diving feints at me as I made my way along the dirt road. Neither did this unduly bother me, as I am accustomed to their tricks. I feel close to them in many elemental ways. Over the course of my years of exile, I have developed many of the same sensibilities that bats possess. It is as if I can see in the dark; my internal radar is unfailing. I can bring the *Clan* into our tiny bay, reef laden as it is, on a moonless night with no running lights. I am also unusually perceptive with people, managing to steer clear of emotional reefs, as well. This is a sixth sense that I have developed, and bats seem to recognize it in me. They play with me; I with them.

Thus it was with some alarm that I realized the bats were no longer simply playing with me this morning. Their dives grew ever nearer, and they flew straight at my eyes. I could see their squinched little snouts—as if a rat's face were crumpled in a sneeze—when at the very last instant of their dives, they flew upward and away. At first, I maintained my steady gait and did not throw up protective hands. That would have been giving in to their childish games.

I saw the glistening fangs of one in the blood-red sunrise; smelled its gamy mustiness; felt the flutter of its wings on my cheek. Then, and I still shudder to think of it, one of the bats alighted on my shoulder, its wings flapping hot air against my cheeks, its birdlike claws digging into my flesh through the sweater I wore. I struck out at it, no longer able to control myself, and as soon as it was dislodged, another took its place. Soon it seemed I was enshrouded by the awful creatures and there was, in fact, a piercing pain at my neck where one attacked me. I gripped the animal, tugging it from my neck, and began running, stumbling along the road. There was a flurry of wings around me, and their piercingly high and fearful banshee cries echoed in my ears.

The one in my hand no longer shrieked, and when I had finally outrun its companions, I stopped and looked down at it. I had crushed the bat in my grip, and the sight of this violence sickened me. I find violence done to helpless animals inexcusable. Though one must admit that this was clearly a case of self-defense, still I could not check my feeling of revulsion at this act. Despite my "notorious" past, I am, at heart, a rather frail creature in this regard. There was blood coming from the animal's mouth; whether it was mine or its own, I could not tell.

In itself, being attacked by a coven of bats is enough to unsettle one. But this had a larger significance for me: It was as if the bats no longer recognized me, no longer felt our old bond. Had they recognized some sort of diminution of my powers? Were they trying to warn me of something? These questions unsettled me more than did their attack.

In the event, I should have heeded their warnings.

The Irish was already on board when I reached the harbor, and she had brought a thermos of strong coffee with her even though I have an extensively equipped galley. It was a nice gesture, however, and the heavy aroma of the coffee when poured filled the boat. Some few fishermen were up as well, preparing for the morning tides. They waved—no one bothered speaking at such an hour. The Irish was wise enough to perceive the custom and kept her verbal responses to a minimum. She noticed the wound on my neck immediately, and when I went belowdecks and looked in the bathroom mirror, I saw two lines of blood flowing down from the bite, just like out of some ghoulish horror movie. It startled Miss O'Brien when I told her about the bats, but hardly incapacitated her. She washed the punctures thoroughly for me and then used ample doses of antiseptic from the first aid kit that I always keep on board. The alcohol burned into my flesh, yet I found myself hoping Miss O'Brien's ministrations would not end: Her fingers, businesslike but soft, felt so comforting on my skin. I almost wished I had more than the one bite from the bats.

She was dressed for the sea today. Where on Sunday she had been demurely outfitted in a cotton skirt, chambray shirt, and open-toed sandals, she was now wearing jeans, sneakers, and a pullover. Her hair was tightly braided and coiled on top of her head. She had, overall, the look of a woman not wanting to be hampered by signs of femininity. For my part, I hoped she was as competent on board as she had led me to believe she was. I do skipper the *Clan* alone on most of my secret night runs, but I usually bring along a crewman from the village for charter cruises. Today, there would be just the two of us.

We set out just as the sun showed full above the village. It was warm and muggy; almost certainly there would be rain by afternoon. We were not five minutes out of the harbor when Miss O'Brien decided to shuck her warm pullover. Underneath was a white T-shirt and underneath that was clearly nothing but flesh.

We spoke little. I set a course for the marlin run just off Cabo de la ____. The water there is deep, and the warm currents bring in the big fish. The water began to look murky with an oily sheen on top as it does before the first rains. The sky was fast becoming herringboned with low clouds. Miss O'Brien seemed to take note of this development, just as I did.

There were no big ones off the cape. I had known that this would be the case the moment I detected the sheen on the water. We fished the area for a time, anyway: The Irish seemed content with the bream we were taking on the smaller side lines baited with squid. Meanwhile, the heavy line from the rod at the stern was silent. Not a bite.

Miss O'Brien mentioned her family again—how much they would love the fishing here instead of battling the Atlantic storms. Either she has her story straight, or there is a large element of truth in it.

But still I was not overly concerned about this. Rather, I spent my time watching the rise and fall of her breasts as she played the lines. Miss O'Brien is a powerfully built woman.

For a time, I simply set the boat at anchor and continued to watch her pull in the bream. A slight drizzle set in and still she continued fishing, her T-shirt wetting through to display the flesh tones of her skin beneath the fabric. I made myself take my eyes from her—I shall not be reduced to voyeurism—and watched instead the graceful swoop and splash of a pelican fishing off our stern. Such birds are of ancient lineage: they remind me of the reconstructions of pterodactyls I saw at the Natural History Museum in Vienna as a child. This pelican dove headlong into the water in search of its prey. A noble animal, but soon the seagulls swarmed to the spot where the pelican had discovered fish. Seagulls are the scavengers of the bird kingdom and would ultimately spoil my lovely bird's hunting. The pelican and the seagull: a mighty metaphor for human life, as well. The seagulls are like the hungry little people, who with their lemminglike natures, flock around the strong leader, then ultimately chase him away by their very number and greed.

I looked back at Miss O'Brien, still busy with her bream lines, and she caught my gaze at her breasts.

"I'm sorry. I'll put my pullover back on."

"It's the rain."

"Yes. Dampens the material. I hadn't meant to be immodest."

"Was I staring?"

"Gaping is more like it."

"That bad?"

By way of response, she arched her eyebrows at me.

"My only defense is that your breasts are quite lovely."

"Damned inconvenient, is more like it. Try sleeping on your belly with a set of these in the way, Señor ____. Or running bare-topped. Or even having a decent conversation with a chap who's a head shorter than you. You can have them, that's what I say. Men like breasts so much, they should have a pair themselves. . . . It's getting cold, anyway. . . . You know, Señor ____, I haven't been absolutely truthful with you."

"A client-relationship hardly calls for total divulgence, Miss O'Brien."

"But it's about that. I mean, as to why I'm renting your boat."

"It would appear, from the carnage at your feet, that you are fishing."

"Oh, that's in the blood. The whole family fishes. But I'm not really researching an article on big-game fishing."

"I rather thought not."

"Actually, I'm writing a book. A novel on the revolution."

"What revolution might that be, Miss O'Brien?"

"You know. In ____."

"Oh. That one. We sometimes get boatloads of refugees from there."

"You aren't political?"

"That depends on what you mean by 'political,' Miss O'Brien."

"Are we getting lexical or just obtuse? You know, political. Involved."

"A leftist, or just political, Miss O'Brien?"

"Have you been watching the pelican, Señor ____?"

"As a matter of fact, I have. It's a lovely bird."

"It dives so wonderfully. All alone."

"Except for the scavenging seagulls, Miss O'Brien. They'll soon ruin its fishing."

"But seagulls have their own kind of beauty, Señor ____. The immaculate white feathers. And no, I do not just mean leftist when I say political. But I do mean having a heart for people. That you want to do things to help the world, to make it better rather than worse."

"Absolutely. That was my whole life. . . ."

"Go on, Señor ____."

"Old sea stories. Very boring."

"You've got a secret, Señor ____. No fair. I told you mine."

"The wind has turned. It's coming out of the southwest now. We should head back in."

"But it's like a bathtub out here."

"The weather is rather unpredictable this time of the year, Miss O'Brien."

"Still, the wind's before the rain. We'll be fine."

"I don't follow."

"It's an old Irish saying: 'When the rain's before the

wind, then your topsails you must trim; when the wind's before the rain, hoist your topsails up again.'"

"Quaint, Miss O'Brien. All the same, I do not want to stake *Clan* on a bit of folklore."

The marlin line rapidly played out with a high-pitched whine of the reel.

"There, Miss O'Brien! Did you see him break water?"

"He's breaking the surface again. How do I get into this damn chair?"

"There, up these steps. Good. Now strap yourself in first. No! Don't touch the drag. Let him have as much line as he wants. Good. Yes, the buckle's there. Now the feet are propped up here. Excellent. Yes, right in the stirrups. You may be here a while, best to get comfortable from the outset. No. Don't tip the rod. Keep it in place. Let him run with the line."

"It's buzzing like crazy. Is there enough line?"

"Don't worry about that. If we have to, we'll run with him. But don't think about that now. Just settle in. Take deep breaths. Grip the rod like this. Good. Fine. It's letting up."

"Only a G sharp whine instead of high C."

"Keep the humor for later. You may need it. Now. Now! He's stopped running. Reel in some line now. Slowly. Take your time. The other way!"

"I thought it was coming too easily."

"I'll untangle the line, you keep reeling in and keep the rod up. Otherwise he'll snap the line. Slow and easy."

"Christ, he's heavy! It's like the line's alive."

"It is, in a way. The fish is speaking to you through the line."

"Like tin can phones when we were kids—Shit!"

"That's all right. He's bound to take more dives."

"All right for you, maybe. I've just lost all the line I reeled in."

"That's the game. See! There he goes! He's breaking the surface again. Lovely. He'll be a fine fighter for you. Hands off the reel now. Let him go with it. Don't fight him when he's running. Let him take as much line as he likes."

———

I watched the Irish fight her marlin for a couple of hours and she showed a good deal of courage throughout. She did not once request that I take over for her, though the grip of the pole showed a viscous smear from popped blisters after the first hour. She was in pain, yet she still joked about knowing now exactly how Captain Ahab felt. I liked her spirit and her spunk.

I am not quite certain how I view these fights. I have seen too many of them in my life. Each person handles the fight differently; some of the pink-fleshed, bloated men who come down here for a week of fishing will hook into a fish like this, and it is as if they must prove their entire lives in this one instant of combat. I pity the poor fish then, cheer for it, in fact. That these men's lives should be so empty as to need filling up by a battle with a dumb and beautiful animal!

The Irish is among the other, smaller category who stumble upon the magnificent foe out of a life entire and rewarding. These few form a bond, a sort of pact with the fish—witness Miss O'Brien's allusion to the tin can phone of her youth. The connection one forms with the fish is one of communication. Fish and fisherman, connected by the 150-pound test line, soon become one. The rhythms of one become those of the other; likewise the hurt and exultation.

With these few people it is not the final kill or capture, not the final gaffing of the exhausted beast that matters. Rather it is the process. The communication, if you will. The Irish has this: She is obviously one of those already proofed by life.

———

"I'm getting tired."

"I know. It's been over two hours. Do you want me to—"

"No. I'm not complaining. Merely explaining."

"More water?"

"There's enough of that about, thank you."

"Not a good day for fighting a fish, Miss O'Brien. We should go in."

"My rhyme was right though, wasn't it, Señor _____? Wind before the rain? God! There he goes again. So close now."

"Rod up! Rod up! Don't fight him now!"

"Fuck!"

"It's all right, Miss O'Brien. There'll be other fish."

"—"

"Come on. Put the rod back in the holder. Get down here. You could use a hot drink and dry clothes."

"Sorry about the language."

"It's disappointing, I know. I've lost some big ones, too."

"I'm glad he got away."

"I know, Miss O'Brien."

"So why am I crying?"

"You're exhausted. Here. Put this on."

"Hold me a second, okay?"

"Certainly."

"I won't break."

"Better?"
"Yes."

We came back into port as the gray sky overhead was turning vermilion in the west. The squalls I feared never appeared, though we were both wet enough after a day out in the heavy drizzle, and Miss O'Brien was all done in from her adventure with the marlin. I did not bother getting the boat completely in order and secured. We were both too tired for that and, besides, we have a very honest village—the local constabulary sees to that. One could leave a wallet outside overnight and find it there in the morning untouched.

It was that quiet, in-between time of day I enjoy so much here: the day not quite finished and the evening yet to begin. Normally, this is my hour for a small drink and settling in for a night of reading, or of working on my memoirs, or perhaps for the monthly game of gin rummy with Cordoba. Tonight would be one for reading, I thought.

We both stood on the quay for a moment. The lights were just coming on in the village beyond the harbor. It is a fine little village, built in concentric rings up the hillside above the water. In the daylight, it is all sparkling white: cubist houses with red tile roofs built all jumbled atop one another. A broad palm-tree-lined esplanade just at the water's edge is home for a few outdoor cafés and restaurants. The crisscrossing strings of lights were on at Hernando's Café.

This scene is very pleasant and has never ceased to fill me with a quiet sort of wonder. Ours is one of the remarkable villages along this coast. Most are poor and tumble-down excuses for villages. But ours is wealthy enough even to support a church with a four-hundred-year-old bell in its steeple and real gold candlesticks on its altar.

We continued to gaze at the village at dusk, both loath to take our leave of each other. For an instant out there on the water, after the marlin had broken the line, Miss O'Brien and I had been linked with each other. I do not mean in any crude physical sense, but in a higher soul-mate manner. We had been in a symbiotic harmony of sympathizer and mourner. For that perfect instant as I held her to me, I was no longer an old man who had been on the run for decades on the edge of the jungle, but was again a young, virile man starting off on the adventure of life.

Miss O'Brien finally commented on the sky, which by now had deepened from vermilion to almost puce. The intensity and variety of color over the bay has a near-frightening quality to it: One imagines that this is what the world will look like in its last instant before extinction. It is a light common to this time of year. I have experienced many such sunsets, yet they still produce in me a feeling of loss, loneliness, and longing. Tonight, as on many nights, I longed for company over a drink; for a consoling voice as the logs burned in the fireplace. Therefore, I asked Miss O'Brien if she would care to have some dinner with me at my place, and she readily accepted. She wanted only to stop by her hotel first to change into some dry things. The Land Rover was ready and waiting for us at the harbor, just as Cordoba had promised it would be. A competent man is Cordoba.

Located on the Calle ____, Miss O'Brien's hotel is far from magnificent, but it is the only one our tiny village has to offer. I myself stayed there my first winter while waiting for my house to be completed. Miss O'Brien pointed out her room from the Land Rover: I was pleased to notice that it was the same large front room I had occupied one winter long ago.

She assured me that she would not be a minute and was almost as good as her word. I barely had time to begin sorting through my memories of the winter I had lived in the hotel—the constant fight with cockroaches and with Señora Alvarado's atrocious cooking—before Miss O'Brien came skipping back to the truck attired in a fresh-looking shirtwaist: quite prim and proper as compared to her fishing outfit.

As I pulled away from the hotel, I saw in the rearview mirror that Señor Alvarado, the proprietor, had come out onto the street to inspect the goings-on. A man of the world is Señor Alvarado. Not much one for gossip, I thought, though he does like to know what transpires with his guests. I do not imagine that we have exchanged more than ten words in the years since I resided there, but we understand each other all the same.

He waved at us as we bumped down the narrow *calle*.

Miss O'Brien was in a festive mood despite her disappointment with the fish. This was serendipitous, for such a mood was the perfect palliative to my own rather melancholy one. Dusk overtook us as we drove. Miss O'Brien's face was illuminated by the green dash lights, her profile taking on a hard, black line. Our headlights bounced ahead of the truck like searchlights as we thumped along the rutted driveway. Now and again a bat would appear in the beams of light: a darting black object in the yellow incandescence. In the absolute blackness of the jungle night, light holds a tightness and cohesiveness of beam that one does not usually notice. The Irish commented on this as I parked the car.

"They should be sucked into the vortex," was the way she put it, referring to our headlights.

We were too late for the wild cries of sunset by the time we reached the house. Early evening and birdsong go together in the snarl of jungle in back of my humble estate. The exoticness of this entertained me for years: I would listen to the screeches and howls, which I had never heard before outside the confines of a zoo, and know I was someplace different. I would be reminded of the path I had chosen in life and its costs.

We walked up the steps to the front door, and when I let us in, there was no mention of tea as on her first visit. The evening had a chill to it.

"Shall I lay a fire?"

"Super. I'd love that."

"First the drinks. You'll trust my judgment there, won't you? My specialty. I call it ____, after our little bay. Nothing sweet, I assure you."

"God forbid."

"You do take a drink?"

"I've been known to. Not to worry. I'm Irish, remember? Sure and we're all fearsome drinkers."

"That's a most pleasant way you have."

"How so?"

"Of reprimand, I mean. Whenever you want to bring me up short, to stop me from being too officious or polite or treating you too much like a dainty lady, you simply go into the stage Irishman act. It's softer that way."

"I really hadn't noticed, Señor ____."

"That's what makes it so effective. It's unconscious. Now for the drinks."

"May I help?"

"Not unless you know how to lay a fire."

"And what do you think? We had central heating in Donegal?"

"Fine. You'll find paper and kindling in the brass chest by the fireplace. Matches on the mantel. How do your arms feel?"

"Like I'm carrying lead weights. Fishing must be great for the pectorals. I'll have to tell my fitness-conscious friends in New York about this. They're always looking for ways to beat the effects of gravity."

"Sorry . . . I can't hear you very well in here."

———

But it is not my intention here to record every word I shared with the Irish. Suffice to say we had developed a rapport, a familiarity, a jokingly bantering sort of friendship. I could not have been more surprised by this unlikely turn of events, or more pleased. But returning to the living room, drinks in hand, I was met by even a greater surprise.

Instead of lighting the fire as she had promised, Miss O'Brien was at my trestle desk brazenly picking through the manuscript of my memoirs! She did not even attempt to feign innocence once I entered but continued thumbing through the handwritten stack of papers. I set the drinks down on the low table between the armchairs, and she looked up at me, letting out a half laugh.

———

"I didn't think you were writing fiction, Señor ____. I thought you said memoirs."

"—"

"I do like it, though. The allusion to Wiesenthal. The teasing fragments of stories all over the place. You have a knack for storytelling, Señor ____."

"I'm sorry you read that, Miss O'Brien."

"Don't be. I think it's quite good. Perhaps a bit of line editing needed here and there, but so far I see no need for major revisions. I'll be curious to see if you bring all the threads together at the end."

"You will be?"

"Yes. . . . Okay, I'm sorry, Señor ____. You look angry. I guess I shouldn't have snooped. But you shouldn't have left the manuscript lying about for anyone to read if you're so sensitive about it. Sensitivity is the first thing to get rid of in this game."

"Yes. A pity."

"Look. Mea fucking culpa. I didn't realize—"

"I think you probably did, Miss O'Brien. At any rate, I can hardly be expected to risk it. Not after all these years of caution."

"Risk what? And will you please stop looking at me as if I have just defecated on the altar?"

"The difficult part is that in our short time together, I've grown quite fond of you. Of course, that was part of the plan, wasn't it?"

"Plan? You're not making any sense. . . . Unless . . ."

"Yes, Miss O'Brien? Unless what?"

"Unless these really are memoirs. Unless you really were an SS man and people like Wiesenthal actually are searching for you."

"Excellent, Miss O'Brien. Hollywood's loss is my gain."

"And you think I'm some kind of Nazi hunter?"

"Journalist is bad enough, Miss O'Brien."

"But this is absurd. I'm only a small-time journalist and would-be novelist. I could give a shit about your past. Especially if you fought against the bloody British."

"Yes. But then you'd say that in any case, now."

"Meeting you was the purest accident."

"There are no accidents in my world, Miss O'Brien."

"Okay. I came here under false pretenses. I already admitted that on the boat today. I wanted to meet you. But not because I thought you might be an ex-Nazi on the run. Christ, that was donkeys' years ago, anyway. The truth is I was looking for a protagonist for my novel. The main character."

"I'm well aware of what a protagonist is, Miss O'Brien."

"And you seemed to fit the bill perfectly, from what the locals have to say about you. Seasoned sailor, mysterious man of the world, displaced European in the New World. I had no idea of what you were really like when I came here on Sunday, only these stories I had heard about you in the village."

"Such as?"

"They made you sound like an adventurer. Señor Alvarado at the hotel and Hernando at the café. They described you as someone willing to take chances in life. I need a character like that in my novel. It's exactly the missing ingredient that I've been looking for. You would be the narrator, the lens through which the light of the action passes."

"It sounds all very fanciful, Miss O'Brien. Maybe you have some of this novel to show me? After all, I seem to have shared mine with you."

"It's in my head still. I won't start writing until I get back to New York. I'll send you a first draft. You'll like it, I'm sure."

"Look, Señor ____, I am truly sorry I snooped. I wanted to learn more about you, to be able to fill you out on paper. I really do not care about your past."

"Yes. I should like to believe you, but I am sure you understand that I must do something about all this. I need time to reflect on the possible ramifications."

"Take all the time you need. You know where I'm staying."

"Yes. Quite. The guest room should do for now."

"Look—"

"No, Miss O'Brien, you look. You have put me in a most awkward situation. Most awkward, indeed. You wormed your way in here under self-admitted false pretenses. I cannot say that I was unaware of the possibility of you being not quite what you said. But that does not alter the fact that you made certain pretenses. You set about building a rapport with me, simply to use me—"

"I honestly like you."

"And then you commence to poke about in my confidential papers. You have put me in jeopardy as a result of your own conniving. You have endangered the life I lead here, my very physical existence. You have lied repeatedly and now, cornered, you expect me to believe more of what could be lies. No, Miss O'Brien, I sincerely believe it is time for you to open your eyes. What would you do with me if the situation were reversed?"

"But it isn't. It couldn't be."

"Let's be hypothetical, Miss O'Brien. Let's say you're an international terrorist. A member of the IRA, even? Say you had done your duty as you saw fit and as you were commanded to do. Then you were forced to run, to change your identity, to hide for years cut off from the land and people you love and fought for. And after all those sacrifices, I, a humble ship's captain with a dubious past, stumble onto your secret identity. You catch me, in point of fact, going through your diary, reading of your former exploits. You do not know me well, but I have been friendly, engaging even. Yet my stories do not ring quite true. I am hiding a piece of me. And this hidden piece could spell your doom. Your fate would rest in my hands unless you took some sort of action to ensure that I would not tell others of your secret life. Do you see what I mean? How all this complicates matters? For, even if you are what you purport to be, even if my Nazi past is more a plus than a minus for a person from Ireland, still . . . even if you are sympathetic, what guarantee have I that you would not speak or write of me at the wrong time and place? That you would not unwittingly give me away? Yes. I see you finally understand. The world is a very serious place, Miss O'Brien. Not a playground, after all. I am not here simply as story material for you to harvest."

"But I wouldn't—"

"Please, Miss O'Brien. You propose the most facile of arguments. 'You wouldn't say a word.' But this is a time for higher analysis. Promises have no power with me. It is certainties that I am after. And I am afraid that you have none to give me. I can't think clearly now. I don't want to do the wrong thing . . . to act too rashly."

"You're beginning to frighten me, Señor ____. And that's not wise, either. I want to cooperate with you. I agree that this is largely my fault. I want to convince you that you have nothing to fear from me. But this talk is beginning to scare me shitless. I mean, it sounds—"

"You are right, Miss O'Brien. All this is most unorthodox. And it must be scaring you. Cooler heads will prevail in the morning. But for now, I must insist that you be my guest."

"It doesn't sound like an invitation to me."

"You may choose to hear it as you like. I do require you to remain here where I can guarantee that you will be incommunicado. Until I—we—decide how to proceed. Agreed?"

"Have I any choice? It's either that, or a wrestling match with you."

"Nothing so barbaric, I assure you."

"Do you always carry a weapon?"

"Always, Miss O'Brien. Old habits die hard. May I show you to your room?"

PART II

Wednesday.

I cannot bring myself to deal with the Irish yet. I sit at my trestle table watching the jungle outside my windows, but I feel cut off from it. It is merely a surrealist painting. This disconnected feeling has not overcome me for several decades, and of course it is Miss O'Brien's doing. Why did she have to enter my serenity and destroy it with her snooping? Why did she have to spread her chaos into my well-ordered existence. My white-stucco home with its red-tile roof no longer feels like a fortress; the refectory table and priceless ladder-back chairs in the dining room no longer look as substantial as they once did. The two leather armchairs in front of my huge stucco fireplace no longer seem snug.

I have just returned from leaving food inside the door to the guest room on the second floor, and barely escaped with my life, for the Irish was waiting for me behind the door with a priceless copy of the Bible in her hands, which I leave in that room for the contemplative. To use such a sacred book as a weapon! The woman is insane. She would have struck me with it, too, if I had not instinctively sensed the danger and drawn back just as the book swept by my face. Miss O'Brien, thrown off balance by the force of the intended blow, tottered drunkenly past me, the Bible still gripped maniacally in her hands. I was able to wrestle it out of her clutches—no telling what she would have done with the lovely old thing—and shut the door against the tattoo that her fists beat on the wood as I left.

Clearly, I must find an alternate form of accommodation for her: She is much too loud and violent to be held in a conventional room. Fortunately, there are heavy metal shutters outside her windows, which I closed last night, locking them from the outside. The door to the room is a massive construction of oak planks held together by wrought-iron flanges. She is secure enough for the time being, but over the long haul?

I am not up to further confrontations; I have no plan for Miss O'Brien. I only know I would like to work this morning. Lord knows I slept little last night with my new guest howling only doors away. Most of the night I spent recording the events of the day and then, unaccountably, I began to think of Miranda. My memories skip and jump like a needle on a well-worn record album.

Through work, perhaps I can find my connectedness once again. The solution to the "Irish problem" will surely come to me. Now for some writing.

The first years here were, of course, the most difficult. A young man, I had biological needs to fill. But I could hardly be expected to take a native woman to my bed, nor could I risk a long relationship with any of the locals of so-called European stock. Instead, I paid monthly visits to C____, the provincial capital, and to one particular establishment there. A very proper and upright place it is, as well. The madam, Señora Flores, has none of the lasciviousness usually associated with the trade. She is very male in this regard: She runs a business, and matters are conducted in a businesslike manner. She will, in fact, interview prospective clients upon their first visit. Quite civilized: sherry and a cigar served in her downstairs study.

There is none of the silliness of half-clad women disporting themselves under potted palms for Señora Flores. She determines, after going through her list of detailed questions with the prospective customer, which of the girls will suit the prospective client best.

Señora Flores's establishment makes one feel at home. It is not as if one has come to her house to perform some outlandish act—for sexual gymnastics there are other houses, most particularly the infamous Pigalle. Cordoba has the quaint habit of referring to that brothel as Pig Alley.

For thirty years, I frequented Señora Flores's business, perhaps once a month on average. Such visits would be only part of my regular trips to C____ to pick up supplies both for the *Clan* and for the house. In other words, these visits were always kept part of the quotidian, for sex is something I have always tried to maintain in its proper place, not allowing it to intrude into one's outer, professional life. Even on my honeymoon, I resisted the temptation to interject it into the range of our normal daytime activities. Sex is a chaotic force: Women live by such chaos, while a man's one impulse, instinct, is toward order. Man and woman are of two different worlds. We rightly have two separate spheres. There should be no talk of sharing these spheres, or of bridging the gap with communication, absurd psychological insights, or even with quasi-scientific self-examination. Chaos and order: These do not compromise with each other. They simply stay separate.

Well, for thirty years, I was able to delegate my sexual appetites to a succession of young women. (It is surprising, or perhaps not surprising depending on one's level of cynicism in this regard, how many of these girls later turned up as wives to some of the wealthiest industrialists and most powerful militarists in C____.) My couplings, far from merely businesslike, were also a far cry from amatory. They were physical and pleasant enough, in fact. Often even quite erotic. This erotic element was enhanced in no little part by the transitory nature of such relationships. In all those years, I never saw one girl more than four times. This resulted not only from Señora Flores's constant turnover of girls, but also because of my own curiosity and self-defense mechanisms. I did not want involvement: I wanted and received ultimate variety.

Then, one Saturday night, I went to Señora Flores only to find her house full of freshly scrubbed and slightly intoxicated rustics: a conference of coffee growers had taken over the entire town for the weekend. I would not have bothered coming into town that weekend had I known of the conference, but once there I was damned if I would let an invasion of hicks throw me off my schedule.

My regular, Rosa—that is, the woman I had seen twice before—was occupied. This knowledge did little to fuel my passion. One has no illusions about such women, of course; neither does one want to look eye to eye with the fellow who has just spread his semen in one's sometimes sexual partner.

I sat for a time in the parlor, quite alone, I thought, and feeling like a man grown too old for such foolishness. I was about to take my leave when I suddenly noticed that sitting there all the while was a very young, very slight woman. I had not noticed her before, as she had been sitting motionless in a chair stuck into the deepest recess of the room as if not wanting to draw attention to herself.

She was a pale little thing, homely almost, with large almond eyes over a hawklike nose. Her cheeks were as sunken as those one sometimes saw in the camps during the war. Something about her helpless, plaintive demeanor attracted me to her, as one is attracted to the sufferings of a poor animal. I smiled; she blushed. Perhaps I had made a mistake? Perhaps one of those stupid, insensitive farmers had actually brought along a daughter or servant who had been forced to wait downstairs while the *padrón* did his business upstairs? But this simply couldn't be, I thought. Señora Flores would never allow such a thing in her establishment. Yet this girl continued to look very uncomfortable under my gaze.

Perhaps it is my age that affects her so, I thought. The thought of coupling with a man in his sixties must be disgusting to this young girl of say, twenty at the most.

At that moment Señora Flores bustled into the parlor, attired in a bright floral kimono, her blond wig slightly askew. Finding me gazing at the youngster, she clapped her hands delightedly.

"So you have finally met! I was hoping you two would hit it off."

"Actually—" I began, but Señora Flores cut me short.

"So sorry we couldn't have our usual little chat, Señor ____. But you see how hectic things are here. All topsy-turvy with the coffee growers in town." She turned toward the girl: "Miranda, take our friend upstairs. There's a good girl. The red room."

Then to me: "You'll find a bottle of Moselle chilling, Señor ____. And please do forgive my seeming bad manners in not greeting you earlier tonight." Then coming closer, Señora Flores whispered in my ear: "She's a sweet child. I would trust her with no other man her first time."

Señora Flores hurried out of the room before I could protest her trust. I felt little inclined this night to the momentous task of inaugurating a virgin. The child rose: She was no taller than the young boy who sometimes cleans fish aboard the *Clan*. She moved listlessly, without a word, toward the stairs. At first, I did not follow, and, from the first landing, she looked back at me, her moist eyes cast down under her long, black lashes. It was not so much a beckoning glance as a recognition. I followed.

Upstairs in the red room, she fussed over the wine. Obviously Señora Flores had instructed her in the ways of the wine steward, though the lesson had just as obviously been inexpertly learned. She managed to break off the cork in what looked to be a tolerably decent '65 vintage of Moselle. Without speaking a word, I took the corkscrew from her trembling hand and pried the rest of the cork out, then cleared the lip of the bottle with a splash into my glass, which I threw into the sink.

"You don't like the wine, sir?"

I laughed and explained what I had done.

"Do you always drink wine?"

She asked this as if such an activity marked me as special, as a man of the world. I must have seemed as cosmopolitan to her as if I junketed around the world on an expense account.

"Not as often as I would like to," I told her and took a sip of the wine. It was too sweet. "It's not the easiest thing to come by here." I put the glass down on the small table with the bottle.

"My father used to drink the local beer."

"Smart man," I said. "The wise and economical minded sticks to what is domestically manufactured, and they have a quite decent beer here."

It was a lie, both parts of the statement, but "he used to" had not escaped me. I wanted to be gentle with the girl.

"You're from the town?" I asked.

She seemed not to hear me.

"Madame says you are a gentleman."

"I hope I am."

"That would be good for me."

She stood near the bed—it is impossible to stand anywhere in the red room at Señora Flores's and not be near that gigantic bed. I was hardly overcome with desire. It was all too pat, and much too demanding of the eventual outcome. Señora Flores, usually so conscious of subtleties, had put us in the worst room in the house. It was one disallowing any function save that of fornication, and rather athletic stuff at that, as the size of the playing field indicated.

Miranda stood in such sharp contrast to the room with its livid red curtains and matching satin bedspread that it made me smile. She was so small and frail looking that it appeared she would shatter if touched. Yet again, I was drawn to her eyes, now half covered with bangs of luxurious black shiny hair that hung down deep over her forehead. She brushed them back with the palm of her right hand and looked at me almost defiantly.

"Do you think you could be?"

"How's that?" I asked.

"Good for me. The first time. I need to learn of love."

This said, and not waiting for my reply, she unbuttoned her blouse and slipped it from her shoulders, revealing silky white skin so unlike the sallow color of her face. It was delicious skin: taut, sweet-smelling, and downy. Her tiny breasts were perfectly formed and crowned with nipples of an elegant pink hue. This was a transformation that suddenly exactly suited the precincts of the red room; a transformation that so excited me that I felt in the grips of another Frau Wotruba.

I see no sense in minutely describing each action of my life. Particularly the "bedroom" scenes. I have no desire to share this part, to risk prurience by depiction. The silky feel of her skin against mine, the weightlessness of her body, the surprise of the rose tattoo on her left buttock, her hip bones jutting against me, a secret provocative region just under her left ear, her big toe scratching along my shin, her tiny hands in the small of my back, these are the impressionistic recollections of that coupling—and of subsequent ones.

But far more meaningful than any of the animal "meltings" we experienced (that was Miranda's way of describing the sexual act) was the connection we developed with each other as human beings. Slowly, incrementally, almost imperceptibly, Miranda became an intimate of mine, privy to my insides as well as my exterior. She was only nineteen when we first met and, despite what Señora Flores said, she was no virgin. That state had been altered by her father six years before we met. I did not care. But I did begin to care *for* her, to miss her even between visits to Señora Flores's establishment. The spectacle of it: me, a man more than three times her age, doting on each word Miranda uttered, suffering pangs of jealousy about other customers so acute that in the end I paid the money to keep her solely for myself. I set her up in a domestic nest: a studio apartment in the hills above the old city. My monthly visits became weekly, and even at that, the intervals seemed too long for me.

Miranda, whose smell still lingers in my nostrils. Just like the lullaby Frau Wotruba sang to me as a child, Miranda's particular scent is conjured up to me every so often, seemingly out of nowhere. In ways, she is in my blood: It is as if I sweat her out of me still.

———

Several days have passed since last taking up my pen. The sea is no longer calm. Autumn tides have begun. This morning, I had to make a special trip to the harbor to secure the *Clan*. Out at the major bathing beach, waves were crashing over the seawall, spilling foam onto the road. Even here at the house, I can hear the waves at night. The rain has been coming in torrents, as well. The seasons have turned the corner.

I have accommodated Miss O'Brien as best as I know how in the guest room, but I now am preparing more pleasant quarters for her in the basement. We shall see. She refuses to adjust to the realities of the situation: It will take time.

Señor Alvarado at the hotel did not seem in the least surprised when I went to fetch her things. He is not the type to ask questions, and of course it helped matters when I offered to pay for the rest of her reservation. Neither did Señor Alvarado comment on my explanation that Miss O'Brien had been suddenly taken ill and was returning to the North. A discreet man is Señor Alvarado.

I must admit that Miss O'Brien, upon seeing me bring her suitcases and portable typewriter to her, broke into a momentary fit of hysteria. I believe she had been holding out hope that such detritus of her life would ultimately effect her rescue. She was unaware of how deeply enmeshed in the infrastructure I am here. She is the outsider, the unwanted one here. This fact only became apparent to her when I brought her things.

"How did you get these?"

"I thought you might need a change of clothes."

"He had no right to give them to you!"

"I also took the liberty of checking you out of the hotel. Such a waste of money."

"You have no right."

"In point of fact, it is said in the village that you were taken ill and are now back in New York."

"How long do you intend keeping me here?"

"—"

"I have friends. They know where I am. My editor, my agent. They'll start asking questions."

"I hope you have been warm enough. Nights turn a bit chilly this time of the year."

The evening chorus of the ravine came in through the open window.

"I can't stand that noise! It's driving me fucking out of my skull. You can't do this. They'll catch you. Look, I promise. I'd never tell. Never. I don't give a bloody hoot what you've done. Please. Please."

———

Of course I feel badly about the situation, too. It is not enjoyable keeping the Irish locked in that room, pointing a revolver at her every time I bring her something—she has attacked me three times already, hiding behind the door, in the closet, under the bed, actually using a fork one time. She is reduced now to eating with a spoon only. Nor do I take any joy in having to stand guard outside the toilet as she passes water. This is surely an insupportable situation. Inhuman, even, to guest and host alike.

The alternative that immediately suggests itself is more than logical, it is prescribed: I should eliminate her. After all, it is not I who has gone snooping into her affairs, thereby endangering her. I did not request that she come into my life and turn up the past. In a way, it is as if she deserves death, as if she has willed it upon herself. Yet I cannot bring myself to do it: to put a gun to the back of her head and pull the trigger. It is a ghastly thought. Or to slip poison into her food. Even if out of earshot, I would "hear" her subsequent retching and gagging for the rest of my life. I suppose I could have Cordoba get in touch with certain of his less-than-savory friends to do the deed for me, but that would rest even worse on my conscience.

No. Contrary to Herr Wiesenthal and the kangaroo court at Nuremberg, I am no killer. Not of defenseless ones, at any rate.

There is another alternative, one that I have already alluded to, and that is to make Miss O'Brien's living conditions somewhat better and on a more or less permanent basis. I need to house her with me long enough so that I will know positively what she would or would not do with the information she now has. Besides, I am coming to rather enjoy the notion of having her nearby for a time. Of course she rails at the idea now: Soon enough, she will calm down and become real company for me. It's strange how quickly one adapts to the absence of loneliness.

To this end, I have begun renovations on the basement room. She hears me hammering down there and asks me what is happening: Am I building her gallows? But I do not answer these sallies. I want it to be a surprise for her. I am outfitting the space quite nicely, as a matter of fact. There really should be everything that a young woman could want in a room. I have used all my designing ingenuity to make it look quite special, unique, cozy and warm.

From a spare single bed, I have constructed a fairy-tale four-poster canopy bed. I even created a frilly border to the canopy out of the flounces of one of Miranda's old dresses. There are no windows in the basement, but I have unrolled some of the canvases I brought with me from Europe: a Waldmüller, two von Alts, and an attributed Rubens, though I rather believe this is from the school of Rubens and not from the brush of the master himself. I also constructed passable frames for these pictures. It has been so many years since I last viewed these glorious things—ironic that it should take the Irish for me to reinstitute my art gallery! The paintings now grace the cinder-block walls of the basement room.

I have covered the cement floor with matting, and atop this, I have laid several of the local woven Indian rugs, giving some gay color to the place. I purchased a leather armchair, slightly used, but with a lot of life left in it yet, and also a standing lamp. These now provide a cheery niche where Miss O'Brien can read at night. There is also a table, rough-hewn but serviceable, and two basket chairs.

The only thing Miss O'Brien now lacks in her little nest is running water. I constructed a little alcove in one corner with a draw curtain on a wire. Here I have placed a chemical toilet and washstand. She can bathe whenever she likes upstairs, but this will supply her with a bit of freedom and independence from me. It also ensures my own privacy.

Best of all, this room is so separate from the top story of

my residence that I can have visitors over without worrying that they will discover my little secret. It is a regular bunker down here in the basement—a romantic notion of mine when constructing the house, a sort of last refuge in case of discovery. In those years, I very seriously considered such a dramatic last stand against Israeli agents who might show up some moonless night. Such thoughts, however, became too morbid for me all alone in the jungle, and I never got around to outfitting the basement bunker properly. For my few intimates, it became something of a joke: my own private white elephant. But now it has finally come in handy.

Tomorrow, I shall introduce Miss O'Brien to her new home. I am as anxious as a small boy waiting to open Christmas presents!

———

The great masters, we are told, wrote, painted, or composed out of pain. What such a good burgher and great artist as J. S. Bach, however, knew of pain—other than arthritic— with his happy domestic life and material success, I am at a loss to say. Nonetheless, it is true that self-expression becomes a palliative to inner turmoil and emotional pain.

What are the great pains we feel? Loss, betrayal, jealousy, unrequited love, sometimes even love itself. Love, of course, is the least trustworthy of emotions, the most fickle, the least responsive to self-regulation. One could well argue, in fact, that all one's life is ruled by the presence or absence of that one emotion, that one feeling wrapped up in the trappings of a four-letter word.

But I digress. Are these memoirs, these stories from my past and present, only a transliteration of pain? Must one truly hurt to truly feel?

I earlier stated that I am a romantic. I am also a sentimentalist. Yet I like to believe that my emotional thermostat is set just this side of maudlin and kitsch. I do not like to think of myself as melodramatic or portentous. But today I hurt; today I write out of pain.

All my good work has, it seems, gone for naught. I became so involved in the redecoration and refurbishing of the basement room that I lost sight of its primary purpose: that of a safe place in which to incarcerate a potential enemy. Instead, I became positively Christmas-y about the project, finding more and more things to make it perfect, relishing the moment when I should unveil the room to Miss O'Brien, savoring her elated reactions to such a wonderful gift, basking in her delight and respect.

Alas, I sorely misjudged the recipient. Instead of praises, my work won jeers; instead of admiration, there was rebuke. First, Miss O'Brien attacked my taste, then, my very sanity. She called me a "death machine," a "breathing cadaver." I cull these epithets from the tape transcription—it is too disturbing for me to reprint it in its totality. One approbation particularly stung:

"You're a necrophile, can't you see that? You want to encase me here like some fertility symbol, some fucking stone Madonna that you can pick out of your collection when the spirit moves you. It's not my knowledge of your past that frightens you, that makes you imprison me. No, you aren't human or man enough to even kill me. It's not self-preservation that motivates you but death. Stagnation. Rot. And you want to make me just like you. But I won't have it!"

At this point, she actually began scratching with her fingernails at one of the priceless oils on the walls—that from the Rubens school. She was like one possessed of a devil, and I had finally to subdue her with an injection—I have a prescription for a powerful sleeping draught that I always keep on hand against my insomnia.

The outburst was horrible, really. After she had calmed down and was sleeping, I carried her to the fairy-tale bed and propped her up against the pillows. (This very same bed that moments before she had reviled as absurd and bourgeois, accusing me of attempting to make her my little doll.) Once lain out on the bed, she looked quite beautiful, like Sleeping Beauty waiting for the prince's kiss. So peaceful and serene, lovely really, with her hair flowing over her shoulders. I touched her face. It was warm, vital, the skin tight. She has freckles on her eyelids, which I had not before noticed. My hand moved down her cheek, across her throat and the strong pulsing artery there. I felt the collarbone under her blue shirt. It was as if she were tempting me, daring me by her very passivity to continue. Her breathing was loud, almost a snore. I unbuttoned the top of her shirt and saw the beginning of cleavage. Here too she was freckled. The skin was firm, warm to the touch. I traced my fingernail along it and watched the skin turn white and then red where I had lightly scratched. I touched the next button, but stopped. After all, a man must live by some principles. Yet after such an unfeminine display of pique, she really deserved no better handling.

No, I thought. *This would be just what she would need to fuel her attacks on me.* So I left her there peacefully sleeping in her new quarters on the bed she professes to despise.

I locked the door behind me, went upstairs, and here I sit at my desk now, looking out at the ravine, thinking about pain and creation.

It is raining. Palm fronds hop to the fat drops of moisture falling on them.

I am afflicted with the I-should-have-said syndrome. Of course, like most men of action, I am utterly helpless in a dialectic. Silence is my best course in a battle of verbal pyrotechnics. But her words stung; I wish I could have parried a thrust or two with my own truths, such as:

"If I am indeed a necrophile, then what attracts you to me? Why thrust yourself into my life, wanting to make me the protagonist of your book, as you insist?"

Or:

"Journalists are the ultimate necrophiles, the only winners in any war. The collectors of woeful tales, the capturers of souls on photosensitive paper. Who but a journalist could stand by as children are shot, calmly recording the event for their voyeuristic audiences?"

Or:

"My stone Madonna is far warmer than you."

I must guard against using the Irish's phrase for my Kreuzberg Venus. Journalists are most adept at labeling things. What seems a harmless description becomes, at one remove, ironic and sinister. I know what she was implying by her "stone Madonna" business. She sees me as the sort of man who does not want to participate in the to-and-fro of emotional life, who is more comfortable by far with the symbols and trappings of love than with the muck of it, the sometimes unwilling flesh of it. The mess and chaos of human love and loving. It is the typical female argument of man's inability to engage on the fullest, deepest emotional level. And it is pure garbage. It is not that man cannot participate thusly, only that most choose not to. Most men prefer a more elevated union.

Yes, there are many things I could have told Miss O'Brien, but she was in no condition to listen. Histrionics cannot be met with reasoned argument. She does not even understand the importance of the Venus for me. She would make me a mere lepidopterist, a collector of objects and people. But Miss O'Brien was possessed by her hormones at the time—there was no possibility of rational discussion. Perhaps after a day or two of injections, she will recover her senses.

My Venus sits in front of me at this very moment: I have taken it down from the mantel for a closer inspection. It is heavy, incredibly so for sandstone. I acquired this lovely artifact from a spa near Melk in Austria, Bad Kreuzberg. Quite by accident, one of the prisoners in the satellite camp at Melk uncovered her while breaking ground for new camp buildings. As ranking officer of the detail, I fell into possession of this prehistoric "lady." Of course, this jumps ahead of my biographical narrative; I shall deal with those years in the camps in their proper place. This simply to explain the long possession of my Kreuzberg Venus. But Miss O'Brien is wrong about her, about my Kreuzberg Venus, on two counts; she says, and I quote: "You want to encase me here like some fertility symbol, some fucking stone Madonna that you can pick out of your collection when the spirit moves you."

Well, she is patently wrong. I do not wish to make Miss O'Brien into an object in my collection, nor is the Kreuzberg Venus a fertility symbol, despite what all the so-called anthropologists say!

As an icon of fertility, I cannot imagine one less inspirational of devotion, not to mention ardor. But I realize that perhaps you, gentle reader, have no idea of what I am speaking of. I refer to the squat, bulbous stone objects that doubtless you have seen, perhaps without quite realizing what they are. Ancient stone carvings—some twenty-five thousand years old, in fact. And the feminist anthroapologists have made much of the fact of these first "ladies" of history. Their provenance is quite widespread over Europe and represents one of man's first three-dimensional plastic creations. And they are immensely, nay, hideously fat. Our intellectuals tell us that they are representatives of Mother Earth, of fertility. Granted, fashions change over the millennia, in body types no less than in clothes. Perhaps in that dark time of perpetual winter when the "Venuses" were created, fat truly was beautiful. But these Venuses are not simply fat—they are quite frankly past their prime. Gravity, as Miss O'Brien joked, has played its cruel joke upon their flesh. No man in his right mind would worship at such a female altar. These statues are, indeed, the best birth control method of all time. Earth Mother they may be, but the mother of one's forebears, rather than one's own children. Venus is perhaps as large a misnomer as is the Irish's "stone Madonna."

In truth, these figures are the Crone—a foreshadowing of where we are all headed. A foretaste of eternity.

My Kreuzberg Venus is to me as the skull was to St. Jerome. Life in the shadows of the gallows concentrates one wonderfully on living, as it must have our Stone Age friends, as well. Such is the symbolic program of the Kreuzberg Venus: a *memento mori* rather than *memento fertilis*.

Writing out of pain; it is what God intended for us.

It is the spring of 1939, a magical time for me. Never shall there be another match for that spring. This was eleven years after the incident with Frau Wotruba. The next crystalline moment—or in this case, interval—that I pick out of the storehouse of my memories. It was a three-fold time of magic for me.

I had just finished my studies and my law exam scores were posted in the university foyer for all to see. The elation of finding the "2" next to my name! I stood by the corkboard where it was posted for a full two hours that afternoon, watching the other students come, their faces white, puckered—as nervous as mine had been when first coming to check on the exam results. Some of these faces brightened as they saw the results. These had passed the first hurdle in life and would be going on out into the great world, as I myself was. Others went even whiter in the face upon seeing their grades. For these, it would be a failure from which they would never recover.

I wondered if these failures saw the "2" next to my name and wished they were me. More than wondered—I rather hoped they did. I had long enough wanted to be one of them: a middle-class university student from a good home. Instead, I was the son of a tobacconist from the Wieden district, for by now, my father had been six years dead, victim of angina brought on, Mother always swore, by the quantities of wine that he somehow managed to consume. Mother had taken Father's life insurance and gambled, investing in a tobacco shop that ultimately supported us quite well. Yet still, the Viennese are very like the British about this point: Money made in trade is not really quite as clean as that from land, the professions, or even from inheritance. Inheritance: Now that is the great launderer of money!

It was that spring also when I fell in love with and became engaged to a woman for whom I was prepared to work and sacrifice that we might start a life together.

Ursula was her name: I knew her by the sobriquet of Uschi. Uschi von Danzel.

The von Danzels, despite their "von," had their status (rather more status than money) from the professions. They were a long line of doctors; ear, nose, and throat was their specialty. Uschi's uncle had, in fact, performed a biopsy on Freud's mouth cancer, a matter of little more than jesting account at the time, but one that takes on increasing importance for me as the years pass. How often the fate of that one Jew touched the borders of my life!

A ranking family, then. One that it would be a great advancement for me to join.

Imagine my surprise when, on the night we announced our engagement, Uschi finally introduced me to her family, and the men were all ranking Schutzstaffel members. By mentioning this, I do not abdicate responsibility for joining the Staffel. Admittedly, having future in-laws in positions of power made my entrance into the Black Corps much easier than it would have been had I submitted my name independently. With someone to vouch for my character and my potential (for it was all I had to trade on in those early days before actively beginning my profession), I was ensured a ranking position after officer cadet school.

But going to the von Danzels' that evening in the spring of 1939, I had not the slightest idea of what awaited me. Uschi had been cautious about introducing me to her family, fearful of their disapprobation. With the successful completion of my law degree, however, I was somebody substantial enough to bring home to dinner without Mummy and Daddy throwing a fit. I should have taken warning from this but was much too naive about the ways of women and the world to take note at the time. I had met one of Uschi's brothers before. We had gotten on all right, as those sharing a conspiracy may do. For that was what Uschi's relationship with me had been at that time: a conspiracy. There had been the usual bantering jokes that men make with each other in vain attempts at creating intimacy. Vain because man is always and forever in competition with other men. He had not worn his black uniform at that meeting: I only knew he was a pharmacy student in his last year and that he hoped to open a chemists shop in the fashionable Josefstadt, for which opportunity he would need no little amount of money. I assumed that, for the von Danzels, this was no problem.

Uschi's father had more or less honorary rank in the Staffel. The brother, Joachim, the budding pharmacist, had gone through the elaborate yearlong training process. Once he passed the crucial racial vetting, he had been accepted into the Clan on November 9, 1938, the date honoring the famous Beer Hall Putsch in Munich fifteen years before. On January 30, another holy day for the party—the date when the Nazis came to power in 1933—Joachim had been accepted as a cadet and was given a provisional pass into the Staffel. Finally, on April 20, Hitler's birthday, he had sworn his oath of allegiance, unto death, to Hitler. At that point, he received his permanent Staffel pass and the collar patches—one oak leaf, in his case. He was now awaiting active service in the coming October, and from that time, he would be permitted to wear the silver dagger that so complemented the blackness of the uniform.

How I longed to wear such a smart uniform! How I longed, after that night with the von Danzels, and spurred by Uschi, to join such an elite club as the Clan!

This was of course no will-o'-the-wisp decision on my part. By the spring of 1939, for quite some time, I had seen the advantages that admission into the Staffel could provide. All the best people were members; the connections one would accumulate with such membership were an absolute requirement for a beginning lawyer such as myself. I do not shrink from absolute honesty: I was a callow, self-centered youth. When I went with Joachim several days later to register with the local Staffel offices on Jasomirgottstrasse, it was with the most material intentions in mind. I joined the Clan more out of a need for what it could do for me than vice versa. Though this self-serving motivation changed radically and abruptly once I put the black uniform on, I must still confess to less than noble intentions at the outset of my career in the Staffel.

But this joining of the Staffel, for whatever naive reasons at the time, completed the triumvirate of exquisite and life-determining decisions I made in that, my twenty-third year.

"Get out of here!"

"You have to eat."

"___"

"You'll feel better if you do. Really. Trust me."

"That's a fucking laugh."

"___"

"You really don't understand a thing, do you? All right, I'll spell it out for you. Why the hell should I trust you? Why should anyone? You're fucking crazy. You've kidnapped me. Threatened me with death. Drugged me. Stuffed me into this paradise of kitsch. Now you want me to trust you. Fine. Fucking fine. Say I'm free to go, then I'll trust you."

"I know what is best for you, Miss O'Brien. In these matters, believe me, I am an expert."

"Oh, I'm sure you had enough experience in the camps."

"If you do not eat, you will sicken and die. At this point, I am not prepared to allow such an eventuality."

"A fucking humanitarian."

"If you do not eat, I shall have to give you further injections and feed you intravenously. It is your choice."

———

"That's better. You look as though you slept well last night. And your appetite is picking up. Didn't I tell you so, Miss O'Brien?"

"___"

"Well, I dare say you'll want to talk sometime. It gets frightfully lonely . . ."

"Yes, *mein Herr*?"

"That. On the wall. You did that?"

"A bit of artwork only. Since you took away the paintings . . ."

"That smell. It's . . . You couldn't have. The lowest of animals wouldn't."

"Don't be squeamish, *mein Herr*. I'm sure you saw worse in the camps."

———

"I'm bored. I need writing materials. Even in your friends' jails, they supply that."

"My friends?"

"You know. Argentina. Chile. Nice places like that."

"___"

"Well? Come on. What harm can it do? And it may placate me. You never know. Keep me from further ventures into the visual arts. In fact, I'll make a deal. I'm changing mediums. No more excreta artworks if I can have paper and pencil. Okay?"

"You promise?"

"Yes."

"It really was disgusting of you, Miss O'Brien. I would never have believed a woman such as you capable of that."

"Even Pope's Celia shits."

"—"

"All right. Sorry. Just get me the paper and pencil. Please."

"Very well."

———

"Still writing? Were you at it all night, then?"

"I slept some. Don't know when or how long. I've gone day-for-night down here. No clocks, no daylight. Nothing to tell me if I should be tired or not."

"You know, I hadn't thought of that."

"How long have I been down here?"

"Not long. A couple of weeks."

"What's it like outside?"

"Fall storms. It's been frightfully wet, actually. Good weather for staying indoors."

"I guess I should be grateful to you. For keeping me dry."

"Do I detect irony, Miss O'Brien? That's a sure sign you're coming around. I would like to think so."

———

The rains have somewhat abated. I have, after transcribing these last dialogues, been thinking about Miss O'Brien's living arrangements. She has not directly complained, but I do see how disorienting it must be living without the benchmarks of sunrise and sunset to standardize one's days. Admittedly, this was not part of my intent in housing her in the basement. Security was foremost in that regard. A soundproof space removed from any possible prying eyes. That was my one intent. I know that sense deprivation is a standard drill with political prisoners, yet that is only an unintended side effect to my primary concerns for safety. I should somehow correct this situation. Miss O'Brien is showing, finally, less tendency to hysteria. Though I know I have written such before only to be subsequently fooled. But now, after nearly a month here (you see, I lied to her—though for her own good so as not to unduly depress her—about the length of time she has been here), she truly seems to have settled into her new life. No more of those terrible incidents with the feces on the wall. No more tantrums. No more attempted attacks with the food tray as I enter. Hardly even a sulk since I supplied her with writing materials. But I know the human body needs fresh air and daylight; we can not long survive without these. Exist perhaps, but not truly live. Following this line of thinking, I have given consideration to converting the dog run at the back of the house. Crudely built, but securely caged, it is part of the residue of my early years here when I felt it important to keep watch dogs. *Schäferhund* primarily, which the English so strangely call German shepherds. They were, ironically, good shepherds for this benighted German. But when they died, I found the loss so excruciatingly painful that it became, in the long run, better to remain alone than to know one would outlive another canine companion.

At any rate, after examination, I have found the dog run is still in good order. Some little repair work is needed here and there, but otherwise it will provide an excellent exercise yard for Miss O'Brien. Large enough to work up a good stiff pace back and forth. It is also built right up to the door in back. Thus, it would be a simple matter to escort her from her lodgings to the outdoor enclosure. Whether or not we can begin with outdoor exercises will depend on her behavior the next few days. After all, I can hardly be expected to countenance a woman's hysterics out of doors. Removed as I am here, there is always the possibility that someone might be passing by or approaching the house. I must ensure that Miss O'Brien will preserve decorum while outside. Ironically, I must trust her before she trusts me.

Cordoba came last night for our regular card game. I must confess that the day had slipped my mind, so busy had I been preparing Miss O'Brien's compound. And he came on foot. He laments that his Ford is well and truly dead this time. He has reached the end of his tether over that car; he has had enough of the constant repairs it requires to stay on the road. He spoke glowingly of my battered old Land Rover, as if he were a suitor talking to the father of the beloved. I hope he has no designs on that machine, for I should hate to disappoint him and thereby lose a fine card partner.

But his arrival by foot and my forgetting what was formerly a most important date on my calendar combined to give me quite a startle. I was still below working on the dog run when I heard his voice. It seems he'd been pounding on the front door for some time before deciding to investigate further. He did not explain himself, but I assume he meant he was afraid that the old German gaffer might finally have checked out, and he might have to force entrance into the house to discover my bloated and stinking corpse. Thus, he had let himself in.

There he stood on the little escarpment over the dog run (one can only get to the back by going through the house; there is no walkway around the steep ravine in back). I was dressed rough in khakis and high boots, warily clearing the encroaching foliage from the compound. Miss O'Brien, if true to her fellow countrymen, would have had little experience with reptiles. I wished to give the little creatures no cover in which to hide. Cordoba smiled that he had caught me off guard. It was the first time in the long period of our friendship that he had done so. But he did not question what I was doing. He is much too subtle for that.

I, however, felt myself go into a cold sweat. This would surely be the test of the basement's soundproofing. There was no way of knowing whether or not Miss O'Brien had heard Cordoba's knocking at the front door, or his calling to me. I doubted if it would be a very profitable night for me at cards, with my mind continually going back downstairs to Miss O'Brien rather than at the card table with Cordoba. I apologized profusely that I had forgotten the card night, for I had also neglected to prepare anything for dinner. Usually Cordoba and I have fish—either fresh or frozen—that I have caught. He supplies the wine, which I now saw in his hand. I would have to throw something together from tins, and I detest doing that. It affronts my sensibilities, and moreover, it reminds me of the hard years toward the end of the war. Rather absurd, living in this land of infinite bounty, that one should ever be forced to consume food from a jar or tin. But there it is. No choice. This sudden realization also brought me up short vis-à-vis my relations with Miss O'Brien. Was I not perhaps becoming overly involved, even to the point of forgetting the all-important monthly card game? Surely such absorption in another was unhealthy. But I had no time to pursue this avenue of self-inquiry. I had to get inside, freshen up, and throw something together for dinner.

First, I made Cordoba a bracing drink—he enjoys martinis. I believe he acquired the taste through seeing American movies, and as I have no idea of how to make them other than from information supplied from the same source, we make a perfect match. I prepared a large shaker of the stuff and left it at his side in the living room—he was seated happily in one of the large armchairs, the national paper in his lap.

I went off to the shower. Hurrying with my toilet, I put on white ducks, espadrilles, and a fresh polo shirt (we keep the evenings casual but festive) and began bustling about in the kitchen. Cordoba did not bother with conversation as long as I was in the kitchen. He never does. Quite content with his martini and paper, he sat quietly in the living room as I concocted a tuna soufflé with asparagus au gratin on the side. The tuna I had put up myself, but the flavor is never so rich as that fresh or freshly frozen. He tolerated it, however; Cordoba was even quite flattering of my culinary skills as we sat down to dinner finally. The bottle of Moselle he brought, by now chilled, went quite well with the dish. All in all, the dinner was fine and put both of us in a good humor for cards. Cordoba cleaned the dishes as is the usual custom, and I set out the green felt cloth and readied the cards and plastic chips.

After many years of vacillating, we have finally settled on gin rummy as our preferred game. For some months, we toyed with Brazilian canasta, basically a free-for-all of canasta in which rules are stood on their head as all else is in that immense, confused country. But, in the end, this suited neither of us. Gin rummy, on the other hand, was fast enough and demanded only a modicum of concentration so that I could get down to the real task of the evening: listening and reacting to Cordoba's lode of local gossip.

A quick bit of background on Cordoba: We would seem, at first sight, to make an unlikely duo. But our connection is quite logical, for Cordoba is not just some backwoods rustic. His father was this country's ambassador to Berlin during the war. Cordoba was, in fact, born in Germany and spent his first ten years of life there. He still speaks the rough Berlin dialect that he picked up from the gardeners and servants at his father's embassy.

The way Cordoba tells it, he spent a hurdy-gurdy childhood given free run of the place. His mother had died in childbirth and his father was much too busy with official business to tend to his young son. After the war, Cordoba's father went out of favor with his government at home; he had been away so long that his domestic power base had eroded. He retired to this sleepy village where he spent the rest of his life drinking Mexican brandy and writing memoirs that never took form. And again, Cordoba was left to fend for himself. He is a man of independent means, though of a very limited amount, I understand. A poet as well, he composes tight little verses of an incredibly scatological nature, which he sometimes favors me with, waiting expectantly for the punch line to sink in. Though he invariably breaks into his snorting giggle before I have had time to register my disgust.

One other thing about Cordoba: He knows my secret. He has some pull in rightist camps of Latin America because of his father's reputation as a Nazi sympathizer. Thus, he is my contact man with the various generals who have employed me from time to time in the difficult years this nation experienced with the left-wing insurgents.

At any rate, this explains somewhat my connection with Cordoba: It was partly a matter of sentiment, for we could speak German together; and partly a matter of business. And then there was also the gossip. It could take so many interesting turns. Tonight, however, I was surprised to discover that I was the chief topic of local gossip. Such had not been the case for many years.

"In town, they say you're in love."

The cards slapped the table as Cordoba dealt.

"___"

"I thought not. Told them they were full of tomatoes. It's the girl. They say you collected her things from the hotel. Some cock-and-bull story about her having to leave the country on account of illness. But there's no record of her leaving, you see. They say maybe she's living here with you. I hope that was not her grave you were digging out back."

He snorts a laugh.

"They say a lot of things."

"Yes, my friend. But I, of course, educated them. I told them Señor ____ was beyond such things as amour. That he only longs for the peace and quiet necessary to finish his memoirs. And that women, as any *hombre* can tell you, do not allow such a pretty condition to come about. Quiet frightens them. Peace they think of only as the absence of war. No, I told them, no one would wish love on Señor ____. He has no need of it. I, on the other hand . . ."

"Just what is it you want to know, Cordoba?"

"There have been inquiries, my friend. The local police have heard from certain parties in the United States, from some literary woman or such. A writer's agent, I believe it was. One cannot, regardless of our lax judiciary here, simply disappear another. Not even you, connected howsoever tenuously with the police as you are. Disappearances are their prerogative. In their eyes, you have overstepped your power. They suspect you of having gotten the woman out of the way in one manner or another—and possibly for very good reasons. That is not the question. The question, the problem, is that they would rather you come to them about such matters. . . . Bad play, friend. I'm collecting aces, remember? Gin. . . . I suppose they would like to be reassured about this."

"She's a guest here. Downstairs. She's writing a novel that is set here. I am giving her a place to work. That is all."

"You sly dog. Is that really all? I remember my father, old as he was, could still get up to tricks if he had enough brandy in him. Enough only; too much and he was like a flower needing water."

"She is a writer. I am playing the part of patron. That is all there is to it."

"Well, we should have her up. A third at cards would be great fun. Do fetch her."

"She does not want to socialize. She works most of the time. Seems she is at a dramatic point now. I even hesitate to flush the toilet lest it will throw her concentration off."

"You sly old dog."

"I assure you, Cordoba . . ."

"No. No explanations are needed. I get the lay of the land."

"And your friends?"

"I imagine they will understand, as well. Tell her to get in touch with this agent though, will you? She is causing a low-level stink. It irritates certain people who should not be irritated."

When Cordoba finally left, I remembered that I had not yet fed Miss O'Brien. Immediately, she sensed there was something amiss. She had heard more footsteps overhead than usual; she was curious, inquisitive. But I had no mood for talking tonight. I simply left the remains of our meal and departed, her questions floating in the air.

Now the complications begin, I thought. As they always do. I will have to do something about this agent and her questions. I cannot afford to irritate Cordoba's friends. I cannot afford to appear ungrateful for their patronage over the years. Complications.

I will put them out of my mind for the time, however. Get back to work on my memoirs.

I sit alone writing now. One lamp only is on upstairs, the green-shaded brass lamp on my trestle table. The room is suffused with soft warm light. Silence like a palpable force emanates from the ravine in back.

We were married that summer, Uschi and I. After our honeymoon—a bike ride through the Wachau, gaping at the terraced vineyards sloping into the sluggish Danube; nights spent at simple inns along the route—I went straight to the Staffel cadet training school at Bernau, just northeast of Berlin. This was my first trip outside of Austria. A strange lightness in my soul manifested itself as our train crossed the former border at Passau. I stress the fact that it was a "former border crossing": For the past year and a half, the Anschluss had made the destinies of Germany and Austria inseparable.

The summer of '39 was one of those apocryphal ones weather-wise. It depends now on which account, whose memoirs you read, whether it was the driest of the century or the wettest. Not even the official meteorological records agree on this point. It is certain that it was much drier and warmer in Germany and on the continent in general than in England.

I remember that day on the train quite clearly. It was only mid-July, but already the first crop of hay was ricked and drying under the hot sun. I shared my compartment with a young boy sitting opposite me. Though only a few years separated us, I looked upon him as a boy. He was continually remarking on the earliness of the crop; I remember that distinctly. His father was a dairy farmer in Styria and he complained jokingly of the burden his "defection" to the Staffel was causing his father—"the old man," he called him. He made sure to lay on the irony thickly with the word *defection*, as he had no inkling whether I would be sympathetic to such a case or not. In the event, he was right to do so. Association with the Staffel was not only a high honor, it was also voluntary. From my initial self-serving motives for joining up, I had already progressed to a reverence, a feeling of being among the select, the chosen. It was apparent to me, however, that this young peasant had joined the Staffel simply to avoid inevitable general conscription into the Wehrmacht. He had taken advantage of the new push in Staffel circles to "leaven" the loaf with other strata of society. The old aristocracy and the technocracy of specialists and university graduates had for a time controlled the Black Corps. I was later to learn that certain people in Berlin were growing nervous about this state-within-a-state organization and that doors had been opened wider to make us a touch less elitist. If this cunning little farmer's son were any indication of the new direction of the corps, then I feared I had made a grave error in joining.

At any rate, it was fortunate the lout tempered his remarks with irony. Had he not, I would have reported him immediately upon arrival at Bernau. Which could have come none too soon, I can assure you. I'd had enough of this peasant's rough humor and looked forward to mixing with men more of my own kind.

Once in Bernau, then, you can imagine my fright when I discovered that the quartermaster was lining us up for accommodation assignments according to order of arrival! I felt an absolute panic: It was bad enough that coincidence had forced me to share a compartment with the loutish youth, but now it looked as though the same coincidence should determine that I share bunk space with him, too. With this Cro-Magnon whose feet most likely smelled of an old barn.

The youth obviously read my discomfort standing in line next to him, fated to be his roommate, for he tapped my arm gently just as I was about to protest to the quartermaster.

"Good luck for me. I'll learn some city manners now."

His ruddy face beamed quite honestly at me, his mouth smiling in a wide arc. He winked and then I knew that he knew, and it made everything all right for me. A small thing, you may say, to make a fellow human being more comfortable by demonstrating understanding and tact. But it was the unexpectedness of the action, the completely sincere manner in which he did it, that was so disarming. Suddenly, this rough youth's features lost their rawness in my eyes. He began to take on the virile blond good looks of the propaganda posters.

"Yes," I finally replied to his overture. "I'm sure we'll get on just fine."

And, in fact, we did. Hannes was his name. Hannes

Friedl, though we all called him Kuh—Cow—after his father's occupation, and also because he forever seemed to be chewing on something.

As it turned out, Cow embodied the philosophy of stoic separation. He never articulated this—he could not have. There was not a reflective bone in his body. But after getting to know him, one sensed in him an inviolate spirit, an apartness. He was not aloof. That is something quite different, quite self-conscious. Cow was always friendly and cordial, though lacking in the social grace and awareness of true cordiality. But he was a natural leader: never one to be dominated by sex or emotion. Not cold, merely complete unto himself.

We were an unlikely duo: he, a burly, tousle-haired blond youth with hands that looked as if they had been invented to fit around teats, and I, a thin, rather ascetic-looking intellectual type, right down to my round tortoise-shell glasses and brown hair combed straight back off the forehead. Yet we formed a bond. He was sincere in wanting to learn the ways of the metropolis from me, calling me "Scholar" and always after me to educate him about which fork he should begin with or the proper forms of greetings for one's superiors, or to tell him, one more time, about the glorious role of Austria in the Reich. Such gifts I thought paltry in relation to those I secured from him: the secret of positioning one's body on the horizontal bar to accomplish the requisite twenty chin-ups (it is in the shoulders and hips, strangely enough, not in the arms; one must thrust upward with a totally flexed body); or the equally arcane technique of goose-stepping (again, the movement is from the hips and is so called, Cow assured us all, because if done correctly you will surely goose the soldier in front of you with the toe of your boot).

Over both these activities, Cow spent many predawn hours with me. It was Cow who prodded me when my spirits and physical stamina flagged; he had energy enough for an entire platoon. Indeed, he was earmarked early on for leadership, if only in the lower echelons, as his peasant background and lack of formal education played against him for the higher officer ranks. In return for an accomplished goose step, I schooled him in a refined cursive signature rather than the half-printed scrawl he placed on all his forms and applications.

Of course, not all the recruits saw Cow as I did. Some, not many, whether out of jealousy or ignorance, called him Cow not out of affection, but to hurt him. They made rude jokes about how his hands had actually gotten so calloused: not from handling udders, but from self-abuse. There was even some repugnant gossip about my friendship with him, allegations, of the humorless joking sort, that I rarely slept in my lower bunk alone. It is true that during a freak electrical storm Cow woke me. Thunder was the one thing that frightened him it seemed, and he was actually terrified that night. He asked—begged, actually—if he could sit on the end of my bunk for a time, and, of course, I answered in the affirmative. I tried to comfort him for a while, telling him of my own great fear of snakes, and that seemed to help. The next either of us knew, it was morning. We had fallen asleep in the bunk together, sleeping head to toe. His feet did not, I was pleased to discover, smell of musty barns, but rather of strong lye soap. A rugged, manly scent. One of the other cadets discovered us in the bunk together, hence the stories. But we ignored them and became even better friends because of them.

Thus it was for the first few weeks of training: drill, drill, and more drill. Harder for me, soft from city living, than for Cow, whose body had been hardened by physical labor. Soon, however, I came alive physically and began to feel that sweet self-power that comes with muscle tone; to enjoy a bounce in my walk and the pull and flex of muscle under my uniform.

In the fourth week of training, a special envoy came from Berlin, Schutzstaffel: Oberführer Heinz Jost, one of the top men in the Sicherheitsdienst, or SD, the security service and intelligence agency of the Staffel and the Nazi Party, and Heydrich's right-hand man. He came to gather volunteers for a special mission and did not have to ask us assembled cadets twice before Cow jerked his hand heavenward, forcing mine up with his other hand.

We were the first to volunteer for "Operation Himmler," as the action came to be known in the history books.

Our names were called by Prokop, our drill instructor, a man who had been heavily decorated in the first war. He was real army, and from the outset, he had made it clear to us cadets that what he was creating was "an elite corps, not a corps of elitists." It was the only bit of wordplay I ever heard Prokop indulge in. He and Cow hit it off famously, both taciturn to the extreme; they could sit over a beer for half an hour without exchanging a word.

It was only when I heard Scharführer Prokop boom out my name that I realized what had happened. I had become a volunteer. This was very unlike me, but later Cow reassured me: "This is no time for faint hearts or second-guessing. Wonderful things are afoot, Scholar. Careers will be made. Now is the day of opportunity. You have all the rest of your life to lie low."

If only he had known how prophetic his words were to be!

"Aren't you going to tell me who your visitor was last night?"

"Card night. An old friend."

"The taxi man, then. He told me about your card nights when he was driving me out here that Sunday. Who won?"

"I have a couple of things to tell you. One, I believe you need to get regular exercise and breathe fresh air. I have, to this end, prepared a compound for you in back. You may walk, sit, write, sun yourself, whatever. I require two promises from you first: you do not try to escape and you do not try calling for help once outside. It would be pointless, anyway. There is no escape from here, and no one is near enough to hear your screams. I shall be watching you closely. Any attempts at either will mean the immediate and permanent revocation of your privileges. Is that understood?"

"You mentioned a couple of things you had to tell me. I assume that is the good news."

"I need you to write something on this."

"A postcard . . . from Mexico City . . . Why?"

"Just write what I dictate."

"Someone's asking for me, is that it? I told you that you couldn't keep me here indefinitely. Who is it? Jeanne, I'll bet. She's the only one with balls enough to cause a ruckus. It is Jeanne, isn't it? Tell me."

"If that is the name of your literary agent, yes."

"I knew it! And she has the meanest friend in the State Department. A brother-in-law."

"But she is not going to bother him, is she? Because you're going to tell her that everything is fine. You're going to write to her and tell her that."

"Not in this bloody lifetime, brother. Why would I want to do something stupid like that?"

"Because if you don't, some very unpleasant things will happen to you. And I don't want that. You don't want that. Some men, very powerful men, you understand, believe you are here. No, don't smile so happily about that. They are not the sort of men who would help a damsel in distress. In fact, they are more the sort to want to rid themselves of a distressing damsel. I speak truthfully now when I say that they are very unscrupulous sorts. Very expert at dealing with delicate situations. If it came to it, they would simply rape and then kill you and make it look as if leftist terrorists had done it. They are men in whom empathy is totally lacking. This you must believe. They suspect—by now they probably know—that you are here. They tolerate such a whim of mine without asking questions, so long as it is purely a matter between you and me. But should your friend in New York cause any sort of questions to be asked at diplomatic levels, well, they would be forced to intervene in our little arrangement."

"—"

"You don't believe me."

"Oh, yes. Quite. That's the usual thing here, isn't it? Women and children die first. The perfect victims for cowards."

"Miss O'Brien, I really haven't the time or energy just now for polemics."

"But this isn't polemics. It's my life we're talking about. If I write your card for you, it will take the trail away from this village, away from you. Why should I do that? Why should I believe you're any different than your friends? Why should I give up my last hope for freedom on your say-so?"

"Yes, I take your point. But you see, I am not like them. Otherwise you would already be dead. I want to keep you alive, to sort this out. I have taken your interests to heart. Witness this room. I know you find it tasteless, but that is a subjective matter. Suffice it to say I did not decorate it thusly to torture you, though you claim that is the net result. I wanted, in my own way, to please you. And your exercise yard. I began it before hearing of the trouble your agent is causing. I have no intention of trading favors. Even if you refuse to write the card, I shall not punish you by taking away that privilege. But I cannot promise you, in that case, how long you might be around to use the yard. I have total power over you, but I have in no way misused or abused that power. Isn't that, in itself, proof of my good intentions?"

"You're amazing. You really don't get it, do you?"

"—"

"The very fact that you have absolute power over me is already a transgression. You're holding me against my will, displaying a gun every time you come within five feet of me, and for this you expect thanks. A pat on the shoulder. I should be panting on my hind legs like a faithful dog, your slipper in my mouth. Well, fuck you! Fuck you and your friends! Are you waiting for the Stockholm syndrome to kick in? For me to love my captor? Don't hold your breath, asshole. Or do. Please do."

"There's no reason for foul language."

"No reason? You and your phony propriety. You and your friends murder six million Jews and then upbraid me for saying 'fuck.' Your friends here want to take me out for a friendly rape-and-kill session and you blanch at the word 'asshole.' Yes, Herr ____, it is high time for foul language, if only to shake you out of your protective cocoon. The Jews should have cursed you all on their way to the showers; it might have finally grabbed you by your short hairs enough to make you wince. It might have at least reminded you of your own humanity, if that is at all possible. If there is an ounce of that left in you."

"The devil you know, Miss O'Brien. The devil you know."

"I think this time I'll opt for the one I don't know. It's refreshing, however, to hear you refer to yourself so. An admission of sorts."

"I'm not asking for yes or no right now. Think about it. I'll need to know by tonight. Think about it carefully. Weigh the pros and cons."

"__"

"Until this evening."

———

I worked the rest of the morning and early afternoon on the compound, clearing brush. And it is fortunate I did, for one bit of brush was giving cover to a family of thin green snakes, the most feared and deadly of our local vipers. I am ashamed to admit it, but, as I have earlier mentioned, snakes are my one weak spot. I mean I literally go to pieces when confronted with one. I am paralyzed with fear; my bowels loosen. And this even with the most innocent garden variety of snake. They are the most noxious of God's creatures, and my idea of hell would be to be trapped in a darkened room with a snake on the loose. I do not know if I should be able to function. Whenever I am in the bush, I make it a practice to wear high boots. There is a certain degree of security in tall boots. Today was proof of that.

Using a long-handled scythe, I was clearing all trace of tall grass and shrubbery from the compound, finishing up the job Cordoba had interrupted. I thought I saw movement in the grass just below the swinging blade. It gave me a start; I stopped the swing of the scythe in midarc. The tail end of a green snake writhed obscenely around the blade, flopping and twisting itself even after death. My heart raced and I broke out into an instant and drenching sweat. I could not move. I simply stood there with that writhing snake section on the blade, trying to catch my breath. From out of the grass, several more snakes darted for new cover. Thank God they were more frightened of me than I of them at this juncture, for I was completely unable to defend myself. I could only watch helplessly as they slithered under the fence and out of the compound.

It took me several minutes more to control myself enough to throw the bloody end of the snake over the fence. I felt quite nauseated and light-headed by this time. Quite absurd, but there it is. My idea of heaven is a country like Miss O'Brien's native one, Ireland, out of which the evil vermin have been driven for good and all.

I went in and had a cup of tea to calm my nerves and then finally returned to finish my work. When I had cleared the area to my satisfaction, I went in and got Miss O'Brien. She looked surprised that I should appear in the middle of the afternoon; dinnertime was my next scheduled visit. Seeing me now, she feared the worst. I quickly eased her mind, however, by telling her that the exercise compound was ready. She had only to give her word not to try to escape while out there or to scream for help once outside.

This done, I led her out into the daylight. She squinted painfully once outside—remember, she had been living under artificial light now for many weeks. She stepped rather hesitantly onto the grass; I assured her that the area had been cleared and was safe. But she said no, it wasn't that. She was afraid to feel the earth again under her feet lest it be snatched away from her again by some whim of mine. This wrenched my very soul, I must admit. That she could believe me to be such an ogre, such a hideous man. I left her alone there, a sign of my trust, and went up to my desk where I am writing these words. I can see her below, pacing, measuring out the perimeters of her new freedom. She is not used to being caged, one can see that immediately. But soon it will be easier for her. Soon the cyclone fence surrounding the yard will become invisible to her eyes. She will no longer approach it, gripping the diamonds of wire in a birdlike claw; no longer stare longingly at the matrix of metal that shuts her off from the rest of the world.

I have watched the phenomenon thousands of times before: the newly initiated rail at their captivity. They pace, they burn inwardly, they put their eyes to the wire so as to have an undisturbed view of outside. But this does not last long. With the strongest of them, such behavior persists only a few weeks, two months at the most. Then a curious thing happens: When they finally realize that there is no release, no escape, they begin to reject the very notion of prison. It is as if the fence is there to keep the world out. It is no longer a limitation of their freedom, but a preserver of it. They become rulers of a postage stamp–size domain. Kings and queens of Lilliput. With no one else about by whom private realities will be tested, Miss O'Brien will, I prophesy, be converted to this belief sooner than others I have known.

She has paced the perimeter twice now. She throws her hands up toward the sky, fingers reaching outstretched. For what? I think she is going to cry out, but no. She is only drinking in the air. She turns around and around; it is like a dance with her arms up, as if beckoning the sky to join her. A smile is on her lips; her eyes are closed in a kind of ecstasy. Then she opens them and is looking straight up at me as I watch her. Her arms drop listlessly to her sides and she heads for the back door. If she had a tail, it would be between her legs. I hear her knocking from downstairs. She wants in.

When I led her back to her quarters, she accused me of spying on her. It was hardly spying, I argued.

"It's so ghoulish. As if you have no life of your own. You only live through me. What did you do before I came? How many other flies have you trapped here? Where are your peepholes down here? I suppose you even watch me on the toilet. . . ."

I made no response. One cannot talk to Miss O'Brien when she is in such a state. I merely closed the door quietly behind me.

She slanders me by such accusations. I believe I have remained a gentleman throughout this difficult situation. It is hardly my style to be a voyeur. The last thing I should want to glimpse is the micturating squat of a female. I know it has been said of us men of the Staffel that we were all sadists, impotent thugs who could find satisfaction only by torturing or watching the torture of others. That, for us, sex was always deviant, and destruction was our only love. This is simply not the case. In my experience, at any rate. The men I served under and worked with were, for the most part, good upstanding family men who loved their wives and children and who proceeded to carry out a difficult and sometimes painful duty without complaint or ire. We were not vindictive; we took no pleasure in carrying out stringent orders; there was no love for any pain that may have been inflicted upon others as a result of carrying out our orders. I feel Miss O'Brien does not understand me. She has made me into a cardboard villain, and that rankles.

I shall set down the rest of those remarkable events of late August 1939 here, as a palliative against Miss O'Brien's thoughtless accusations.

So now we two and some eighty other graduates and cadets were transported to yet another training camp. Herded and trucked in the dead of the night, we were not allowed even to write family members and tell them we would be incommunicado for a time. We were sworn to secrecy in the dead of that starless night, secrecy unto death. This command I am now—or will be with the publication of these memoirs—directly and with conscious knowledge disobeying. Most of the story has already been pieced together by historians and journalists anyway. There is little left for me to protect.

For two weeks, we remained at this new camp. None of us knew where it was; we could only surmise distance by how many hours we had driven from Bernau. Neither were there any leaves to visit the local village, whatever that might be. Entertainment of sorts was brought in for us: Beer was rationed to two half liters daily, and women were trucked in twice a week. I did not bother with them. I understood their necessity but could not condone their services. Cow was happy to use my chits for this pastime as well as his own, and I found myself becoming almost jealous of his spending his free time with prostitutes rather than with me.

Our days were taken up in a new sort of training: We volunteers were broken into three separate groups, the smallest of which was hand-picked by a certain Staffel officer—Sturmbannführer Helmut Naujocks. This officer hardly appeared to be the dashingly romantic type of a Skorzeny: He was slight and wiry looking and sported a pencil-thin mustache such as an Italian waiter might affect. Yet there was an air of absolute confidence that wafted from him like aftershave. This attracted one to him. Word had it he was to be in charge of the most delicate phase of the operation. Remember, at this point none of us had a remote clue of what the overall operation would be, let alone what the most delicate or vital part of it was. Europe, though arming itself in preparation for the war everyone believed inevitable, was still at peace that summer.

Naujocks made an appearance the day after we were transferred to the new camp and chose six of the older hands—not one cadet among them—and trucked off with them to God knows where. I never saw a one of those men again, though we coordinated our subsequent operation with them.

Thus we were two large groups of men remaining, groups Viktor and Redux. My first inkling of what was in store for us came when we in group Viktor were issued uniforms in drab olive, very unlike anything a German soldier wore at the time. These uniforms were ill-fitting and evil-smelling.

"Polish uniforms," Cow announced.

I told him I thought this was a damn silly charade. It was obvious that the Poles, belligerent and arrogant over the Danzig corridor, would be our natural enemies in the coming conflagration. But this playing war games unto even wearing the uniform of the enemy—this was going a bit far.

"I don't think it's a game, Scholar. I think it's dead serious. Working behind the lines. That sort of thing."

I realized in that instant that Cow was right and wondered at my own naïveté. Admittedly, such a thought filled me with fear. Insurgency work was the most dangerous of all: If captured wearing the uniform of the enemy, it meant the firing squad. And there was always the risk of being killed by friendly fire. I began to regret allowing Cow to volunteer me. Especially so since Cow, a member of group Redux, had not been issued such a uniform!

The third day at the new camp some chaps arrived in a six-wheeled Mercedes. They looked very crisp and in control in their high boots and shiny-billed black caps. Two of these higher officers began drilling group Viktor using Polish language commands. We learned only the most basic ones. To this day, I can still recall the rough-throated accents of the younger of our interpreters. He drilled us for six straight hours under a blistering sun until we reacted automatically to Polish and German commands interchangeably, until the Polish no longer sounded foreign to us. But not before three in our platoon had passed out from heat prostration.

The next long days of training blended one into the other. We were unaware of happenings in the outside world: from the increasing international crisis over the Polish Corridor to the Moscow-Berlin nonaggression pact. Nonetheless, there was speculation among many of us that there would be war before autumn. We needed to move on Poland before the September rains set in and slowed down the advance of our highly mechanized Wehrmacht. No muddy roads could be allowed to retard the advance of the Blitzkrieg, for Poland would have to fall quickly so that we could about-face and deal with England and France to the west.

We waited every day for traveling orders, but as August neared its end, we continued undisturbed with our incessant marching and drilling, orders barked out at us in both Polish and German.

I saw little of Cow, for group Redux, dressed in Wehrmacht uniforms, drilled separately from us. We could sometimes watch them during our own breaks, and their drill seemed not much different from ours, save that they were commanded only in German.

Then one day our tedium was broken by the arrival of two transports. I thought our time had come; now we would be sent into action. But to what action and where? This was the most infuriating part of all, for all we had learned thus far was how to march to orders in Polish. We had received no special training in detonations, hand-to-hand combat, or reconnaissance—all skills needed for insurgency work.

The two new trucks were not for us, as it turned out. They remained in the center of the compound until the midday meal was ready, then closed metal platters and buckets of food were brought out. I happened to be standing guard duty near one of the trucks when the flaps were thrown up in back. The food was quickly and roughly thrust in. I caught a glimpse of the interiors: there, in each of the transports, were a dozen or so men in ragged clothing, their heads shaved and ankles manacled together. It was their eyes that I remember. They were enormous, staring mournfully out of skeleton faces, and the men fell on the food ravenously. Enough for only three men had been supplied for each transport.

Early in the morning of the twenty-fifth of August, we were transported far to the east; we knew the direction only by the sun's position. We still had not been advised of our destination nor, more importantly, of our purpose. All I knew was that I was weary of the Polish uniforms. Groups Redux and Viktor traveled together; I could see that Cow wore his Wehrmacht uniform with not much more pleasure than I wore my Polish one, but I would have felt better about the whole affair had we been wearing the same, regardless of whose.

It was a warm day, but for obvious reasons, the flaps were all down on our trucks. Under the canvas, it was sweltering and most canteens of water were quickly emptied. Cow kept me from immoderate use as he sensed it would be a long trip with no stops. Some of the others followed our example; most, however, thought us fools for suffering needlessly. Surely we would stop soon. It was inhuman not to.

It was late afternoon by the time we finally stopped. For eight hours we had been cooped up in the truck, and our legs had turned to mush sitting confined so long. When the sergeant threw open the back flap we stumbled out of the truck, blinking into the sun. What greeted us outside was an expanse of rolling, sparsely wooded countryside. Farming country, with not a trace of human habitation nearby. Flies buzzed angrily overhead; I could hear a lark in the distance melodious and pure. It was like landing somewhere in the steppes, I said to Cow.

"Or in the middle of Poland," he replied as a second transport with more of Redux men pulled up alongside us, raising a cloud of dust.

I looked at Cow, shocked at first. He smiled, but not to minimize the suggestion. Things fitted together in my head quickly then. A little later, just as Sergeant Prokop began to fill in the particulars, the penny dropped. The truth of the matter finally became apparent to me. I was amazed I had not seen it all along.

Cow and the rest of the thirty or so men in Wehrmacht uniforms were led off down a dusty dirt road into the setting sun. At the tail of his column, Cow suddenly turned and waved to me, a gesture very out of character for him. The rest of us, in Polish kit, remained where we were, wishing we could be with the others. After all, no one chooses to be on the losing side, even in play.

Dry rations were broken out and we partook of these gratefully. There was also a new ration of water passed around; it seemed this had been kept stored under the very benches of the transport where we had sat so long. (Which rather brings to mind a tasteless bit of humor my Miranda was fond of repeating: "I could have passed my life in near starvation in our run-down village if I hadn't finally realized that I was sitting on a gold mine." She would always slap her delicious little bottom as she said this, in case any listener misunderstood.)

While we drank thirstily and then ate, Sergeant Prokop further detailed the plan for us. Until nightfall, we were to stay in position where we were, just inside the German border. There was an audible sigh at that statement, for most of us had thought as Cow had, that we were already inside Poland, and we had been waiting for the Polish border patrols to chance upon us. By cover of darkness, we would move west, toward a small forestry station at a place called Hohenlinden. We had been assured that the German couple who habituated there had been removed. We, disguised as a band of marauding Polish army regulars invading the Reich, were to shoot the place up, perhaps even start a fire, and eventually be surprised in our villainy and exchange fire with Wehrmacht troops, who were, in reality, group Redux. The point was, our leader stressed, this would be friendly fire. We were to return it by shooting into the sky; our rifles were never to be aimed parallel to the ground. As he put it, we wanted no balls up here, no freakish accident of German killing German.

Theatre, I thought. Pure and simple. A child of Vienna, I had a sense for that art form, all right. No "balls up" indeed. Especially when I was wearing the wrong color uniform. With Cow gone, however, I had no one in which to confide these thoughts.

We would, Prokop went on, be taken prisoner by the German troops, and then be transported quickly out of the region. All this just in case any of the locals stumbled onto our game. This had to look real. No German was to be spoken. Only the few words of Polish we had. The forestry hut was close to a village, but far enough from the border that we would not attract the attention of bona fide Poles on border patrol.

Private Schmidt, one of the few men I ever met who exactly filled the Nazi description of the perfect Aryan specimen, and who was still a bit miffed at being chosen as a Pole despite his blond good looks, now spoke up: "But if we're carted out of the area, what proof will there be that the raid ever took place?"

"The burned forestry hut for one," the sergeant said. He had asked for questions, yet seemed loath to answer this one. "Also, there will be certain . . . incontrovertible proof left behind for the press." Prokop did not look us in the eyes as he spoke.

Schmidt pressed the point, but the sergeant was finished with question-and-answer time. For the next hour, we sat around smoking and growing more and more nervous. This would be the first action, staged or not, that most of us had ever experienced.

I do not think I shall ever forget that sunset: It seemed to go on forever with the sun turning blood red as it finally slipped down over a far knoll to the west. Atop the knoll was one lone sycamore tree, its bark changing to brilliant red in the dying light, and the sun appeared to melt or drip onto the question mark of that tree. None of us really wanted to see the sun go away, for that would signal the beginning of our adventure, and it was as if the communal will of us twenty young men held the glowing orb suspended above the earth. There was something powerful yet terrifying in the exercise of this communal spirit and will, a manifestation of *Volksgemeinschaft*, for it was unspoken yet recognized by one and all.

It was just the other side of this knoll, Sergeant Prokop said as he investigated his map, that we would find the forestry station. This gave a double import to that tree and the fading sun.

When finally we moved out, there was not a man among us who did not feel an incredible sense of relief at finally doing something. The waiting had taken its toll on us. The evening was full of the sound of crickets and the occasional high-pitched hoot of a field owl on the hunt. A sweet earthy smell came up with the cooling of evening, carried on a slight breeze. I was grateful for the coolness, for I had not stopped sweating since early in the morning upon first donning my uniform. Moonless, the night sky was sprinkled with stars undimmed by artificial lighting anywhere on the horizon. We followed the dusty track that earlier I had watched Cow tramp along.

I was pleased to be walking. Sergeant Prokop occasionally barked out orders in Polish, just in case some farmer was out late in his fields. Up the distant knoll, we marched, past the sycamore shaped like a question mark, and then down the other side into a copse of chestnut trees. Ahead of us, we finally discerned the black silhouette of a building, massive and solid in the darkness, its blackness even deeper than that of the night. That darkness could take on such a visible manifestation was a discovery to me, unaccustomed as I was to moving about in it. This was a revelation, this understanding of the relative mass of light. I still remember the slight shock. I was elevated to another plane by the realization: slight irony implicit here, for most reports of such peak experiences mention the accompaniment of white light. From Swedenborg to Gurdjieff, this inclusion of white light is pretty much standard drill. My revelation was accompanied by the opposite—darkness as black as the uniform of the corps.

For a brief instant, I was not a plodding foot soldier heading for his battle, but rather a messenger of some higher consciousness, in tune with all around me: the trees, the darkness, the very slope of the hill. They were a part of me, I of them. It was the glorious world unity achieved when one is doing one's duty totally, faithfully, from the heart. So far removed was I now from the callow cynicism and selfishness that had initially prompted me to join the Staffel. I had become now one of the unit; I had found my mission in life.

My reverie was sharply halted by the crack of rifle fire. The man in front of me jumped backward into my chest, knocking us both over like bowling pins. I spluttered a protest and started to shove him off me, but my hand came away wet with a warm sticky substance I knew at once to be blood. I rolled his body off me and it made a gurgling sound. He had been shot in the throat. Blood pumped freely from the wound. This I could see despite the darkness. Flies or mosquitoes buzzed over my head and something struck the ground nearby. *Thwump.* I realized these were not insects but bullets, and I stayed down. I had no time for reflection, but knew I must get off the exposed roadway and find protective cover in the woods. I rolled several times and then crawled on my belly off the road. I could not make out where the fire was coming from at first. I felt only dizzy and disoriented, rather helplessly clutching the foreign rifle to my chest as if it were a crucifix and I a boy of seven waiting for First Holy Communion. Another body rolled onto me. It turned out to be Schmidt, the asker of uncomfortable questions. His presence, normally an aggravation to me, was now quite reassuring.

"It's coming from the fucking house."

It took me a moment to realize what he meant. Then I saw the orange-red explosions of shots being fired from windows in the forestry station.

"The bastards!" Schmidt shouldered his gun and shot into the blackness in the general direction of the building.

It was something to do; action as opposed to inaction. It removed the impotent fear brought on by only reacting to the situation. Shouldering my rifle, I felt I was putting a template onto events. I was taking charge. The first shot recoiled painfully against my slack shoulder, for we had been given little drill in weapons use. I cried out aloud and Schmidt thought momentarily that I'd been hit. I braced my shoulder thereafter.

I doubt that we exchanged more than a hundred rounds on both sides. Strangely, I gave no thought to who might be firing on us. In Germany, the "enemy" was obviously other Germans, yet this thought did not arise in the several minutes of the battle's duration. It was enough that they had fired on us, shooting at least one of our number. This made them, whoever they might be, the enemy.

I must have fired off a good dozen rounds, all that was in my clip, and then ejected it and inserted a second, but held my fire as shooting from the forestry station seemed to have stopped. I sensed movement to our left. Voices. Confused shuffling of feet. It seemed the rest of our comrades were in retreat. I did not want to call out in case these sounds were not from friends but from those who had opened fire on us. I heard the choked gurgling of the man lying on the road. He had not yet died and I wanted him to so as to still his grotesque sounds.

There came a loud voice, almost familiar. I could not make out exactly what it was saying, but there was authority in it. The tone was both reassuring and frightening. I made sure the second clip was securely inserted and held my rifle at the ready. Schmidt broke wind in a most ungracious manner and did not even bother to apologize. I had the urge to move away from him and his fetid innards but did not want to make any noise. The voice grew louder and then there was a body attached to it. At that very moment, more shots rang out from the house and Schmidt let off several rounds, giving away our positions. I heard heavy footfalls approaching us.

"Stop shooting! Cease fire!"

It was the same authoritarian, vaguely familiar voice. And then I saw the gun and the uniform. It was not ours. It had been a trap. I swung around to the approaching figure, leveling my rifle straight at his middle. He continued to approach, his voice booming out in the night. Stumbling over the wounded man in the road, he came lurching across the road toward us. My finger pulled off two rounds: the first one spun him full circle and the second sat him down hard on his ass as he held on to his bleeding middle.

It was only then, recognizing the characteristic slump of the shoulders as he sat, that I realized with a visceral shock that it was Cow.

Well, to paraphrase Sergeant Prokop, it certainly was a balls up. The worst had happened: We of the Staffel volunteers had fired upon each other, and for real. There were casualties and confusion. The first imperative was to clean up the mess before our border patrol should stumble upon us. We had no idea what was happening or what had gone wrong. All we knew then was that we had to clean up and clear out.

Only later did we get the news. The invasion of Poland, Operation White, of which Operation Himmler was only a small part, had been called off at the last minute. Hitler had canceled it because of startling news: That very day, the British had formalized their mutual defense treaty with Warsaw, and that prompted the comic buffo statesman Mussolini to go back on his assurances to the Führer that he would come to the aid of the Reich in case of war. Hitler thus had no choice but to call off the Polish invasion—for the time.

This decision, however, came at the eleventh hour, quite literally, and too late to stop our groups from moving into place. The old couple from the forestry building had thus not been evacuated as planned, and the old man, hearing our movements in the middle of the night, expected the worst. Seeing the uniform of one of our number who had gotten close to the building, the forestry man had opened fire with a World War One Mauser, starting the firefight in which groups Redux and Viktor—stumbling toward each other in the darkness—quickly became involved.

This was a setback, but not a total failure. The operation had not been discovered, despite all the confusion of the night of August 25–26. We of the Staffel were still in shape to go through with another staged raid when the Führer decided the time was ripe. We did not have to wait long. Five days, in fact. Hitler had, by now, had time to assess the new situation: Mussolini had been brought around, and if, now, the Poles were backed up by a written agreement with London, so what? It was worth the risk that the spineless English would not go to war over a simple border dispute.

There were also outside urgencies at work: The fear of autumn rains was one, as mentioned before. But more important was a further outside exigency: 1939 was the year of Hitler's fiftieth birthday. He was determined to begin the war in Europe—the cleansing war—that he knew it needed. It should begin when he was at his half-century mark so that he would have time to lead it to completion and see Germany into the millennium thereafter. Once and for all, we Germans would fight to end the vicious policy of encirclement practiced upon us by our neighbors from the time of Frederick the Great of Prussia on.

So when word came that we would again see action the night of August 31, there was not a sad face among us. We were ready, and everything this time went according to plan. The dress rehearsal had at least accomplished one thing for us: It had made the real thing possible. We "Poles" were captured by the "Wehrmacht" troops; we put our hands over our heads and were led off to waiting troop transports. These transports were, however, not empty when we got to them. What looked to be lumps of clothing in the beds of the trucks first needed to be unloaded before we got in. But it turned out these bundles of clothing were actually bodies of men, dressed very much like we were in Polish uniforms. These men were alive; one heard a groan occasionally as they were lifted out and carried toward the Hohenlinden forestry building. A good fire had been started there now, and its flames danced up into the dark sky, a brilliant garish orange. I could see the men clearly as they were lifted out of the transports. They had the shorn hair and emaciated features like those I had seen earlier at our training camp when the food was handed them. They were, in fact, I realized with a start, the very ones I had seen just the week before.

We all watched as these men were unloaded; other Staffel personnel whom we did not know did this business. No one looked at another, no questions were asked. The bodies had to be carried from the trucks as if they had been doped. They were taken to a grove of trees within the circle of light cast by the fire, and there propped against trees, their backs toward Poland. Once the lot of these were unloaded, we "prisoners" were ordered aboard and the canvas tops were removed so that any of the local villagers awoken by the fracas should be able clearly to see Polish prisoners of war being carted away from the scene. The trucks started up and, simultaneously, a sudden sharp roar came from the forestry building where perhaps a can of gasoline had exploded. The trucks were put into gear. Bumping down the dirt road away from the border we heard automatic weapons fire. We all heard it, but no one commented.

Early in the morning, we invaded Poland, Hitler crying out to the world of the Polish atrocities in Upper Silesia, showing photos of Polish soldiers killed in this action on German soil. His speech that day was impassioned, moving, filled with outrage. I almost believed it. In two more days, the entire world was at war.

———

"Hungry? I made a bean soup. . . . I thought the fresh air might have given you an appetite."

"I accept. The devil I know, I mean. On one condition."

"Which is? Eat before it gets cold."

"I want to think . . . to believe I can trust you. If I'm going to write off my only chance of help, I want to feel you will honor what you say. I want to understand you, to know what makes you tick. Before I write the postcard."

"__"

"Is that so much to ask?"

"I'm listening."

"I want to read your memoirs. I want to get inside of you. Know what kind of man has power over me. Know whether you really are different from those friends of yours or not. I have to do this. I have to have some sort of feel for you. Otherwise, you might just as well call your friends in now."

"__"

"It can't matter now, can it? I mean, I know the worst. I know your name and that you are a wanted war criminal. What else matters? Why keep the memoirs from me now? The particulars are of no consequence. Either I would inform on you or not. That's the fear, right? Tell them, the Israelis, where to find you. So you might as well let me know the full story. It can't damn you any more than it already has. And maybe, just maybe, it will breed some understanding between us."

"I'd like that."

"You would?"

"Yes, Miss O'Brien. I think I would. But this friend of yours. She is persistent. She is causing problems right now. How long will it take you to get to know me? You see, the problem is with others, not just between you and me. My friends want no complications."

"I've thought of that, too. A compromise. I write to her, telling her not to worry."

"Fine."

"But not from Mexico City. The postmark must be from here. A postcard of the waterfront. A short note saying I'll write later. That everything is okay. Then later, after getting to know you, then the Mexico City card."

"—"

"It takes the pressure off outside complications."

"I'm not sure . . ."

"Or weren't you serious about developing an understanding between us?"

"I was. . . . Am."

"Then? She already knows I'm here. Reconfirming that would do you no harm. And it would buy us time."

"Miss O'Brien, I am tired of being misunderstood. That is why I have been writing these memoirs in the first place. And I think I would like you to read what I have thus far. I think the time has come for that."

"Deal?"

"Deal."

PART III

Several things at the outset: know that I detest the 'blame-it-on-mommy' syndrome as much as I do Freudian psychology. They are both aberrations, bad reads. Freud was a great explorer, a miserable clinician. But if you're going to dabble in either or both, at least get it right.

You made the point about the stranglehold quality of the female (archetypal) in Viennese turn-of-the-century society. But you want to have it both ways: to simultaneously revile that matriarchal tradition and to get your jollies from it (vis-à-vis Frau Wotruba and your infantile sexuality with her). There are many things about the first sixty pages or so of manuscript to which I draw exception. But perhaps the most blatant was this sexual adventure with Frau Wotruba. What is startling here? Not the fact of sensuality, to be sure. We all experience this extreme eroticism of prepubescence. Sex is the one thing, it would seem, that we are all prepared for from day one. We have a hard-on for life; it is a blind urge to be satisfied by anyone and everyone. Neither is the fact startling that this fully grown woman is dominated by the same urgency that controls the youth. There is, in fact, an extreme honesty in her portrayal. There is no doubt that this happened: She is much too real to have been invented. She is much too human to be mere fiction. Her need and her outlet are not bothersome to me. I am not shocked, though I see how such an invitation could lead to certain warps in the sexuality of the little boy: be the passive recipient, the object to be rubbed against.

And this is what I do find startling about the scene: that the connection between the all-powerful matriarch and Frau Wotruba has not been made. The boy's mother comes in for a full dose of scorn on that account (she controls when and where the boy goes out; how much wine the father will drink). This mother is the supreme warlord of the tiny flat. And the boy distances himself from this woman, who may or may not be hiding the castrating shears behind her skirts, early on. Yet, having spoken so sentiently about women in Vienna, it is too bad that you did not see who the real matriarch was in your life, for this role must go to Frau Wotruba. It was she who dominated you, who sent you wild with her rubbings. She used you for her satisfaction only—which, when you come down to it, is what sex is all about.

We're not talking about love here, but pure sex. By the end of the relationship (I assume that was finis when your parents discovered you together?) you have rebelled: you now appear to be in control. Yet you noticed she still enjoyed her satisfaction of you— she still employed you for her enjoyment. The stakes had been upped. You were more a participant, but had the situation really changed? Don't you think she may have prompted your sadism simply to make a stale situation fresher for herself? To spice up the act somewhat? Were you actually in control, or did she simply lead you to believe you were? And being, as you thought, in control, weren't you even better as a sex partner than before?

A statement of belief apropos all of this: The dynamics of man and woman together are the basis of all relationships, all things political in the world. The conjugal is the fundamental political map; look at the sex of any age to determine the political climate.

And what of the day your father jumped into the fountain and could not get out? You were perceptive enough to see this for what it was: the knocking down of the man who stands in the way of your own manhood. Every boy must see his father with his pants around his ankles in order to see the man-ness of him: the father's humanity and thus his ultimate frailty. If we must, this would be the penultimate act in the Oedipal play in Freudian terms. The father, competitor with the son for the love of the mother, is laid low. His power, his vitality, his very masculinity is destroyed. Which leaves the boy as sole contender for his mother's heart and bed. Which comes in the final act. But there is something amiss here. If it is true that Frau Wotruba, and not your mother, is the real matriarch in your life, then what are you not telling us? And why have you left us dangling about your parents' reaction to the scene they witnessed: your spunk all over the woman's hair; her tits hanging into your face? For I sense that you're not coming back to this scene. You have moved on in your chronology to early manhood. And what, too, of your father's real demise as opposed to his symbolic one? You mention his death in an aside. That of course is your prerogative. But I have the feeling this hides something. You are not allowing full disclosure. Such a course is not necessarily required in literature. But you have led us to believe that such will be the case with your writing. Anything less, therefore, than complete honesty is unacceptable.

Do not misunderstand me: This is not a problem of style. I have very few criticisms apropos your way of writing, though it strikes me you are a trifle stuffier than need be. Perhaps it is the language problem. Why, indeed, do you write in English? Why not German? Especially when writing your memoirs, it would be assumed you'd want absolute ease of expression. I am positive that your choice of language is no accident. I await your explanation on this point.

———

I reproduce Miss O'Brien's handwritten critique of the first part of my manuscript in full. It awaited me the very next morning as I delivered breakfast. I read it drinking my coffee. It angered me then and still does now. I suppose I should be gladdened that she was interested enough in my words to take them seriously. They work for her. They describe a life to which she has no other introduction. Strange, when I began these memoirs, I thought of sharing some elemental truths with a large anonymous audience. Of reaching out to this ur-public from the wisdom and loneliness of old age and telling them the truth about a certain period of history and about a certain man involved in that historical movement. As such, my dream was sublime; there was a degree of grandeur in the thought of reaching those nameless thousands who might read my little book.

Sharing these things with one other person, however, is a different matter. One is made to feel more responsible for one's words when the audience is limited and known, rather than when it is vast and amorphous. This accountability is something I never reckoned with. This calling to account by Miss O'Brien is what smarted at first. This must be how every writer feels about every critic: Who are they to judge when they do not put their own intellectual and emotional viscera on the line? They are seagulls to the artistic pelican.

After reflection, though, I have decided that Miss O'Brien is different from these carrion. She is, like it or not, intimately bound into my life. She is not looking at my work from an artificial, stylistic point of view, but from that of one employing ultimate personal honesty as the benchmark. She has a vested interest in that: She needs to know how capable I am of telling the truth so that we might call a truce on that score. My initial rancor then softens at this realization. I listen to her voice, reread her criticism. I cannot stomach the constant referral to the Jew Freud. His doctrine sickens me. As one of his own kind once said, Freud's work is a symptom rather than a cure of the contemporary malaise. Oedipus be damned!

All the same, Miss O'Brien is perceptive. I was not intending to go back to the family scene: I thought leaving it at that dramatic point would be more effective. After all, what could I relate but how Frau Wotruba threw the cover over me, turned her back on my parents' air-gulping startled faces, and buttoned her bodice quite calmly. How she did not bother with dissimulation but walked out wordlessly, her hair still flowing about her shoulders. Walked out never to return to our flat, leaving me to explain, as best as I could, what all that naked flesh had meant.

Thank the deity of your choice, Maria awoke in the midst of Father's subsequent harangue, and neither of my parents had the heart to continue the conversation in front of the virginal little girl. In the morning, it was as if nothing . . . and everything . . . had happened. No word of the transgression was mentioned, yet disapproval hung in the air like the sour smell of boiled cabbage. Something had ended between Father and me; some near intimacy of maleness was cut dead before fully developing. No longer did we go on our Saturday afternoon outings together; there were no more clumsy attempts at the friendship of equals from him—which was fine as it had only made me nervous, anyway. But I felt a loss that I am even today unable to describe.

At first, I thought the trade-off more than worth it: a view of Frau Wotruba's breasts and an explosion at my groin were more than compensation for the loss of Father's attentions. As the months and years wore on, however, the bargain seemed ill-struck and far too one-sided.

You were right, too, Miss O'Brien, about his death and about the true competition for the real matriarch, but not in the silly Freudian framework you insist upon. This I will presently relate, painful as it is for me.

By the by, I can easily tell you why I write in English, even though it comes over stilted at times. The reasons are twofold: First, I would like to reach as large an audience as possible with these memoirs. English reaches nearly four hundred million as a primary tongue, countless millions, if not billions, more as a second language. What I have to say is too important to trust to translators and their helpful mistakes. Second, I avoid German so as to avoid any possible sentimentalizing on my part. I want meaning to come with difficulty, not with ease. Thereby all memories will be conjured up, not just the comfortable ones. I abhor selective memory: It is at the very heart of what is kitsch. These words are as much confession as memoir.

We left the Hubertusgasse not many months after the incident with Frau Wotruba. In my mind, the two seemed to relate directly to each other, but I know this was not the case. It was not a matter of cause and effect, but rather something Father and Mother had been planning for quite some time. I had actively fought against any such plans as removal to a new district. As miserable as I was in the *gymnasium* where I was enrolled, still I was more fearful of change. With the inherent conservatism of youth, I wanted to cling to the known, even if it was making me miserable, rather than opt for another situation and all its uncertainties. But after my being discovered with Frau Wotruba, I suddenly longed for change: anything that might replace the awful silence in our sitting room at night.

We moved to Ungargasse one bright day early that summer. School was just out and I was helping with the packing and hauling, hoping to restore some of the old feeling between Father and me. But he only gave me carefully worded directions for packing, spoken as one would to a person with a brain defect, and set me about my tasks, which were largely independent of his own. We had movers come for the large pieces, so there was not even the need for Father and me to lift something in unison. Yet, I held out hope that moving to Ungargasse would somehow change things. I could not understand his reaction: I expected disappointment, but this was worse. Father reacted to the thing as one would to a deep betrayal.

The new flat did one thing: It supplied privacy, an unknown commodity at Hubertusgasse. I had an alcove off the sitting room, a triangular space just large enough for a three-foot-wide bed and a night table. This was closed off by a length of paisley cloth reaching from floor to ceiling. It was a far cry from the Chinese screen I had lived with for so many years.

As tiny as this alcove was, I felt fortunate for it; it was my space. I could do with it as I pleased, within reason. All I needed to do was draw the curtain to shut my life off from prying eyes. Upon the night table stood an electric lamp with a massive lead base molded to look like a scallop shell. Next to the lamp was an alarm clock that I seldom used because of the frightful tocking reverberations it set up in the alcove. Behind this, like a talisman I kept by my bed summer and winter, was the snowy bubble of Stephansdom, St. Stephan's. And always, and increasingly so as I grew older, were the books into which I would escape from the present. I'm afraid my reading list was not very original. It might even have been a trifle retrograde, for my favorite novels of all were those of Karl May and the adventures of his heroes Shatterhand and the Indian Winnetou in the American Southwest. Winnetou, I must confess, was my favorite, for I had all the typical youth's fondness for the exotic free life of the Indian. For years together, I imagined, as I walked down Vienna's cobbled lanes, that I was a sleek-footed chieftain on the hunt of bobcat and invading white men. My sympathies lay altogether with the Indian cause. From Winnetou, I learned the fear of encirclement, of encroachment on one's land by lesser peoples, just as was happening to us Germans and Austrians by the peoples of the east. Hitler, another fan of Karl May's, was perceptive enough to understand this threat, as well, and to act upon it!

Other books I enjoyed as a youth: mainly history and historical romances. Anything I could lay my hands on about the Holy Roman Empire or stories from the Norse sagas (these came in one of the first paperback editions I had ever seen, its front covered in the pigeon footprints that I later learned to be runic writing). There were also the Corti biographies of the Habsburgs, which I think still stand the test of time.

And, by mistake, one time I purchased, with *Groschens* dearly saved, a battered old volume of *The Memoirs of Josephine Mutzenbacher*. I had no idea what the book was about, only that it was written by Felix Salten, the creator of *Bambi*. I had once overheard a schoolmaster of mine laughing about this fact but could not decipher what the joke was. At any rate, I bought the book, to the surprise and lightly concealed disgust of the female proprietor of a dusty secondhand bookshop I frequented off the Graben, but could find no indication it was written by Salten. Beginning it, I was painfully shocked at what I read. Far from being some Pygmalion-like tale as my teacher had been saying (or perhaps it was in the truest sense), the book was actually a pornographic novel based on the sexploits of a famous Viennese demimonde late last century.

It seemed there was no disgusting vice in which Josephine would not partake if the price or the size of the codpiece were right, and the list of her partners was awesome: from the coal man to the aristocrat to her priest and even to her biological father. I forced myself to read the book through, just to inform myself of what things my school chums found so enlightening.

I wish I could say I did not find it titillating; on the contrary, it was most arousing. One wonders about our sanity, our very health when perversion becomes the grounds for sexual arousal. I have since talked with many other men who have read that book, and most of them were delighted with it. They found it "dear" or "charming." I am flummoxed at such descriptions: They found the erotica humorous rather than debasing, cute rather than crude. I guess there is no explaining men.

That book, in fact, so aroused me that it got me thinking once again of Frau Wotruba and her breasts. I also began wondering about that secret moist furry place my hand had begun to explore between her legs—at the very apex of where her legs and trunk met. Josephine Mutzenbacher made it very plain what that region was. I was now equipped with not only an anatomically accurate description of it, but also a vast assortment of sordid names for it, as well. I wanted very much to touch or gaze upon a woman's "pussy." This became an all-consuming urge with me after having read this prostitute's memoirs. I forgot all about Winnetou for the time being and put the fight with my father clear out of my head. I even left off worrying about my new school, which I would start in the fall. I had only one goal, one purpose in life. I went to sleep thinking of it and awoke thinking of it, usually accompanied by a painful erection.

This continued throughout June and July and into August of that year, 1928. There were no walks in the country for us that summer, for the vacation money had been spent securing a bigger flat. And it was a hot, humid, and unbearable summer. Occasionally, Mother would take Maria and me to the bathing beaches of the Old Danube, a blind arm of the river with no drainage. The water was thus thick and warm, but it cooled us nonetheless. After swimming, I would lie on my back in the prickly grass under the baking sun, feeling rivulets of sweat build up and finally roll off my belly, between my legs, and even this sweat was charged with eroticism. The mind and consciousness are at once infinite and all too finite, full of caprice and stodgy as hell. It could conjure up pictures of sensuality enough for the rankest of orgies. Like the Cyclops or unicorn, the woman's yoni took on mythic proportions in my mind: the omphalos of the cosmos. What a lovely instrument of pleasure it was in these fancies: like a breast, but inside out. It would be soft and sweet smelling and would envelop my stiff prick like a fur muff on a cold day. Thus is the imagination. But as the mythic proportions of fabulous pussies soared in one part of my mind, the other hemisphere, the clerk of the cerebrum, was sifting through pragmatics: With whom and how? *Fine to daydream*, this accountant reminded me, *but let's get on with it. Let's get our hands and glands on one*, he urged.

But, I complained, I was only a child. Who could I find to let me indulge this passion?

Do I have to do everything for you? this tidy man of sums said. *You know very well who. You know very well how.*

Like I say, the mind is at once so fanciful and so mundane. All these images, these fantastical apparitions of a woman's love seat, to be reduced to four square centimeters of Frau Wotruba's person. Yet, that now became my target, my goal. It was required, and quickly, before summer vacation ran out, for not again in many months would I have time enough to myself to accomplish my task—sex had already become associated with labor because of that miserable scrivener's suggestions.

With the aid of hindsight, it is as if the whole of the summer had been building to one day late in August. It was a Wednesday. I remember this because the paper shop across the way from our apartment house had half-day closing on Wednesday. I wanted to stop for a card, something to carry, some excuse for the visit, but the paper shop was closed. I almost turned around and went home again, but then saw the candy shop next door was open. In that lush chocolate enclave I used up the few *Groschens* of pocket money I had—now I would have to walk rather than take a tram to her apartment—on Schweden Bombe for the frau. I bought three: two with coconut covering and one plain chocolate. Not half a block from the candy shop, I stopped and ravished one of the coconut-covered candies. I bit ravenously into the chocolate: I still remember the luscious silky sensation of marshmallow oozing about my teeth and gums. Soft and warm as I imagined Frau Wotruba to be down there. I felt no remorse; after all, she would have two of the sweets all to herself. The sun glared off the cobbles and the sidewalk. I could feel the heat through the soles of my leather shoes. The air was scarcely breathable, contaminated by diesel fumes and horse droppings. Ours was a fairly wide avenue, but as I set out into the outer districts, the streets narrowed and the air became scarcer and scarcer until I felt I would no longer be able to breathe, until I felt as if I were suffocating.

My heart pounded so furiously in my chest as I approached Hubertusgasse that I felt sure passersby would hear it. Reaching our old street, I could only stand outside the apartment building where we once lived and where the frau still lived, stand there for minutes on end, unable to bring myself to ring the portier's bell for admittance. The portier would ask my business: She was an evil old shrew who would see through my lie—which I had not yet even concocted—and would know that I had only come to touch Frau Wotruba's pussy. I felt myself getting hard even thinking of this word and so had to wait more minutes for the erection to subside. I walked down the street a few buildings, conjuring up a series of disgusting thoughts in order to lose tumescence. Across the street, I saw Herr Braunstein come out with his little dog on a lead. Half-day closing meant he was not at his frame shop this afternoon. I quickly turned my back to the street, for I did not want him to see me there. The thought of this nattily dressed little Jew calling out to me and announcing my presence to the whole neighborhood was enough to make me lose the erection. By the time his dog and he had reached the corner, I was in condition to ring the portier's bell.

Just as I turned to head back to the apartment building, however, I saw my father walking up to its door. He inserted a key and entered the main door as blithely as if he still lived there. He had not seen me, and I could only stand dumbfounded on the street watching the door close in back of him.

I could not understand this. Not only did he no longer live there and was, therefore, no longer entitled to the sacrosanct house key, but there was also the fact that he should be working. He had no half-day Wednesday as some shopkeepers did. He should be hard at it in Hütteldorf where he had told us his crew was repairing track the whole summer. I could think of only one explanation for his presence here: some terrible thing had happened. An emergency of some sort. Frau Wotruba! She was ill, or perhaps dying. And instead of feeling remorse and sympathy for the poor tortured soul, all I could think of was that now I had lost my chance to touch her. I ran to the door but was unable to reach it before it latched itself. I had no choice but to ring the portier, who took her time in coming. She finally recognized me and allowed that a message from my mother to Frau Wotruba was grounds enough for letting me in. Having no time to prepare the lie, it came out quite well, I thought. I thanked her and raced up the familiar stairs, along the dark passages with their communal sinks. Frau Wotruba's flat was on the fourth landing and I was out of breath by the time I got to her door, and sweating heavily to boot. The dark passage was cool compared to outside. I leaned against the wall for a moment, feeling the coolness of the plaster permeating my shirt. Old apartment buildings and churches: those were our air-conditioning in those years before climate control.

I was about to knuckle on the door when I heard voices coming from the partially open transom overhead. Laughter. A man's voice, and then a woman's. The voices held none of the urgency I would have associated with an emergency. They were playful rather than alarmed. I stopped my hand midway to the door and listened. The man's voice belonged to my father; there was no mistaking the deep gruff tones. But there was something new in it that I had never before heard: a lightness, a softness, and an almost tender playfulness. This was a tone he never exhibited to his family.

Perhaps it was he who was ill? I listened, entranced, to the soothing sound of this never-before-heard tone of voice, and then Frau Wotruba laughed that full-throated laughter of hers that made one smile uncontrollably. I wished I were inside her flat saying the things that were making her laugh so exquisitely. And then the question finally arose: What was my father doing in the flat coaxing her laughter? What business had he with Frau Wotruba that did not entail emergencies and that allotted him a house key? Such keys were not easy to come by in Vienna. It is not like the Americas where one simply goes to a hardware store and has a man grind out a duplicate whenever you want one. No, in Vienna, one must have a note from the owner of the building, or at the very least from the portier explaining the necessity for a duplicate to be made. Locks are meant to be respected in Vienna. The key my father kept with him was surely not our old one, for it had been duly returned to the portier the day we left Hubertusgasse. That meant the key he was using was most likely Herr Wotruba's house key. Father was using the key of her deceased husband. What else of the dead man was he using?

The question was half formed in my mind when sounds from inside answered it. They were speaking louder now; perhaps they had moved back toward the kitchen, onto which the apartment door opened. I could hear her distinctly.

"But why, Max?" (That was my father's name.) "We're such good friends. Why spoil it with that?"

Then my father's voice, still tender, though the gruffness was beginning to come through: "It won't spoil it, little birdie. It'll make it better, more. You'll see. Just this once."

"But it's just me down there . . . just me the same as you see here. We shouldn't."

"Oh, come on."

A sound like the smack of lips.

"You'll like it."

"No, Max. Stop it. Please. Why can't we just be friends?"

"After. Afterward we'll be friends. Now come on. You let that little runt of mine have his way, yet you keep me, a big healthy man, away from it. What kind of woman are you, anyway?"

There was silence for a time. I looked around frantically for something to stand on. I did not want to miss one instant of this. Near the communal basin was a stool upon which sat a large and dusty rubber plant. I put the plant on the floor quietly and moved the stool to the door. Standing on it, I was just at eye level with the transom, and looking in I saw part of Frau Wotruba's back. She was wearing a blue-and-white-striped housecoat that I had seen her wear many times. The material was coarse like mattress ticking. Father's hand was clearly visible on her back, rubbing up and down her spine, and lifting the housecoat farther up her legs with each seemingly innocent rub. She was no longer protesting. She wore half-hose reaching only to her knees. These were revealed as father persistently kneaded the housecoat upward. Abruptly, he stopped kissing her and held her out at arm's length. I could see neither of their faces through the tiny crack in the transom, only their decapitated trunks. Frau Wotruba shuddered as he continued holding her away from him, then came a loud snort from Father, followed by a girlish giggle from Frau Wotruba. I thought for a moment that he had left her, for his hands were no longer upon her, though she continued to stand very still. Suddenly her housecoat slipped off her shoulders, spilling in a pile to the floor. She stood in brassiere and underpants with those half-stockings still on. Her flesh looked all goose-bumpy despite the warmth of the day. Then Father's calloused hands appeared in back of her again, undoing the brassiere and then pulling down the underpants. These last left lines around her waist and at the bottom of her buttocks. She helped him by stepping out of the panties very slowly, as if in a dream. And I was amazed, once divested of clothing, at how lithe she appeared. I felt my own breath coming in short gasps now, my own urgency building. I became so dizzy I almost fell from the stool and had to exercise great self-control to be able to keep watching.

Frau Wotruba's back was still to me, tiny and triangular, the spine ridged with muscles. The knobs of her spine stood out distinctly and her behind was high and fine, for she had never carried a baby. Just above the rump, at the small of her back, were two dimplelike impressions on either side of the spine. I could not take my eyes off the fold of her buttocks leading downward, downward to that secret spot between her legs. She, unwillingly it seemed, slowly moved her feet apart, opening her legs. Strands of dark hair curled out of the base of her buttocks. She arched her back as if in pain and gurgled some words I could not understand. The muscles of her buttocks went taut. The fingers of a sun-weathered hand suddenly appeared down there, cupping her, holding and rubbing her.

I felt about to burst, but the extreme eroticism of the

moment was tinged with betrayal. Betrayal both from the frau and from my father.

Father turned her now and came around in back of her. He was still fully clothed, but his penis was sticking out of his pants, a great red angry sausage with thick black hairs bursting out of his fly at the base of the thing. He made poor Frau Wotruba bend over the table, her breasts crushed against the oilcloth covering, and then he placed that ugly penis between her legs and it disappeared. This seemed to cause her great pain or great pleasure, I could not tell which. She stuck her hand into her mouth as if to stifle a scream. Father moved his hips and out popped his sausage, glistening wet.

Then Father began moving back and forth more and more quickly, sinking his shaft into her and then withdrawing it. Frau Wotruba, at each entrance and exit, emitted little gasps, like a choo-choo train climbing a steep gradient. Still she bit her knuckles. Then her hips began to move, too, uncontrollably and spasmodically. She pumped them around and around, up and down as Father gyrated back and forth like a belly dancer. His face got redder and redder; a vein pulsed and expanded on his forehead until I thought it might burst. I was surprised they didn't knot up his wurst with such movements. Her frisson—the same she had with me when I gently rubbed her breasts—happened and suddenly her hips were still. But this did not stop Father from continuing to batter at her buttocks like a siege weapon at the gates of a Mussulman fortress. This went on, the slap of belly against rump, until finally he shouted out "Jesus, Mary, and Joseph!" and rammed very tightly into her, gripping her hips against his with such force that his fingers seemed to bite into her very flesh. They held together like that for a long moment, then Father pulled away from her and his penis was all crumpled now, no longer alert and angry, but a peaceful thing that occasionally jerked upward as it continued to droop. It was as if it did not want to lose its stiffness, its strength. It did not want to reassume the quotidian function of micturation and encumbrance inside tight-fitting pants. It wanted to hold on to this other existence, this life at the edges of experience.

Perhaps it is romanticizing the event years after the fact, but I remember then, at that very moment as a young boy watching the act for the first time, that I felt the mystery of it; I saw the magic of the penis for the first time. And I hated him, my father, for it. For being the one to have Frau Wotruba, to steal her away from me. I hated him all the more because of the size of his instrument. She would never be satisfied with me now, after she had that massive thing inside her. Mine was a pencil in comparison to his. If before I felt mild disgust with Father, from that day until his death two years hence, I felt active jealousy and hatred. He had both shown and ruined the magic for me. He had been the one to get there first. There was no thought of the fact that he was betraying Mother with his activities. Such bourgeois morality has never played a part in my ethical system. No, father's was a betrayal of a much larger scale: He had betrayed his own son's sexuality. This stung at the very heart of me—it killed something inside of me. Some remnant of feeling I held vis-à-vis Father. I believe that day in August I truly left my boyhood behind.

———

Cordoba called unexpectedly last night. It was not our card evening. I shall not transcribe the taped conversation. He merely handed me a letter postmarked from New York. It had been opened. I quickly pulled out the cream-colored linen paper and read the message for Miss O'Brien. Her agent had been mollified by the postcard sent from our village; she was looking forward to seeing her once again in New York.

"Don't be so long between letters again," she wrote by way of closing.

My gambit would not, then, keep the woman at bay indefinitely.

I was all smiles, but Cordoba only frowned at me. It seems our mutual friends are not pleased with my compromise. They do not want any trail leading to their country.

"They are becoming very nervous, my friend," Cordoba told me as he was leaving. "Very nervous."

This morning, I showed the Irish the letter and told her of Cordoba's warning.

"Let them sweat, the bastards."

This was her only comment. No Mexico City postcard until after she's read more of my manuscript. There is no cajoling that will work on that score. So be it. If she is unconcerned for her well-being, why should I lose any sleep over it?

But let me not be detoured from my major purpose: I wish to show explicitly what transpired during my years in the corps. That is what is of value here; enough of this other wallowing in sentimentality—the small bourgeois aperçu. This is not a chronicle of small struggles, awakenings, and disappointments, but of sweeping, magisterial world history. Indeed, the very world hung in the balance, not the paltry emotions of a twelve-year-old boy. And I was part of that movement which shook the very foundations of the world.

Thus, back to the movement. . . .

———

As planned, Operation Himmler gave us the opportunity we needed to dispose of the Polish problem. We invaded on the first of September; by the third, we were at war with both England and France. It was unfortunate that they felt the need to interfere in a border dispute between neighbors, but there it was. There was no going back, and within a matter of weeks, we had completely subdued the foolish Poles who fought us so ludicrously with sabers and horse cavalry while we rolled across their countryside in Panzer divisions and the Luftwaffe strafed and bombed them from the air. It was war practiced as it never had been before. A new word had to be added to the dictionary to describe such a lightning-quick attack: *blitzkrieg*. Apposite, both for the speed with which it transpired and for the fact that much of the attack did come from the skies, like lightning, or like the judgment of the old gods upon lesser evolved races. It was a purifying war, a holy war. We Germans were the modern Crusaders. Those were inspirational times, uplifting, ecstatic. No one can truly understand those times who did not live through them.

No one can have an accurate picture of the Nazi movement without knowing what went before: the shame of Versailles; the runaway inflation of the twenties and thirties; the destruction of the very fiber of German intellectualism by the poisonous theories of the Jews Freud and Einstein. Those two between them, the first with his unconscious forces, the second with his relativity, killed the world of certainties and moral exactitude upon which Western civilization is built. Little wonder then, amid the resulting anarchy of the thirties, that the Nazi Party, with its reestablishment of tried-and-true feudal values, its resurgence of law and order, and its belief in a quasi-Christian morality ("quasi" in that it blended the pagan with more orthodox traditions, not the least of which was Judaism itself with its sense of apartness, the chosen people)—little wonder then of the groundswell of support we experienced: from the displaced little people to wealthy industrialists, from the military to the university. We were in the flow of the time. We, in fact, created both the current and the time. To be a part of that movement—to be, indeed, among its leadership—those were heady times.

I went back into training for several months following Operation Himmler and the onset of the war. From the start, it was tacitly agreed that I should not be part of the Waffen Schutzstaffel, which fought alongside and, more often, in advance of regular Wehrmacht units. My law degree, my interests, my connections (why be less than frank about this?) all pointed toward a higher administrative posting for me. Which was fine. I am not an overly brave man. I do in a pinch, but the action at the Hohenlinden forestry station demonstrated to me my own limitations. I am a man of moral action, but physically, I am, like most men, shy. Not cowardly, but certainly one who is frightened under fire. My skills would be better used and my fatherland better served in administration.

By late fall of '39, I was in Berlin on the Prinz Albrecht Strasse working as an assistant at Amt IV of Foreign Intelligence at Staffel headquarters. Lord knows the qualifications I had for such a position. I was, in fact, adjutant to Major General Heinz Jost, the man who had come to our training camp at Bernau and asked for volunteers for Operation Himmler.

I was soon inducted into the SD, the security branch of the corps, and wore the silver SD lozenge emblazoned on the cuffs of my black tunic quite proudly. Jost came to rely on me heavily. We at Ausland SD were responsible for a network of agents in foreign countries, for deciphering and interpreting their cables, for keeping up our end of the show and not letting the Gestapo or Abwehr scoop us. That autumn, our biggest coup was the capture of Captain Best of the British mission in the Netherlands whom, via a double agent, we enticed to a meeting near the border. It was a fine bit of work, a real shoot-'em-up cowboy type of abduction, as we had to chase him right back over the border into neutral Netherlands and kill his bodyguard to capture him. All this right under the noses of the potato-headed Dutch border guards who did absolutely nothing to stop us! Himmler was ecstatic at the news, and Heydrich sent promotions all around to those involved. I began the process that would ultimately elevate me to lieutenant colonel by the end of the war. At this time, I won my lieutenant's bars. But it was not only for my planning on the Best affair. My strength lay in organization, and that became apparent to everybody at headquarters. I knew how to find the people needed for a job and how to keep them busy. There was a sense of great things in store for me.

I wanted very much to succeed in my new position, for by this time, my wife, Uschi, had joined me from Vienna and we had set up household in the suburb of Wannsee. The small villa I took for us was above my means, of course, but by this time, I had learned the importance of presentation. One must act the part one wishes to obtain. It is that simple. The villa was, in fact, a trifle superior to that of my boss, Heydrich, who lived in Grunewald, another nearby green suburb, and to that of the chief of the Abwehr, Admiral Canaris, also a neighbor. With all the fervor of the petit bourgeois graduating into the middle class, I went for ostentation.

The villa was rented before Uschi arrived. It would need all the interest her dowry earned to pay the rent; we would have to eat, clothe ourselves, and entertain on my meager salary. Uschi was not happy with the arrangements from the very first. A member in good standing of the upper middle class, she had no need to prove her membership status. Far better, she suggested, that we take a commodious flat in town that was within our means. After all, she reminded me, we had not arrived yet. We had hardly earned the right to flaunt all the privileges of the station. Those would come with time.

She had patience; she could afford to. But I, who saw the world from the bottom up, would not be lulled by her arguments. I knew how chimerical history could be. What I wanted, I wanted right now; let the satisfied make do with patience, let them trust in history. I was paying the ultimate price for my prizes. But I could not explain this to Uschi, nor could I even say that I understood how she felt about the villa: *Burgher als Edelmann*—the bourgeois acting like nobility. I could even laugh at my own ambition, but not with her. We unfortunately disallowed each other the ultimate comfort of total, naked honesty, one with the other. If there is one thing I could imagine a marriage to be good for, it would be this comfort, this release from the worldly roles that we assume. But this I was unable to do with Uschi, nor she with me, which was a great sadness for us both. I maintained the role of the stolid silent anchor, she that of the frivolous, gay, spritely girl. Such roles had obvious advantages during the early days of our courtship; they made for simple straightforward dealings with each other.

But they lingered, they continued past the point of usefulness. Now we were as two marionettes. There was no ease between us; we were only players in a very bad farce and neither of us knew a way out. The villa in Wannsee was cold and cheerless with only the two of us habituating it, and I began finding reasons for staying later and later at the shop. These were now the months of the Sitzkrieg, the phony war as the English call it, but still it was wartime. Uschi could hardly complain that I, a soldier in uniform, was not spending more time with her.

No, there was no ease, no comfort there for either of us, in even the most literal of ways. Uschi was a woman of very limited libido. Which is not to say that I am the eternal Don Juan, but she found the entirety of the sex act somewhat disgusting. Ultimately she refrained from even a casual kiss or cuddle in fear that it would lead to more.

And thus we lived for months on end, avoiding each other, happy for the work that would take me out of Berlin on occasional inspection tours, for by this time, I had been transferred to another and most important posting: Section IVA, 4b of the Schutzstaffel desk under a man named Eichmann.

"I read the rest of the manuscript."

"Quick reader."

"There's very little else to do here."

"You've your own writing."

"That accounts for four, maybe five hours. Then there's the other twenty. Can we talk?"

"Of course. I should like that."

"I was hard on you about that Wotruba thing. And I think it helps. I assume you're going to rewrite, I mean reorganize, the materials rather than include my criticism directly in the narrative?"

"___"

"I'd advise it, anyway. What's the old dictum? Everywhere at work and nowhere apparent. I know these are memoirs, but still you don't want every nail and joint visible. Writing is like cabinetmaking, not carpentry. If you're going to do it at all, you must agree to the code: You must not diminish the world of letters by your contribution. The old Latin saying for doctors holds with us, as well. *Primus, non nocere*. First . . ."

"Do no harm. Yes, Miss O'Brien. I know my Latin, too. But you surprise me. Such conservatism. Such pomposity. And about mere words."

"There's nothing mere about words. They're the one thing that matters to me. And no one demands that you elevate literature by what you do, or that you make revolutionary changes in form or content. But you must not belittle it, reduce it. You must not take it down. You understand that, don't you? I'm not talking simple style here, for some of the best work in letters is done by amateurs. Those who have a story that must be told, any way they can tell it, rather than those old pros who have to tell a story, any story will do. Like a traffic warden and her quota of tickets for the week. You do see that, don't you? I know you do. For your writing at its best has an urgency. It cannot be stopped. It must come out. I respect that, and that is why I attack when you present me . . . us . . . with less than candor. That's the betrayal I was speaking of in my note to you. You make a bargain with the reader when you use the confessional mode. You're not allowed to break that deal by using less than total frankness. Trouble is, though, you're playing a game somewhere in between much of the time. You've enough verbal skills to seem polished, and enough frankness to seem confessional. But in between all that, you dissemble and revert to stuffy writing. That's a problem. A definite problem."

"But you like it, don't you?"

"I'm sorry to say I do. It would be easier for me if I didn't. I'm taken with your writings. You display a full character, pimples and all, even if you don't realize you're doing it. It's a gold mine for researchers."

"How do you mean pimples and all?"

"I don't want to make you self-conscious."

"How do you mean? Aren't you going to eat at all? It's getting cold."

"You spice your beans enough to keep them hot for hours. . . . I mean that, in many ways, you are an intellectual naïf. Others would examine their writing for hidden messages. For the Freudian slip, or a connection to the Jungian consciousness. But I honestly believe that you do not know more than the few obvious buzzwords about depth psychology. I mean that you're a tabula rasa intellectually, so that your experience is not filtered through any intellectual apparatus before it is served up to us."

"Miss O'Brien. What are you getting at?"

"Take Cow, for instance."

"He was the most straightforward one of us all. He had no need for silly Jewish head games."

"I don't mean Cow himself. Rather your relationship with him. Again, you revealed it yourself quite unconsciously."

"Revealed what?"

"If you're going to be like that . . ."

"All right. Sorry. But please do not be so elliptic. I am a

stubborn old German. Ossification has set in. I need things spelled out."

"Okay. But you're not going to like it. There was an obvious homoerotic content to your friendship. Take the incident of Cow falling asleep in your bunk."

"It was the lightning storm. It scared him. Can't a man have a close friend anymore without the onus of fairy being leveled at him?"

"And the feelings of jealousy you experienced when he went to the camp prostitutes, using your chits as well as his own. That's suggestive of more than simple camaraderie, don't you think?"

"What is your point?"

"Operation Himmler. The first go-round of it when you killed your friend. I assume he died, for you do not mention him again in the manuscript. He simply disappears. You voice no remorse, no sadness. Heady symbolism there. The belly shot and all. And your very first shot of the war at a potential enemy. To shoot one's silver bullet is, in American slang, to lose one's virginity. The penetration of the bullet. Destruction of that which is unattainable. I assume Cow did not share your inclinations? There's nothing wrong with it, you know. It's not a sickness, not something to hide from the world."

———

She is a witch. She takes every fine noble intent and twists it to her own perverted ways. She questions, questions, and destroys by her questioning—like Turandot, only more malevolent. Perhaps like one of those goddess-witches in Russian fairy tales who always pose the series of life-threatening questions to weary travelers.

Of course I cared for Cow; of course I felt horrid about his accidental death. That I have not written of it does not mean I have something to hide, but only that I will not wallow in sentiment or false guilt. I shot Cow, yes. But quite by accident and without erotic intent!

How ill must the Irish herself be even to see the possibility of such a relationship from what I wrote. Attempting honesty, I am rebuked for homoerotic tendencies. Yet if there is not some such psychological overtone to what I write, I am assailed by the very same vituperation for lack of candor. She puts me in a no-win situation. What is so surprising to me is that I have allowed her to do so. She is my prisoner; I have no need to deal with her at all. I started this for her own good, to give her something to do and because she asked me. I confess to having been swayed by flattery. She professed to like the first pages. At that time, she talked in the jargon of publishing, of line editing. Nothing of content. Yet that is all I have received from her thus far. Criticism upon criticism on the content only. She wishes to engage me in debate over the very basis of my life's work; thus she must deconstruct me incrementally. This has now become apparent to me: her sinister plan. I am wise to her now; I shall not go into our friendly little discussions anymore without my own store of ammunition. It is her turn, now, to share.

———

But first, I relate the following incident to demonstrate how far off the mark O'Brien is. It was January 1933, the very day, in fact, when Hitler came to power in Berlin. In modern histories, I see the proper way to refer to the beginning of the Third Reich is "the day Hitler seized power." This from German historians wishing to avoid any shared blame. "Seized" be damned. He was duly elected by the German people to the Chancellery. They also write of the period in the passive voice, ever a popular mode for the gutless historian, but done to the extreme when writing about the Reich, to imply that all this was done to Germany; the Nazis were oppressors and not representing the true German Zeitgeist.

In 1933, the Nazi Party is still outlawed in Austria. Vienna has clandestine cells that show their muscle on occasion. I am attracted to these sturdy youths in their crumpled trench coats and riding boots. They are full of a virility that is otherwise sadly lacking in Vienna. A most proper city is Vienna, a place-for-everything sort of city. I am not a Bolshevik as a youth, not the sort of anarchistic personality who would tear down the structures of society just for the fun of it. But even then, before more exactly identifying myself with the National Socialists, I know I want to see some of the old stodgy ways replaced, to let a breath of fresh air into our stuffy city.

On this bitterly cold January day, the Hitlerians are out in force, celebrating the victory of their leader. "Austria next!" is their chant, and it rings in my ears as I walk the windswept Ringstrasse toward the university. The police do not interfere with the demonstration today; they dare not provoke an incident on such an emotion-charged day. This is an early indication of the new hands-off policy toward the Nazis now that Hitler is legitimated by elected power in Germany. So the Nazis stride brazenly down the center of the boulevard, obstructing cars and trams alike. Yet the motorists are strangely quiet; no one dares honk his horn at the marchers.

"Austria next! Austria next!"

This, the tramping of boots on cobbles, and the cawing of the Russian crows in the parks, are the only sounds to be heard.

I stop for a moment in front of Café Landtmann to view the procession. There is something hypnotic about it, the fanaticism of young men in a ragtag assemblage of uniforms and trench coats. The interstices of relative quiet between chants is punctuated by the sound of their boots on the stones of the street. I stand where the café terrace is located in the fine months; customers inside have their faces pressed to the windows watching, watching.

One elderly gentleman, quite distinguished looking with a fresh white carnation in his lapel, smiles at me. It is one of the law professors at the university. I do not know him personally and have not yet had a class from him, being only in my first year at university, but I know him by sight. He is well respected in his field, one of the brighter stars in the law faculty firmament, an expert in constitutional law. Austrians have seldom proved talented at jurisprudence. Perhaps this is a legacy of Habsburg paternalism, perhaps a result of the Viennese penchant for "what-if" living. In a city ruled by the god of stodginess, the intellectuals take refuge in dream worlds and idealism. Freud is the biggest dream merchant of them all. Wittgenstein, too. Arguments spun out of air. No practical value. Those are the legacies of the city. Schoenberg and company, as well, with their antimusic. Theorizing, theorizing. Never creating anything usable. Applied physicist Ernst Mach was the only so-called brilliant Viennese to give the world something lasting: He left behind a benchmark of speed relative to that of sound. I bring these names up to illustrate my point: Austrian theoreticians of jurisprudence follow in the same nonapplied, non-reality-bound tradition as those other intellectuals. Yet law is the most reality bound of all disciplines. Or should be.

Professor Haberloch, the man sitting in Café Landt-mann smiling at me, had somehow avoided that terrible tradition. He had been a first-class trial lawyer in his day. It was he who won the suit for Lieberman AG against the government, a groundbreaking decision setting the limits of culpability for private corporations. He was a brilliant tactician and had the accompanying strength of brilliant elocution. He could explain complex points to a jury or judge alike without making either feel patronized or manipulated. In short, Haberloch was every fledgling law student's hero. He still kept a limited private practice even though he now taught full-time at the university.

His lectures on criminal law were attended by half of Vienna it seemed, for they were far more than mere lectures. They were events in which, by his very power of speech, Haberloch made one feel in the presence of great authority. His talks encompassed the entire spectrum of creation: He could make law appear to be the sun around which the planets of ambition, love, sadness, longing—around which all aspects of life—revolved. Some of these lectures I had sat (or rather stood, they were that crowded) in on, and I had been impressed by the man's charisma, like all the rest of those attending.

But there is absolutely no reason that man should recognize me, a face out of the multitude. It is unmistakable, however: He continues to smile at me in a very knowing manner, as if he sees right into me. He nods once and indicates a free chair at his window table inside the café. I am already late for my geopolitics course, yet such an opportunity of talking to the great man one-on-one is not to be missed. I enter the door and push aside the heavy felt curtain that serves to catch drafts at the entrance. He has risen from his chair. I think for an embarrassing moment that I have misunderstood his gesture. But instead of preparing to leave, as I thought momentarily, Haberloch pulls out the other chair for me. I move to the tiny marble-topped table in a dream and make a bowlike nod of respect to the proffered chair. The place is rich in the smell of roasted coffee, cigar smoke, and hot chocolate. I cannot look at the great man for a time, for I am too embarrassed and tongue-tied. I watch, three tables distant, a group of well-to-do pensioners playing Tarok. I start, shocked, when I realize that one of these card players is the onerous Dr. Freud, who occasionally makes such a stir in the press with his psychoanalytic theories. Haberloch notices my glance of recognition and smiles. It is as if he wants to initiate me into the world of great men. Me, a first-year student at the university who still works afternoons and Saturday mornings in his mother's tobacco shop!

He asks me if I would like a cup of coffee and I say yes, that would be very nice, and I still cannot believe I am sitting here. Or cannot understand what he could want with me, but suddenly I blurt out how honored I am, a simple law student, and how much I respect his work. It comes tumbling out of me without grace or much coherence. And he smiles again, quite pleasantly, at my accolades. I feel his strength even in his silences. Power emanates from him palpably. My right leg begins to move nervously: My heel taps and jerks my knee up and down like a piston as I sit poised on the edge of my chair, brittle as a china cup in expectation. Coffee is brought. It is a mélange, I remember, with a liberal dose of chocolate powdered on top of the creamy froth. I do not know why I should remember that detail. I look at the coffee nervously for a moment and he tells me it is his treat. That he remembers how it is to be a poor student. And I feel a comforting kinship with him after this remark. I quit wondering why this distinguished, almost famous man is wasting his time on me. With that absolute arrogance of youth, I assume Haberloch is lonely and thinks me to be an interesting-looking fellow to chat up. He is unorthodox enough in his lectures to make such personal behavior an accepted eccentricity. I drink the mélange contentedly. My foot slowly stops tapping.

He begins to speak of the auspicious day we are experiencing. But he says this with bitter irony. I do not reply one way or the other; I do not want to disagree with this man of the world, but I nonetheless feel drawn by the bond of shared youth to those followers of Hitler in the streets. They have passed by, but traffic is still backed up behind them. I smile at the thought that ones so young could have the power to bring the staid old grown-up world of breadwinners and bureaucrats to a halt.

Haberloch talks of today as the "death of law"—I remember that phrase exactly. How the Führer principle would soon be established and we would be back to the old feudal days of the law as the consensus not of the people or of tradition, but of one man powerful enough and tricky enough to have gained power over the rest. There is a great sadness in his eyes as he speaks, and I notice for the first time that he is not drinking coffee but brandy. He does not ask me where I stand on this issue, and for that I am thankful. Instead he lectures on about the rule of man being replaced by the rule of one man; of how the kaiser principle has ruined the German-speaking peoples with too much paternalism. He says that those young street toughs are right: Austria will be next. We will embrace the

National Socialists like a whore her richest customer. His voice raised with this statement.

I feel he must be a bit tipsy to talk so in public. The men at Freud's table turn for a moment to see who is creating the stir. This embarrasses me. I want suddenly to be elsewhere. Haberloch drains his glass and apologizes. He calls the waiter to pay his bill. I am about to say that I must be on my way to class. We get up to leave, and as we stand, I am about a head taller than the great man. From the stage or podium, he has always taken on the proportions of a giant. His hair, so white and thick when seen from a distance, is, at closer inspection, tinged with yellow. He is suddenly, in my eyes, an old and embittered man out of step with the times and using solipsism and casuistry to defend his outmoded position.

Once outside, he apologizes again for his outburst and calls me his young friend. Regaining his composure, he also wins back some of my respect. He breathes deeply of the chill air, and it seems to brace him better than the brandy. Squaring his shoulders, he looks once again the influential and thoughtful man he is. I repent my traitorous thoughts of only moments before. We stand for a moment there in front of Café Landtmann: I feel it is my part to await dismissal. But Haberloch continues to take in deep breaths and look into the brilliant blue sky, a sky that only extreme cold can create: that blue which is as hard and pure as a mountain lake.

He tells me suddenly that he would appreciate some company today. He has had bad news and would be most happy if I could see my way to stay with him a little longer. It is such a straightforward and honest request that I can hardly refuse. He looks at the satchel of books I am carrying and says that he will make it good with my professors. I need only tell him who they are and he will have a little word with them. We begin walking into the Inner City from the Ring. I have no idea of our destination, but it is a pleasant day for a walk. It is by now early afternoon and the shops are reopening after the long lunch hour. We stop occasionally in front of a men's clothing shop or an antique dealer and Haberloch investigates the contents of the display window minutely. At more than one shop, the proprietor recognizes Haberloch and comes out in the street to see if there is anything he can help the great man with. His aura of importance is completely reinstated in my eyes.

Finally we enter a fine ("noble" is the way the Viennese describe it), large apartment on Habsburgergasse. There is an oak and plush elevator in the stairwell that we take up to the third floor. Haberloch, who has a villa in Hietzing, tells me he keeps a pied-à-terre in the city for those late nights working when he just does not want to return home. Here, he keeps his files, and now it seems he needs to fetch one before a late-afternoon court appearance. His simple pied-à-terre turns out to be an elegant flat much larger than the one that I share with my sister, Maria, and my mother. I have noticed this about influential and wealthy people: Understatement forms the very core of their self-deception.

We go into one of the grand rooms off the entrance hall. It is set up as a study with a leather armchair by a ceramic stove and rosewood desk in the projecting bay window. It is cold in the flat, for Haberloch has not used it for some time. He pours out two brandies from a crystal decanter—to ward off the cold, he says—and I sip at mine. I am no fan of the fiery taste, but do not want to appear the callow youth, so I continue to sip as he picks through a wooden file cabinet by the desk. His back turned toward me, he apologizes once again—needlessly, I think—for his outburst at the café. But it is true, he says. We in Austria shall surely be next. He turns, and his face has a strange, rather pleading expression. He says (and I remember his exact words) that such thinking is defeatist. He wishes it were not so, but he can see that all he has so stubbornly and painfully fought for is soon going to be swept away. He wonders why any individual then should cling to outmoded codes of honor if, as he sees, the state itself is about to forgo such a code. It is the ultimate breakdown of mores, he says, and he feels he should no longer play the little boy with his finger in the dike. He laughs strangely at this turn of phrase and then approaches me, coming right up close to my face. I can smell the brandy on him.

"You don't know what I'm talking about, do you?" he says.

I am uncomfortable, that is all I know at the moment, and make no reply. We stand thus for a full minute. He looks up into my face with real force and with gray eyes that single one out, isolate one and penetrate. I have never looked so closely into a man's eyes before and I feel somehow locked to him, under his power, and I know something new and rather terrifying is about to happen. I notice his breathing now as he stands so close to me, and it comes raspy like that of Frau Wotruba at those certain times we had together.

Suddenly, he tosses back his head and laughs. It is ironic laughter, but not cruel, and then he slaps me on the back, telling me what a capital fellow I am and to pay no attention to an old man's mental wanderings. "I shall need a keeper before it is all over," he says.

We finish our drinks and he tucks the file into his brief-case—a quite smart one out of the softest calfskin, not rough and horny like the old pigskin one I carry. Before we leave, he claps me on the back again and says he could use a bright young student like me for legal research. His last assistant has done the unforgivable of becoming a high-class lawyer in Klagenfurt—would I be interested in the position? "Take your time," he tells me. "Let me know next week."

I am ecstatic at the suggestion: to team up with this famous man at the very beginning of my studies! It will mean instant success for me. Just imagine the connections one could accrue through such a man. Yet there is also the inexplicable discomfort I feel in his presence. I thank him for the offer and promise to let him know my decision by next week. We leave, taking the stairs as the elevator only carries passengers upward. Outside the house door, he indicates that he is going to the Federal Court. I must catch a late lecture at the university. He makes a comic Heil Hitler salute at me; I blush and merely nod.

As I walk down Habsburgergasse in a daze, a fellow student catches me up. It is Hofnagel, whose patrician family also has a flat in this street. Normally, when we meet at the uni, he manages to cut me, but today he is suddenly solicitous. He is out of breath as he comes alongside me. I am surprised by his sudden interest in me, even that he knows my name, until I realize he must have seen me and Haberloch together and this has raised my stock in his eyes. He mentions, as subtly as he can, that he was not aware that I have such important friends. He says it in a way that I take to be condescending. Hofnagel is tall and stoop shouldered and wears a faint finely trimmed mustache. He brushes at it continually while talking to me. His statement is a challenge, as if to say that I probably accosted the old man in a grasping petit bourgeois attempt at securing some pull with the powerful. This constellation of priggish patrician

J. Sydney Jones

assumptions angers me and I blurt out to Hofnagel that I have been offered the position as the great man's research assistant.

"Oh, that is rich," he says. "That is just fine. I didn't realize you were one of those," he says.

But I do not understand him. Perhaps Haberloch is a Jew? I have not thought of this possibility. I try to decide whether to bluff it out or not, but Hofnagel sees that he has me at a disadvantage.

"But you have no idea what I mean, do you?" he says. "Impossible. I had no idea there were any pure naïfs left."

And then he takes great pleasure in explaining to me just what it is that half of Vienna knows about Haberloch: Namely, that he is a homosexual, and that the sinecure of his research assistant carries with it rather more responsibilities than can be accomplished in a law library.

"I am sure you understand me, old man," he finishes.

And as we approach the university, he manages to pull ahead of me so that his other fancy friends will not see him talking to such a lowly and naive person as I.

Needless to say, I did not take the proffered appointment, though I was greatly amused to learn that the snob Hofnagel himself accepted it later that year. The families were somehow connected; young Hofnagel must have capitulated under pressure from his parents, regardless of what others would say. What an object lesson for me: The absolute disregard for self-respect that the upper classes display when advancement is in the balance. Of course, I am not saying that Haberloch and Hofnagel committed any indecencies, but still . . .

At any rate, Hofnagel's unsolicited information explained the extreme discomfort I experienced in Haberloch's presence. Now I knew the type and was duly on my guard against them. A small incident, one might say, but if I had even the slightest inclination toward a life of sodomy, I should surely have availed myself of this opportunity, for the reward of it would have been high indeed. In the end, I did not need Haberloch's help, and, as events turned out, would have been hurt by association with him. We shall have occasion to meet up with Herr Haberloch again in these pages. . . .

———

"You don't look well."

"I feel the shits."

"You didn't eat your supper last night."

"___"

"You've got to eat."

"You aren't listening. I feel the shits. I can't eat. I think I've got a fever."

"You're just imagining things. A form of hypochondria. Many prisoners experience it. Too much turning inward."

"I forgot. You're the fucking expert on prisoners, aren't you? You've made it a lifetime hobby."

"I didn't come to exchange evil words. Eat your breakfast or you will become ill."

"Screw you. I already am ill."

"And your time is up. About the next letter to your agent, I mean."

"But I haven't finished reading. You haven't given me the rest."

"It's right here, along with your eggs. Now I've kept my part of the bargain."

"I can't eat. I'm sick."

"We'll see."

———

The Irish goes out for a short time today, and admittedly, I notice she is unsure on her feet. Perhaps she really is ill?

But it is a lovely day. The sun is still high in the sky and very warm. Usually, I rather like watching her in the compound during her exercise period. Yet, today, she mopes about listlessly, then sits on a rock holding her freckled face into the sun.

She makes the situation more difficult and uncomfortable than it need be by not simply accepting it. It is as I said before: Giving up and giving in are the two things women cannot do well. With the proper mind-set, she could take this entire affair as an opportunity rather than a punishment. She is finally free to write all day long just as she chooses. I am sure this is what writers yearn for: such an opportunity to hole up and write that novel that they have been promising themselves for so long. In a way, as I said to Cordoba, I am acting as her patron. But she just cannot see it like that.

She sits so placidly in the sun. Here is the cat in her once again: so feline and sun warmed. She barely bestirs herself for minutes on end. I think today would be a good laundry day with the sun so warm. I must get the Irish to change her clothes. The khakis she is wearing look as if they've been slept in. I shall talk to her after the—

———

I must explain the abrupt ending in my previous diary entry. As I was musing to myself about the Irish and her hygiene, she simply fell over. She fainted.

Three days have since passed. It has been awful.

I was skeptical of the Irish's faint. I let myself into the compound warily, armed with my syringe, and went over to her. She was breathing strangely, like a dog panting on a hot day. I felt her pulse: It was racing, and her skin was hot to the touch. It was a fever and not sun induced. I put my syringe away and lifted her eyelid and saw that her eye was cloudy and dilated. She truly was unconscious. I did not panic, knowing immediately what must be done. It was the same fever I'd had upon first coming here. Most Europeans, in fact, suffer from it initially. Many die. It is the rite of passage to this colony.

Miss O'Brien is a tall, sturdily built woman. I tried lifting her, but to no avail. Dead weight in my arms, she was also too ungainly for me to hold. Gripping her under the arms, I dragged her indoors to her room and laid her on the bed. As I did so, she emitted a loud liquid sound from below, followed by the most repellent odor. It was already in her bowels, then, and from that, most die. Perhaps it would be a blessing, I thought. Nature making the decision. But I could not just leave her like that; I was compelled to do as much for her as I could while she still lived. I knew what the course of the disease would be: a fever high enough to split her head and simultaneous diarrhea that could kill her with dehydration.

The odor was horrid. I breathed through my mouth and pulled her down from the bed and dragged her upstairs to the bath. There I stripped her clothes off and wiped her like an overgrown baby as she lay on the bath mat. Then I filled the bath with cold water and lowered her in. I propped her head up so that she would not slide under and fetched a squeeze bottle I once used to force-feed a pup whose bitch had died. As she lay in the cold water, I forced the nozzle into her mouth and made her drink. She choked at first, coughing and spitting, but did not regain consciousness. Then finally she began drinking the water, emptying the bottle. Just as soon, she voided herself in the tub. I drained the water, cleaned her off once more, and filled the tub again. This process I must have repeated ten times that first afternoon, and finally, at sunset, I began to notice a drop in her temperature—from 104 to 103. But she was far from being out of danger and was even beginning to eliminate blood.

For me, these hours were spent in a blurry nonreflective haze. I was exhausted and dreaded the long night. Light from the sunset poured into the bathroom, turning the tile and tub a fiery red. It threw shadows of the window sash across Miss O'Brien, making the sign of the cross on her breasts. Her face was not contorted or twisted in pain, but looked very peaceful and far away. Her breasts half floated in the water, two misplaced fishing bobs rosy in the sunset. It had been many years since I had the chance to simply appreciate looking at a woman's body. Don't get me wrong: I was not being a cheap voyeur at this point. I felt a true intimate of the woman, as much as if we'd slept together. And then, once more, she voided herself and her eyes opened momentarily, consciousness flooding her at this most private moment, and she looked at me pleadingly, her face full of shame.

I kept her wrapped in cool wet sheets all that night up in my own room, handy to the bathroom, and rigged up huge diapers out of bath towels and pillow slips. I forced water into her at intervals, but the swallowing also activated her sphincter and the water was passed out of her almost as fast as it entered. I fell into a fitful sleep at one point toward morning and had the dream I have not had in years: the Eichmann trial in Jerusalem is running in full Technicolor in my head, but I am Eichmann and I must listen to all the lies of those supposed survivors of Nazi persecution. It is a terrible dream, not because I feel any guilt, but because no one believes me when I rationally and logically tell them that I had little knowledge of such events. That I was, at first, a simple transport officer responsible for getting people and things from point A to point B. After all, if I were guilty of the horrendous crimes they say I am, would I not dream about the victims? Would I not see newsreel footage of bodies stacked like so much cordwood just as the Allied propaganda machine served up after the war? And if I were such a beast, then why would I be degrading myself so by helping the Irish, a woman who directly endangers my life? But the prosecution says this line of evidence is inadmissible.

I awake sweating and crying out, "But it's true I tell you!" Then I see the gray pellucid light that comes just before sunrise and I recognize the Irish's form on my bed, and I know things are all right. I have only been dreaming and I go to her, thinking I will need to change her diaper once again, yet there is no vile odor coming from her. She is bathed in sweat just as I am. A good sign. I insert the rectal thermometer: even better. Her temperature has dropped to 101. The fever is breaking. I replace the diaper and wrap her now in dry sheets and a warm blanket. She seems to be aware of my ministrations, for as I gently wipe her forehead with a damp towel, she sighs and then falls into a sound and contented sleep until midday.

———

"Your bed's nicer than mine."

"You must be getting better."

"How long has it been?"

"Only a few days. You've been very ill."

"That's good to hear. I'd hate to feel like this if I were healthy. Have you been having your way with me?"

"Miss O'Brien!"

"Only kidding. It feels like I've been sodomized by the entire Albanian army, though. Don't you think I'm a bit old for diapers?"

"—"

"Thanks. That's what I should say. It's just that I'm a little embarrassed."

"Don't be. There is no such thing as propriety where illness is concerned."

"No, I didn't mean about the fever and the diapers. I meant about saying thanks to my captor. That's what embarrasses me. Why did you do it? If you'd let me die, your problems would be over."

"I thought of that. I guess I've gotten used to having you around. You needed help. There wasn't much choice."

"Do me a favor?"

"Certainly."

"Get me a pen. I'll write that postcard to my agent now."

It is true, I should have let nature take its course. Miss O'Brien asked the correct question: Why didn't I? I still have no answer to it. I have gotten used to having her around; that is a fact. But one becomes accustomed to all sorts of things, both good and bad. Propinquity—forced or otherwise—brings about feelings too often confused with liking or even love. Yet man is a creature of habit. Thus anything threatening to disrupt habit is fought against, even that which threatens a bad habit. Realizing this does not mean that I am not controlled by the principle. Though I do not rule out the possibility of a true attachment, I do leaven it with the pragmatism of propinquity. To this must be added another possibility: During the days of nursing her, I rarely associated the being and personality of Miss O'Brien to this sick person. There was no way I could turn a blind eye toward her. She was sick unto death. It was impossible not to do all I could to help her. That is the paradox: She is my enemy, yet I must save her life!

There is a resonance here between my treatment of Miss O'Brien and that of the inmates of Mauthausen, the concentration camp where I served during the war. There at Mauthausen, in the winter of 1944, I decided to let nature take its course, as opposed to my intervention in the case of the Irish. Diphtheria struck the camp, a particularly virulent strain as it turned out, and by the time it had run its course, it had killed some forty-five hundred inmates. There was little enough one could have done under the best circumstances. What little medicine available was reserved for frontline soldiers and camp guards. Yet, in the end, it was my name on the order deciding not to aid the prisoners whatsoever. Even had there been adequate supplies, I would have acted the same. For in this case, it was right and proper to let nature proceed in its ineluctable cleansing process. In this, I was merely acting in good faith with party doctrine. The parallel with Miss O'Brien is this: In the case of the Mauthausen inmates—Jews, Gypsies, social undesirables, and hardened criminals—the patient was Europe and the disease was the inmates themselves. I acted as automatically to save civilization as I did to save the Irish. About this I am unrepentant, nor should it be otherwise, despite the *in absentia* judgment handed down against me at Nuremberg.

———

Things have begun to return to normal around here. Miss O'Brien regains energy every day. Yesterday, she elected to move back to her own quarters. I helped her down the stairs, but otherwise she is becoming quite steady on her feet once again. It was quite touching to see her face as she returned to the familiar surroundings of her room. We have, suffice to say, come a distance since the time, nearly two months ago, when I first introduced her to her new home. I do believe it would be safe now to return the paintings to her walls.

She walked about the room, touching her things. At her work desk, she simply stood and felt the wood of the table-top with her palm. She said not a word, but I knew what she was thinking: that she might never have survived to come back to this room, that what she had seen as her jail before now had the comforting and sheltering effect of home. One becomes used to so much in this world. I, for my part, am very happy I helped her through her illness. It took that to establish trust between us. If that was the price to be paid, I do not find it too high.

Today as I write, Miss O'Brien is once again in her compound. The sun at this time of year does not reach the back area but for a few hours at midday. The jungle growth blocks its light as the sun approaches its southern winter course. Winter. A laughable concept here, though after so many decades I do not know why it should matter anymore. How bizarre to think I have spent the greater part of my life here on this coast, backed up against the jungle. I, who love snow and the festivities of winter more than any man I have ever known. The ironies that life dishes up!

Christmas approaches. I do not know if the Irish is such a one as to celebrate the season. I shall have to inquire. As a sign of her trust, she has let me take one of her short stories that she has worked on while here. She sits now in the midday sun reading my memoirs, while I sit up here, having looked at her story.

What she has created here is really quite remarkable. I am a bit at sea as to know how to interpret the work, however. The title itself is quite something: "I Have to Tell You What I Know Before I Know What I Have to Tell You." I am not sure I understand this at all; I must confer with Miss O'Brien about it. This is the story, if you could call it that, of a sort of gigolo, a young man who has great success with the ladies. He falls in love with an older woman. This woman is, at one point, described as "someone whom the feminist battle had killed, but who advanced to fight the proper dentry."

Now I ask you. What in the world does this mean? What is *dentry*? I assume I am in the precincts of some new and weird modern fiction techniques. All right. I persevere. Little really happens in the story itself. It is told in conversation, somewhat like the transcripts of my tapes. Asterisks litter the text, however, and correspond to footnotes—this is the only way I can describe them. These are at times completely unintelligible mixes of abbreviated words; sometimes little cartoons in boxes at the foot of the page that in a way seem to throw light on the woman's character, or the man's, but do not seem really to have anything to do with advancing the story.

And the story is simply this: Here is one woman (hardly worth the fight, I should think) who will not allow the man easy access to her body. She forces him to admit first that he wants her, that he needs her.

"Though she was dead from the sexual battle herself, she knew how it should be waged."

Admittedly, there is a power to Miss O'Brien's rather understated, spare prose. It is almost lyrical without attempting to be so. The footnote to this particular aperçu is a picture instructing us, I assume, on how to win love: three monkeys of the "hear-see-speak no evil" sort with the caption "Fight, love, and live" beneath them. Another cartoon, its meaning totally lost on me, shows a bus with a smirk on its front radiator like a face, and a destination board on top with *Dentry* on it. This fixation with dentistry or oral hygiene (or is it some form of the Greek for *tree*?) is evident throughout the story. And when the young man is trying to woo the older lady—he has by now rented a room in her house—he is shown to be frying cold clotted rice in too much oil in a white porcelain dish over a low flame. This being the first literal concrete detail in the story, it must obviously have meaning, but I'm damned if I can figure it out. Sounds like some silly dream she had one night and transcribed it word for word. An eerie quality to it.

The lady now listens to the young man's subtle wooing without responding.

"Until now I have made no advances," he continues into her silence.

She is stubborn. She will not let him use that speech as meaning everything. She wants him to spell it out, if only for himself.

In the end, after playing by her rules and admitting his love for her, he is unable to perform.

————

"A very interesting story."

"You didn't like it."

"That's not what I said."

"I don't expect you to like it. Most wouldn't."

"I thought the footnotes clever."

"They weren't meant to be clever. They were meant to hurt, to sear into your guts. Clever is for novelists."

"___"

"___"

"I thought you drew him quite well. The poor chap's utter confusion at the antics of the older woman."

"Oh, Christ! Look, do you take everything in the world at its surface value?"

"Yes, I do, Miss O'Brien. I am not a miner. I leave grubbing around the pits to the colliers. When I read a story, a book, an essay, I like to know what it is the writer has to say. If he or she has a clear conception, then they make it apparent to their readers. If not, then they should remain silent until they have sorted things out for themselves."

"'*Wovon man nicht sprechen kann, darüber muss man schweigen.*' That sort of thing?"

"You surprise me continually, Miss O'Brien. But yes, precisely. One should learn to hold one's tongue about that which cannot be expressed in words, rather than fussing and fretting about it all over volumes of works."

"Like you and your memoirs?"

"I don't follow. Those are different altogether. A very realistic laying down of the facts. . . . Why do you shake your head?"

"I don't know how to get through to you."

"Be direct. Tell the thing simply and openly. All this symbolism, Miss O'Brien. The metaphor. The private language. I simply do not understand."

"But don't you see? That's the point! You aren't supposed to understand everything. Not up here, anyway. It works down here. Not with reason, but with your guts.

That's the idea. It makes you wonder rather than feel self-satisfied at understanding."

"But what, pray tell, is wrong with understanding? What is wrong with plain talking?"

"How can I tell you what you have to know before I know what I have to tell you?"

———

It is 1941. I am stationed in Vienna, quite an advancement. I am now a Schutzstaffel obersturmführer, and via my job in Section IVA, 4b, I commingle my destiny with a man history knows only too well: Adolf Eichmann. I am his assistant, as it were, at the Central Bureau for Jewish Resettlement; our offices are found in a suite of rooms in an old Rothschild palace on Prinz-Eugen Strasse. Initially, we get along fine, Eichmann and I. We are both Austrians; we understand the courtesies. Besides, by this time, Eichmann is seldom in Vienna. Much of the time, his duties are taking him to distant parts of the far-flung Reich.

My work, organizing the transport of Viennese Jewry, is all-encompassing. I take great satisfaction in solving problems of logistics and transport that others say are insoluble. Indeed, my colleagues take to calling me the Problem Man. I solve, rather than make, problems.

By now, I have learned the subtle art of simulated subservience. I have made it my trademark to know how to work my way through the state bureaucracy. My legal training helps here: I understand the hypocrisy of written laws, of constitutions, and how to get around these impediments.

In ways, it seems strange to be back in Vienna. After only two years in Germany, I am already feeling the German impatience with Austrian *Schlamperei*—a legacy of our quasi

Mediterranean Catholic heritage. The city resists organization, punctuality, order—all the virtues of the Reich. To find it so is a bit of a shock to me, having always seen Vienna as the most cosmopolitan of cities. Perhaps it still is—but after Berlin, Vienna pales in my eyes. It is, if this can be the case, much too feminine of a city for my liking. I appreciate the masculine charms of Berlin more: the Brandenburg Gate, the magnificent broad Kurfürstendamm, or Unter den Linden stretching from the Tiergarten to the Royal Palace. True, Vienna has her Ringstrasse, but even this is described by cognoscenti as a necklace around the Inner City, a most feminine adornment. And the rabbit warren of old streets in the First District unsettles me now, where once, as a child, I had found them rather romantic. I look at things from a tactician's point of view; I would just as soon Haussmannize Vienna as look it. Baroque lanes no longer fill me with a deep sense of rootedness in history. I care not that Mozart once trod these very cobbles, that Beethoven and Brahms lived in this house or that. Such considerations no longer pertain in the modern world. The free flow of traffic, of goods, materiel, and people is the goal of the modern world. That is how I saw it then, and largely how I see it still. Things that impede free flow are obstructions to be dismantled, destroyed, blown up—be they buildings, narrow lanes, or other people. Life is a magnificent procession: There is no room in it for backward looking, retrograde thinking, or for sentimentality. And Vienna is the capital of sentiment. The City of Dreams, it is called. The Phaeacian paradise with a chicken in the pot every Sunday, where the wine flows freely and the women are all insouciantly sweet. How laughable, how frivolous this reputation seems in 1941 when faced with the monumental tasks of war. I suppose I write so strongly about the procession of life, the meaning of life lying in the free flow of traffic, because those were my concerns during those years.

Sixteen-hour days are nothing for me, nor are six days a week to boot. I am at the center of the chaos that is Vienna. Presented with a tangled ball of string the size of Manhattan, I have the task to unravel it. That is what the work feels like; and when one loop of string is pulled free, it only tightens and knots another. Sisyphus, then, and the stuffed bureaucrats of the Municipality are my carrion birds, forever pecking at my innards.

Forgive the melodrama, but that is sincerely the way I felt in that period of service in Vienna. The wonder is that we were able to round up the several hundred thousand Jews residing in Vienna, that I was able to secure transport for their shipment and resettlement in the east.

Uschi, I regret to say, was very little help in these labors. In point of fact, she even questioned the advisability of our racial policy. She liked putting on aristocratic airs: Her family's *von* was granted at the time of Kaiser Franz, when one of the Danzel men became a minor court physician because of his impressive work with phlebitis, a disease from which one of the royal charges was suffering at the time. Of course, a physician could not be at court without the vestiges of belonging to the aristocracy. The rest of Uschi's family were quite humorous about their titled status, very droll, but Uschi latched on tighter and tighter to this *von* as the years of our empty marriage increased. She turned into something of a snob, in point of fact, and thought it her duty to protect those less fortunate than she. This noblesse oblige attitude of hers extended even unto the Jews and would be expressed at the most inconvenient of times, as would her opinion of Hitler himself, whom she described as a *tapezierer* and *anstreicher*, a mere paper-hanger and house painter, because of the rumors of his down-and-out days as a youth in Vienna. In general, this was the feeling of the entire von Danzel family. Though two of them had accepted the colors of the Staffel, they tolerated Hitler as some kind of comic hero who would fade away after the Nazis finally came onto the world stage; after the New Order had been firmly established.

Such a conversation was broached only once in my presence. I quickly put an end to it by a rather pointed comment; namely, that all we men in the room had pledged our very lives to this man they were ridiculing. Whereupon a long silence was punctuated by Frau von Danzel accidentally knocking her Lobmeyr crystal wineglass against her Augarten porcelain plate as she lifted the former. As for Uschi, I simply disallowed her to speak on the subject in my hearing.

So there was little support for my work at my villa, the big empty house on the Hohe Warte. It was Uschi who went for ostentation this time, who had to have the representative villa in the posh northern suburbs. It was a strange reversal for us: In Berlin I had been the one to play the role of newly arrived, swanking it with the Wannsee villa and the accounts at all the finest shops on Unter den Linden and Kurfürstendamm, all grossly above our means. Uschi had been the condemning one then, scornful of my typical middle-class delight in wealth. I embarrassed her, I do believe. One accustomed to living with fine things finds the delight in them by others to be slightly bad form. Lord knows why it is that, to truly exhibit class, one exhibits nothing, or if anything, just a disdain for it and its accoutrements. It is a policy of understatement that we inherit from the British, world advisers on all things to do with snobbery. The very suburbs we lived in, so proudly adorned with the finest villas and mansions in the world, we referred to in English as the "Cottage" district, as if to describe a twenty-room edifice on two acres of grounds as anything more than a humble cottage were in the worst of bad taste, just as with the lawyer Haberloch and his "simple" pied-à-terre.

And, of course, during my sojourn in Berlin, I had not a clue about such artifice and was thus forever inviting colleagues to my Wannsee villa. Uschi would blanch at the mere use of the word. I would handle the Sèvres vases in the entry hall and tell visitors how much they had cost. This was enough to make Uschi want to cry. Perhaps I knew better, yet I loved the feel of those pieces and the knowledge that my talents and hard work had won them for us.

But now, in Vienna, all this had changed. I was immersed in my organizational work; I cared little where I lay my head down at night or what I ate, let alone what I ate off of. But Uschi, back in her hometown, wanted to put on the dog. Hence the "cottage" in Hohe Warte; hence the Hoffmann furnishings, the tapestries on the wall by Kolo Moser and his wife. Uschi's penchant for Jugendstil was a trifle unsettling to me. The Wiener Werkstätte had, I must admit, turned out some lovely designs. But have you really ever attempted sitting in one of Hoffmann's chairs? Impossible! One even risked the damning epithet of "decadent" having so much of that fin-de-siècle production around. There was something not quite right about furnishing a house so in 1941. The proper furnishing for a villa such as ours should have been Empire, or at the very least Biedermeier: something solid and eternal in oak. But Uschi cared not about such things; it was Jugendstil she loved, and thus, the entire house, even down to her bathroom and bedroom, were done in that style.

One ironic aside, that this villa had formerly belonged to a Jewish banker and had become ours only because of the racial laws that Uschi purportedly detested, did not diminish in the least her passion for the place. She became as house-proud as a washerwoman with a new municipal flat. But none of this did I throw in her face: It was part of our unspoken agreement.

Agreements: We soon hit upon the compromises of our marriage. Two paragraphs above I mentioned "her" bedroom, for by this time we both understood that ours was not to be a deeply physical union. We had, instead, agreed to present ourselves in the best possible light regardless of what occurred in private. To the outside world, she was decorative, if not a trifle eccentric in her tastes and beliefs. But that was allowed as she came of a good family. In many ways then, from the outside, she appeared to be the perfect wife for a young and promising Staffel officer. I did not mourn the lack of love; I had no time for such sentiments in those hectic years. We lived separate lives, Uschi and I. I did not inquire how she spent her hours away from me, nor she of me. So, "her" bedroom then.

My sleeping accommodations were much more frugal: a simple single bed in an unadorned back bedroom of the villa. More often still, I slept on an army cot in my office in town. I was often reminded in those years of the old emperor, Franz Joseph, and of his wife, Sisi, the elusive Empress Elisabeth. He the tireless old civil servant, and she the frivolous wife. He had no more support in that quarter than I did. She was forever wandering across Europe avoiding the poor old man. He, too, slept on a simple cot and by day did his duty to his country. Uschi had not yet taken up gymnastics as the empress had, though it is true she had become a devotee of the game of golf. She was, in fine weather as she told me, generally to be found at the exclusive golf club in Lainz. Not that I ever looked for her there. And I had yet to find my own Katharina Schratt—someone else to comfort me as the emperor had in that actress. Another difference: the empress had at least presented Franz Joseph with a son. Uschi was an iceberg in that respect. An iceberg does not give birth. Uschi was too worried about her figure to participate in such activities as childbirth.

But if there was no support at Hohe Warte for me, I found it elsewhere: from my mother. Her work as a parent should have been done. After raising me and laboring hard for all those years so that I might get a good education, one would assume that she could sit back proudly and simply be pampered. But Mother was not like that at all. She was one of the few to recognize the emptiness of my marriage, and she tried to see me through the struggle of those years. Mother already had burdens of her own, for sister Maria was a special case. At nineteen, she was turning into a striking black-haired beauty. Her eyes were a bright blue, but one had only to look into them to know something was amiss. Despite the color, those eyes shed no light. They were all spatial color; they emitted nothing of their own. Only reflective surfaces. She had always been a simple child, Maria. But as she grew older, we began to understand that this was not a mere act, not an affectation. She was to be a little girl forever. Thus Mother was destined to be a mother for the rest of her days. I hesitated in bringing her more problems, but I think she found my occasional afternoon cake-and-coffee visits a relief in her routine days. Lord knows they were for me, too.

Perhaps the most difficult part of my work was the constant requests by friends and acquaintances to help a "good

Jew." Everyone seemed to have their good Jews; we all knew one or two. There was the little watchmaker on Ungargasse who always had candies in his pockets. Like Brahms, he would walk the streets followed by a troop of children who knew of his tricks, for suddenly he would toss up a veritable snow shower of sweet mints. Or the tobacconist from whom Mother had bought her shop. This lady allowed Mother to pay her over several years, interest free, because she knew we were a fatherless family. A Jew nonetheless. Even Hitler had his favorite Jew: Dr. Bloch in Linz, who had treated the Führer's mother in her fatal illness. This Jew doctor survived the war, living almost in sight, so to speak, of the camp where I spent the final years of my Staffel career, Mauthausen.

Only I, the bureaucrat in charge of resettlement of the Jews of Vienna, was disallowed my good Jew. They were made a logistical problem for me; success and failure were easily differentiated in my monumental task. Numbers pure and simple directed my actions. Each good Jew decreased my statistics; ergo, there was no such thing as a good Jew. These were my orders; such were the terms of my appointment. One hardly brands Franz Joseph a war criminal for putting into effect the awesome train of events after Sarajevo that led to World War I. Yet I, a humble bureaucrat, suffering from my burdensome work as much as others, am hounded to the ends of the earth for putting into action orders over which I had no power whatsoever. Franz Joseph could, I suppose, simply have ignored the assassination of Archduke Franz Ferdinand. He had no great love for this nephew, after all. But I had no such easy avenue open to me. I was caught in the middle. I do not hyperbolize either when I speak of the suffering the duties caused me. There was one instance especially in which I should have liked the luxury of having my good Jew.

It happened in this way. It was fall of 1942, not long before my posting to the concentration camp at Mauthausen. A glorious autumn, and the heat stayed with us well into October. Fine balmy days with the leaves tumbling out of the trees almost in slow motion; the parks full of the golden rain of them. One particularly warm day, my mother approached me for a favor—a thing she did not, as a rule, do. I thought I had made it clear enough both to her and my sister, Maria, how difficult the whole business was for me. I have found the task presented to me an enormous responsibility; I spent countless sleepless nights wondering about the destination of these hapless people, for—contrary to the later decision at Nuremberg—I was merely a "bearer of orders" and not a "bearer of secrets," as the bureaucratic jargon had it. I had not been told anything explicitly about the Final Solution. I was not a cognoscenti of the new language rules. My brief spoke of "resettlement in the east." As far as I knew, that is exactly what it meant. It was only after the war that all the information came out on the true meaning of this terminology. Of course, I had my doubts at the time. I could not imagine what all those Jews would be doing in the Government General of Poland. They were urban Jews and had been for centuries. To expect them, overnight, to revert to rural ways and to survive on the land—well, such questions frankly were not part of my orders, yet I thought of them nonetheless.

And then when my mother came to me that one day, her face drawn and rather mournful looking, I knew that she had come for the favor she had never yet asked.

"It's Frau Wotruba," she said without any preliminaries.

My orderly had, unbeknownst to me, kept Mother waiting the better part of an hour in the outer office. She was excited and flushed.

"Easy now, Mother," I responded. "What is it about Frau Wotruba?"

But I knew. In a way, I think I always knew. After all, what Aryan woman would carry on so with a mere boy and then compound the sin by carrying on with the boy's father? She was a woman without shame. She did not know the meaning of the word; and it is exactly that absence of shame in what is otherwise a worthy race that sets them apart from the family of man. I listened as Mother explained. We were in the Rothschild Palace office. I tapped the loose piece of star-pattern parquet under my desk. It was an irritation, that piece of unglued parquet. My windows were open; the light summer drapes fluttered in a breeze. A car horn sounded; there was the rattle of a streetcar in the distance. I wished I could be out in the fresh air; I wished I did not have to hear what my mother was preparing to ask.

Frau Wotruba had received resettlement orders, it seemed. A *Mischling*, second class as it turned out. These mixed-race cases were lower priority, and thus, she had lasted until the very end of the Jewish evacuation, most probably thinking herself to be safe. And after all, she knew, via my mother, of my important work and must have counted on my protection. Yet this was all the more reason for me to be hard and unmoved. I had to be the example by which others patterned their professional lives. Were I to allow personal considerations to creep into my decision making, I should be no better than any of the pettifogging bureaucrats we had rid ourselves of when we put an end to the Republic. What indeed had all our sacrifices been for if I allowed myself to make an exception? All these thoughts passed through my mind, along with a remembrance of the warm embrace of Frau Wotruba and of our private times together. The softness of her bosom, her exquisite shudder of delight as she rubbed against me.

And then my mother told me how sorry she was that she had asked, but Frau Wotruba was frantic. She had pleaded. . . .

"You mean she sent you here?"

"How could I refuse the poor woman, son? How could I? Granted, she was not always upstanding with us. But then her poor husband and your father were such fast friends."

Just like a Jew, I thought, *to presume on old connections in order to get them out of a fix!* This knowledge steeled my heart to the woman and I told Mother that there could be no exceptions. There was simply nothing I could do. Mother actually seemed relieved at this. From that day on, she looked at me in a different light. No longer was I her overgrown son. Now, I had become a man in her eyes. I had stood firmly by my duty. Only cowards and Jews attempted to wriggle out of theirs.

I do not know what became of Frau Wotruba. I assume she was lost somewhere in the vast hordes of Jews sent to the east. She was a very frail creature, really. I doubt she could have survived resettlement for very long. I feel no sense of guilt that I could not help her; I like to think that had she known the full extent of my devotion to duty, she would not have asked for any help. She might even have found my devotion to duty a manly virtue, as Mother did.

———

"What's this?"

"A text."

"Why do you insist on calling it that? Is it a story? An essay?"

"Yes."

"Really, Miss O'Brien, you can be most infuriatingly vague. Isn't it typical that amateurs such as myself are the ones to safeguard the sanctity of forms? I refer specifically to your latest creation. Shall I call it a text, as well?"

"As you will."

"I'm no critic . . ."

"They always say that before they assume the role. You don't have to be. I don't write for the critics. I write for the people."

"Neither am I a Catholic any longer, though the smell of incense and the brushing sound of a priest's cassock filled many of my earlier days. Mass at Stephansdom, the sound of the organ filling the immense space."

"Exactly what is your point?"

"I just think you come awfully close to the edge with this one."

"The edge of what?"

"Of decency . . . good taste."

"Shit! That old war horse again, is it? You know, Herr ___, I find that when people run up against something they don't understand or that makes their hair bristle or that churns their guts uncomfortably, they let themselves off the hook by crying about bad taste and propriety. We've gone through all that old argument before."

"The title, even. 'The Annunciation.' Isn't it rather a sick joke? And then the scholar, this fellow named—"

"Kaltmann."

"Exactly. Rather tedious symbolic stuff, don't you think? Hardly worthy of you. 'Cold man.' The precise, scientific sort."

"You said it, I didn't."

"But you've played the tricks. You've been unfair to us.

Exactly what you accuse me of. You give us this character, we get to know him quite well, and then you have him destroy himself over such a trifling matter."

"You think it was?"

"Who cares about Sogdian dialect, anyway? Some absurd ancient Near Eastern tongue."

"You seem to, for one. At least you're agitated about something. You see, he had to kill himself to keep the secret. He couldn't trust even himself to keep the secret from the world."

"But what's so earthshaking about it? So he translates this old rendering of the Bible. Where is that passage, anyway? Yes. Here: 'And thus Mary, wife of Joseph, found herself with child for the third time, and this one, unlike the others, was born living, to be named Jesus.' And over this sentence, over this piddly footnote to history, you will have us believe that this Kaltmann chap, a man who spent his entire life breaking the linguistic code of the language this fragment was written in, that this sort of man would hang himself over the discovery of such a piece of information? Absurd."

"Pain is relative."

"Which means?"

"While the debunking of the Virgin Mary myth may seem a trivial historical footnote to you, for Kaltmann, it signaled the shattering of his well-ordered universe. I mean, it is the central male myth, isn't it?"

"I can't follow you at all, Miss O'Brien. Sometimes it's as if *you're* talking Sogdian."

"It's at the very heart of the way man views woman. We live by extremes. The archetypes of Mary and Eve. Polar opposites. Mary the virgin, who is neither soiled nor sweaty. She has not given into crude animal sexuality. She is the pure vessel. The white light in a crepuscular world. She has no other meaning or function than that of bearing a man child who becomes a messiah. A repeat of your Viennese mother and the pasha son."

"But with the subsequent loss of one's own independence, Miss O'Brien."

"Exactly. For there's the flip side. Eve the spoiler. The whore. The clipper of hair and testicles, no matter the name given to her. Mary Magdalene, Judith, Salome, and all the other idols of perversity you men have created. You carry around a symbol of that yourself. You put it on your wall."

"You mean my Rubens."

"Judith and Holofernes. A lovely subject. Call her what you like, Judith or Eve, the idea is the same. I suppose I could have had poor Kaltmann translate that scene from the Garden of Eden, had him discover that it was Adam and not Eve who ate the apple from the tree of wisdom. Man, the toy-maker and putterer who will never leave well enough alone. It wasn't woman, after all, who opened the biggest Pandora's box of all, unleashing the atom. It will destroy us all sooner rather than later, but no one is yelping about the evil inside of man that he must always tinker about with things. It is man who does not listen to that tiny voice inside us all counseling, 'If it works, do not fix it.'"

"But what has all this got to do with Kaltmann?"

"It would be as if you discovered that you were illegitimate, perhaps. That your mother had you by another man. It was that sort of betrayal for Kaltmann. It brought his universe tumbling down around him. And he had nothing to replace it with. An uninventive man, to be sure, and not an uncommon sort. For Kaltmann, it was the woman as either virgin or whore. When he found that Mary was an elaborate hoax, then all that he was left with was the whore. It comes

J. Sydney Jones

from thinking in extremes, and it starts right here, right here with this one man and one woman together. There seems to be no middle place for woman. There is a virgin or whore polarity, played out in modern terms in career woman versus mother goddess and howler at wolves. Man and woman is the fundamental political unit, and it is sick. That's why all politics is sick. That's why the world is on a course of self-destruction. It's pictures like Rubens there. It's men like Kaltmann. It's policies of hate and extermination. And all because we, you and I, man and woman, are at odds with each other. The old battle, the virgin and the whore."

"I'm supposed to see all this in Kaltmann?"

"Oh, do piss off! You're not supposed to see anything. You're not supposed to find parallels in the story with our own situation. You're not supposed to understand. Feel maybe. Understanding is a tall order."

"If you're going to be like that."

"No, wait. Don't go just yet. I didn't want to talk about the story. Look, I need to get out for a while. I'm going crazy in this one room and that chicken run out back. Just for a drive. Or maybe a bit of fishing on your boat. Don't shake your head. I've got it all figured out. I'll be disguised. People won't know who I am. I'll wear some of your clothes, hide my hair in a cap. What do you say? I'll be so good. No funny business, I promise. Just a change of scenery. You can trust me. What do you say?"

"We'll see."

———

Dear Herr _____,

"I take up here your persistent argument—indeed it may be the theme of your memoirs—about the chaotic force of sex and

the female as representative thereof. I haven't heard such errant bullshit since slogging through that old pederast Plato. Though I think you've put the argument in a nutshell: So long as we, men and women, continue to view each other as polar opposites, the fight will be engaged. The fact of the matter is that we are all a continuum, a color spectrum of energy. For reasons mostly to do with former biological necessity, women tend more toward one end of the spectrum and men toward the other. But it is impera- tive to remember always that we are parts of one spectrum, not two distinct ones. We are slide trombones at A and G, respectively.

But let's backpedal to Plato for a moment. It was his group of gormless twits and sycophants who encouraged the old fart to his extremes of thought. The Greeks, Plato foremost among them, were hung up on one problem: how to make the goodness of a good human life secure from the vicissitudes of happenstance by using reason as a controlling agent. Reason would be the buffer from all 'outside' agencies that could fuck up love or friendship or object ownership. It was always this tuche, as the Greeks called happenstance, that could knock the good (i.e., both the artificially ordered life and happiness as attained through living) right off its track, never mind the terminus to which it was headed. And never mind what Kant might have to say about the invulner- ability of the ethical quality of life from mean old tuche. Then goodness, for Plato, is a fragile condition, a compulsive child who needs the rarified air of the mountains and no disruptions, please! A child who must at all costs avoid the debilitating stress of appe- tites, feelings, emotions. These must be warded off with fingers in the sign of the cross. That was the price of complete immunity to tuche. All passions were suspect and thus suppressed. They might undermine one's personal dedication to rational self-sufficiency. That is the paradigm Plato imagines for us at the peak of his argument in Phaedo, in the Symposium, and even in the Repub- lic: rigid self-control, denial of emotion—a life of self-sufficient contemplation where unstable activities and their objects have no intrinsic value. Well, we all know that this led Plato and his followers down the merry road to sodomy—no messy emotions there. Just get it up, get it in, and get it off. Slam, bam, thank you, man.

This is the light by which I read your argument of order versus chaos. And I find it spurious. To begin with, your Nazi search for order unleashed the most chaotic period in world history. By attempting to suppress, on a megascale, all those nasty complications of appetite and emotion, you fueled a perversion of them on a scale never before known to the world. By suppressing love, you unleashed hate; by boxing up passion, you fed sadism; by bottling up emotion, you flooded the world in necrophilic urges. So much for your new order; so much for your thousand-year Reich. It was the culminating point of male ascendancy, of the male urge for order and control, and it all but destroyed the world. In a history that views the man-woman struggle as paramount, this was the turning point. From Plato—who was writing at a time recently converted from the supremacy of women—to the Third Reich. Those centuries delineate the time of male dominance. The pendulum has now begun its return swing; those days of male order at all costs are on the wane. That is probably the only good to come out of the Nazi period. It took the male argument to its logical and absurd extreme and showed us all just how empty it really is.

The good life is not one that protects itself from tuche, but rather embraces it. The good life is one of constant change; it cannot be static, for that is not life or living. The good life is not one that views appetites and feelings as chaotic and therefore undesirable forces. The good life is a mixture of rational self-sufficiency and passion, of ethics tempered with emotion. It is not a life represented by the logical either/or symbol, but by the Boolean symbol of overlapping circles. Inclusion rather than exclusion.

"A most intriguing hypothesis, Miss O'Brien."

"I don't hypothesize."

"A guru, then?"

"It's quite clear to me."

"You write forcefully. Most convincingly."

"That's because I believe in what I write. As I said before, I have stories that need to be written, not merely the need to write stories."

"That is what you think I am doing with my little narrative."

"You say that, I don't."

"But . . . ?"

"Well, you have become less convincing lately. Have you thought about my request for an outing? I'm going fucking stir-crazy here."

"How do you mean, unconvincing?"

"Jesus! I wish I'd never started this editor shtick with you. Unconvincing, like bullshit. Like words put down on paper to fill space, not to fill minds and hearts. Like cacophony."

"But where? At what point? I thought you liked it."

"The early parts, yes. Frau Wotruba. There were scenes there that made me believe. That made me see and know you. Even some of the early Staffel stuff. Cow. But now you recite cities where you lived, but not really what you did there. I mean, are you a bad fucker or not? Eichmann came clean finally. Even before the Mossad caught up with him in Argentina. Remember the *Life* articles? The interview for posterity? It was all there. He convicted himself long before his trial in Jerusalem. But he had the guts at least to own up to what he had done. No repentance, mind you, or recanting. If anything, he was pissed he hadn't been able to finish his job. To deport every Jew in Europe to Auschwitz.

But you, you promise confession and all we get is that hackneyed old line of '*alles von oben*,' 'doing my duty,' 'true to the Clan.' But what about you? And if you were so enamored of the Nazi cause, why not tell us about your wondrous career? Enough of insipid Uschi and of your mother with her cakes playing surrogate wife. What about your job? What about the days in the Palais Rothschild in Vienna?"

"I wrote that. I even told of my hard decision vis-à-vis Frau Wotruba."

"That. That's not telling anything. That's wrapping up loose ends in the narrative. Like Chekhov: a gun introduced in the first act needs to go off by act five. So you took care of Frau Wotruba. But it's all offstage. Don't you see? We don't feel it because you don't. It's just words."

"I was Eichmann's man in Vienna. It's all in the memoirs. It was I who was responsible for Jewish resettlement in the early forties."

"Wait. Let's talk English if we're going to talk English. 'Resettlement.' That means moving, settling down somewhere else. Creating a new life."

"That's what it was called."

"I don't care fuck all what it was called. That was all part of the Nazi big lie. Playing with language. The language rules, *Sprachregeln*, where nothing meant what it traditionally meant. 'Resettlement,' 'Jew-free zone,' 'special treatment.' All the euphemisms that meant killing, murder, homicide on a grand scale."

"You seem to know much about the period, Miss O'Brien. Are you a student of it?"

"—"

"You display more than an editorial interest, it would appear. I do not recall mentioning *Sprachregeln* in my manuscript."

"I am a student of life, Herr ____."

"Yes. Quite. So you advise me to reveal all. Confess my deeds most thoroughly. Name names."

"Or not at all. You're the one who wants to write this. Either do it honestly or forget it."

"A most severe ethical system. But what of your honored *tuche*, of the happenstance of life? The soft corners of it, the rounded edges, the fuzzy areas of morality. Your Boolean symbol rather than either/or?"

"___"

"In truth, Miss O'Brien, I believe the two of us are closer in spirit than you would ever like to admit. I believe we are both uncompromising, true to our ideals. Unshakable. If we are at the opposite ends of your energy color spectrum, still our lights shine brightly enough."

"The outing. Have you thought of it?"

"I have, Miss O'Brien. And I shall let you know."

"And the other?"

"Yes. Quite so. I nearly forgot. Here you are."

"___"

"What is it you find so amusing, Miss O'Brien?"

"I'm just trying to imagine your explanation for these at the local drugstore."

"Actually, I had a supply of them sent from the capital. More anonymous that way."

"How many months' worth, Herr ____?"

PART IV

"They are such fine tens you have, my friend, that I shall build on them. And three aces, four jacks. I fear I am out."

"—"

"Your mind is not on the game, my friend. Have the tentacles of love ensnared you? Have you finally succumbed to female charms? That is what they are saying in the village. No one sees you about anymore. Your boat has not even yet been soundly moored for winter. People wonder if you have died or are simply too weak from nightly calisthenics to get out of the house. Don José at Café Candide even speaks of a wedding, of how he shall be the logical one to cater it. Octopus, bream, all manner of shellfish, and the most lively of Bolivian white wines."

"Don José is a fool. And I wonder at your sagacity, Cordoba, in repeating such inanities."

"Another hand?"

"I think not. As you observe, my mind is not on the cards tonight."

"My friend, I worry about you. It is this woman, is it not? She has some hold, some power over you. You do not look well. You are too much shut in of late. Altogether you have taken too much upon yourself with this woman."

"Out with it, Cordoba. Have your friends been whispering in your ear again?"

"On the contrary. Your last postcard seems to have done the trick. The Mexican police will now have the missing person's report on her—last reported location, Mexico City. That is all as you planned. My friends can live with that. They are still miffed at you for taking individual action, but no longer clamor for your hide."

"That's reassuring to hear. Then what is it? Why the sudden concern?"

"I hate to lose a good gin partner, is all."

"What a bastard you are."

"Men are bastards. All of us, even the legitimate ones."

"And supposing I am truly in love with the woman. Which I am not. But just let us suppose. You, I imagine, would do everything possible to scotch the affair, just so as not to lose a partner at cards?"

"Put like that it does sound petty. Yet there are few enough halfway cultured people in this godforsaken place. Few enough with whom one can exchange a friendly word, let alone share a fine dinner. Such things are worth fighting for, yes. And look at you, my friend. You are a shambles. You have not shaved in days; there are bags under your eyes large enough that my father could have packed his diplomatic wardrobe in them. You are as gray as the herring gull and as tired looking as an old sea turtle. If this is the result of love, give me celibacy any day."

"___"

"A word of advice, my friend. In seriousness now. Get rid of this woman. She will kill you in the end. I do not know what power she has over you, but whatever it is, you must destroy it before it destroys you."

"Nonsense, Cordoba. She's proven quite helpful editing my memoirs."

"You haven't let her read them, have you?"

"She wouldn't sign the postcard unless . . ."

"Yes?"

"She said she wanted to know me. To see if she could trust me. Believe in me as a man."

"I see."

"Now don't go getting Jesuitical on me. What the hell is it you see?"

"I see that you two are locked in mortal combat. You know that you can never let her free now. Before—reading just the first pages of your memoirs—perhaps. Perhaps that was only an accident. As I say, journalists are naturally snoopy. But now that she has pried into your total life, has begun to edit for you . . . well, now you can never be sure."

"Damn your eyes! Be sure of what?"

"Sure that she is not playing the double game. That she did not come down here expressly to worm her way into your life to win conclusive proof for her Israeli masters."

"Be serious, Cordoba. Who would take such a chance? How could she know that I would not kill her out of hand?"

"Yet still, now you can never be sure, my friend. Can you? Tell me, does she, at times, speak quite knowingly of the Reich? Does she, in heated moments of conversation, know a trifle too much for a layman?"

"__"

"I see by your eyes that I have struck oil. Perhaps such well-informed arguments did not strike you as being out of character at first. After all, you have spent your life with such facts. The Reich was a reality for you. But for this woman . . . She was born after the war. She has no direct personal experience of it. Remember that, my friend. All information she has of the war will have come from her own study of it. She had to make the conscious decision to learn about it. The inevitable question then is: Why? And once you ask why, then the worm of doubt has entered your mind. You see, you can never set her free now. You two are handcuffed together for eternity. Unless . . ."

At the behest of Miss O'Brien, some leaves from my Staffel scrapbook (translated of course):

```
SCHUTZSTAFFFEL PERSONALITY EVALUATION
Religion: Has none
Race: Nordic
Personality: Self-assured
Appearance Out of Uniform: Unfailingly correct
General Character Analysis: Objective, sociable,
    clever, ambitious
```

It is the "clever" that rankles. Surely this was Eichmann's adjective, pejorative in the extreme in the original German, meant to rein one in, to put a curse on one so that no other Staffel department would have me. Eichmann above all hated losing his trusted subordinates. As Miss O'Brien says, if it works, do not fix it. That was Eichmann's lifelong motto.

```
Training: Expert in legal disentanglements;
    quite knowledgeable on the Jewish question
Special Characteristics: Knows his way through
    the state bureaucracies, whom to contact and
    whom to avoid
Sports Activities: Received the Special Decoration
    of the SD
```

I passed a physical exam, that is all. I had no desire to do well in competitive games, though Uschi urged fencing on me.

```
General Note: A good organization man and faithful
    follower
```

Another Eichmann description, surely. This meant to put the kiss of death on my promotion past major of the Schutzstaffel.

```
SCHUTZSTAFFEL PROGRESS AND PROMOTION REPORT
SS No. 323498        6.2.39
Party No. 2038692
```

Station	Rank	Performance of Duties
Bernau Academy	Kadet SS Schütze 3.9.39	Willing, cooperative, somewhat reserved. Took part in Special Action Himmler, for which he was awarded Cross of Merit, 2nd Class.
Berlin RSHA 1939-1940	SS-Rottenführer 1.10.39 SS-Scharführer 2.6.40 SS-Oberscharführer 9.9.40 SS-Untersturmfuührer 1.1.41	As member of SD, performed diligently and loyally all duties assigned in accordance with RSHA requirements, assistant on Foreign Desk, Amt IV, Foreign Intelligence. Work on Foreign Desk is exemplary. Fine organizational/clerical talent. Also acute facility for resolution of delicate legalistic problems.
Vienna 1941-42	SS-Obersturmführer 20.5.41	Assigned to Department IVA, 4b, Jewish Affairs. Quick grasp of problems at hand. Ready hand at untangling antiquated Austrian legalities. Diligent worker. Loyal party man. Question arises over unstable domestic situation.
Mauthausen KZ 1942	SS-Hauptsturmführer 13.12.42 SS-Sturmbannführer 1.10.43	Administrative Officer of major Austrian Konzentrationslager at Mauthausen. Unfailingly diligent and uncompromising in fulfillment of duties to Reich and humanity. Iron Cross awarded 8.9.44 for outstanding and unfailing troth, loyalty, and exactitude.

```
CEDULA DE IDENTIDAD
No. 212430

_____

Firma del interesado
    Certifico que don _____ que dice de
estado _____ que lee y escribe si y cuya
fotografia, impresion digito-pulgar derecha y firma
figuran al dorso, es naciado el 23 de Mayo de 1916
en el puebla de _____ Provincia de _____
Nacion Alemania que tiene I m_____etms, de esta-
tura, el cutis de color blanco, Cabello rubio.
Barba afeit. Nariz dorso recto.

    Base bajada. Boca medi. Orejas meds. Mat.
_____ Distrito _____ Div. _____
Observaciones _____

    Abril 3 de 1947
```

The above was my identity card issued when first I came to this godforsaken strip along the sea. But why grouse? The country has been good enough to me. You, gentle reader, will surely forgive me if I have left many blanks. I am still somewhat schizoid on the point of my exact physical whereabouts. I assume I shall sort this out sooner or later. Perhaps on the second draft.

———

"Chickens are laying again."

"I'm not really hungry. When can I get out of here? No kidding, it's driving me batty being closed in like this. I'm not used to it."

"Eat. Don't start all that again. You don't want to get ill."

"Why not?"

"I don't want to have to coax you to eat."

"You mean force-feed me."

"I mean coax. If I had meant the other, I would have said it. Stop putting words in my mouth. Or on my papers for that matter."

"I'm not so sure, Herr ____. I mean, I'm not sure you ever say what you mean. Too many years of dissimulation. It becomes a habit."

"Eat. I'm still considering your suggestion. An outing might be nice for both of us. But do eat, Miss O'Brien."

"Okay. I'm cooperating, see? Knocking off the top of this five-minute egg. You do them perfectly, you know."

"Years of training."

"You're wrong about me. You wrote when I first went out into the compound that I'd be like all the rest. Pressing my face against the cyclone fence and no longer seeing it as a prison but as a refuge from the world. That's not me. I'll never be like that."

"I was generalizing from what I witnessed at Mauthausen."

"It won't happen to me. I won't let it."

"Eat. I brought you something to read."

"And I you. We'll trade. Mine's a new story. What's yours? Records? Forms? This is your SS history. You're going to do it like this in the book? And that's all?"

"What more do I need? What more do others want to see?"

"But where is the heart of it?"

"Metafiction, Miss O'Brien."

"But this isn't fiction. It's your life. It's your only chance to tell your side of things as fully as possible. Don't you care about that?"

"___"

"Isn't there any more?"

"More of what?"

"For example, look at your promotion record. While in Berlin you skyrocketed. Promotion after promotion in a couple of years. But all the time in Vienna and Mauthausen you only get three. Why? What happened? Did you top out? Did you fuck up? What the hell happened? Tell us the story of that."

"Hardly a story. Or hardly worth telling. Mainly it has to do with Ricardo Klement—"

"Alias Adolf Eichmann."

"Another surprise. You do know our history."

"It was on the news nightly when I was a kid. The gray-faced man behind the protective glass. Speaking German in that irritating monotone and the rather too animated tones of the interpreter. The men and women weeping in the courtroom as evidence was given."

"Yes. To be sure. But what I refer to was all my years prior to 'justice in Jerusalem.' My years in Berlin were productive because I was not yet directly subordinate to Eichmann. My superior in Berlin, Jost, was only too glad to receive some bright suggestion from his junior officer. Those were the years of intensification vis-à-vis the camps."

"You mean the building of the concentration camps?"

"Yes. And it was an organizational nightmare, I can tell you. The pure numbers alone were mind-boggling. I was always rather good at such things, schedules and the like. But in my Berlin years I learned I had another talent, one more, shall we say, of a psychological nature. The very name of the camps tells a lot. Concentration. Thousands of Jews, Marxists, Gypsies, and other enemies of the state were concentrated in one spot. So we in the Staffel and SD, though not directly responsible for the administration of the camp system, were up to our necks in the actual day-to-day running of them. And with such a concentration of bodies, one had recourse to devising control mechanisms. After all, we could hardly spare enough Waffen Schutzstaffel from frontline duty to patrol the camps if the inmates became truly desperate. They outnumbered us quite significantly. And it thus fell partly to me to devise strategies whereby the inmates would not become desperate."

"Strategies?"

"Gambits. Psychological tricks, as it were. It was imperative that neither the inmates nor their relatives and friends should have doubts about what resettlement meant. If the fever and contagion of fear broke out among the Jews of Europe, then our entire enterprise could have broken down."

"Enterprise? You mean the Final Solution."

"Yes."

"You admit to it, then? The reality of the Holocaust. You won't play games with history like the French revisionists, claiming it was all Allied propaganda."

"As I said earlier, I was not of the highest level of the bearer of secrets. I had my suspicions, certainly. But all I knew for certain was the task set for me. If the Jews of Europe suspected the nature of the Final Solution, it would make rounding them up a near impossibility. Transport to the camps would become an exercise in hell, and life inside the camps themselves would be one of constant warfare.

My job in Berlin was to see that such would not be the case. And I confess I did quite well. And my exertions were appreciated. Once in Vienna, on the other hand—"

"What tricks? The showers?"

"No. That was Hoess's. The camp commandant at Auschwitz. A matter of individual initiative, and quite effective as it turned out. Mine were of a subtler nature, actually. You know of my love for music. How it is playing constantly upstairs. Well, I know firsthand the calming effect of music. The normalizing effect it can have on the most bizarre of situations. Thus, I had every transport to Auschwitz greeted by the camp orchestra. They played Viennese waltzes as their fellow Jews detrained and were separated for the main camp or for Birkenau. This arrival was normally a most chaotic time. But once the orchestra was initiated, the new arrivals were calmed and lulled by it. A small innovation, yet it made everyone's life so much easier."

"Marvelous."

"You asked. You needn't be sarcastic when I respond to your requests. It seems obvious perhaps now, but then . . ."

"What else?"

"I don't like to boast."

"Please do."

"That ploy took care of the new arrivals. But we also had to think of those Jews awaiting transport to the east. We needed to calm their fears and apprehensions, and we could hardly send an orchestra to every ghetto and shtetl in Europe. But the post, that was a different matter. We simply had each new inmate fill out a postcard for friends or relatives where they had come from, saying their new homes in the east were fine, and that there was nothing to worry about."

"Let me guess. The date was left open. Just like mine from Mexico City."

"__"

"Just like mine, Herr ___?"

"That was different."

"How?"

"We have a bargain. It was done in good faith on both sides. You must believe that."

———

I feel badly about that slip. It puts Miss O'Brien on guard quite needlessly, for all that chicanery is behind me. In fact, she would not have needed to know about it if she had not pried it out of me herself. It was quite frankly not something I was going to include in this record. I scored high points for innovation at the time. One must remember what the years 1941–42 were like. The second front was opening in the East: a global war now and all the consequent transport problems that it wrought. Troops, materiel, supplies. The trains were rolling to and fro with our boys all over Europe and the Balkans. And in the midst of this, the Führer ordered that the solution of the Jewish problem be put into effect. As I say, I was not aware of the total meaning of that solution at the time. I had not been a participant at the Wannsee Conference, where so much of the policy was hammered out, though, ironically, it took place in a villa just around the corner from where my wife and I once lived. All I knew was the problem that adding the Jews of Europe to the transport lists would create. Anything I could do to lessen that problem was obviously my duty. Under the historical lamp, of course, my gambits appear cynical betrayals, less than human. But such is the chimerical nature of history. Had we Germans won the war, I would have had streets named after me. As it is, I am fearful to even use my own name.

But I do not want Miss O'Brien to feel about me as the Wiesenthals and the soft liberals of the world do. A foolish desire, perhaps, an old man's whim. It hurts that she feels deceived by me. Tonight, I will show her how much I trust her: We will have a candlelight dinner together upstairs. A sort of prelude to the outing she keeps demanding. I must also find some time to read the new story she exchanged with me. But not this afternoon. Too many things to do in preparation for the dinner, for it is Christmas Eve, a fact that I am sure has slipped her mind. Not mine, however. I never forget Christmas. It is my favorite of all the yearly festivals: the winter solstice, the birth of Christ, the rebirth of the sun. She will be surprised. I have decorated upstairs like something out of Dickens: streamers bedecking the rafters and a wizened fir tree in a corner adorned with red bows and white candles. Cordoba fetches me one from the high mountain pass in the center of the country each year—for an exorbitant price, I might add. But worth it to me. I have champagne on ice and a rum punch brewing. Fish instead of goose, but there is one's health to consider. I would lay snow on, too, if humanly possible, but I am afraid that is out of my control. All in all, the place is quite festive looking. I do hope Miss O'Brien assumes the proper mood for the evening. No gifts, of course, for I am afraid that would only embarrass her, as she has not had the chance to purchase or make one for me. I am all aflutter just like Scrooge's Mr. Fezziwig. Oh, I do so love Christmas. . . .

"That was lovely, Herr ____."

"I'm glad you liked it. White fish is one of my favorites, as well."

"It's another world up here. I'd forgotten. It seems so, so big. I needed this. Merry Christmas."

"We'll leave the dishes until tomorrow."

"I don't have to go down just yet?"

"No, no. Just clearing away the clutter. A brandy?"

"Umm."

"I take that as an assent?"

"Yes. A double assent, please."

"You're in a very festive mood, Miss O'Brien."

"Champagne does that for a girl. It's been a long time since I've even bothered putting on a skirt, let alone doing my hair."

"You look quite lovely."

"I'm sure you say that to all your girls."

"____"

"This is so unreal. I mean, here I am, here we are, exchanging coy small talk when I should be looking for a heavy candlestick to knock you over the head with."

"Why unreal? To my mind the realities are very apparent. We are behaving quite well under the circumstances."

"But I don't want to behave well. That's what happened to the Jews. Good manners and false hopes destroyed them. Why do I sit here sipping your brandy as if I'm at some quiet bistro in the Village? What's happened to my rage?"

"You'll forgive me for saying so, Miss O'Brien, but it's part of the syndrome I described. One begins to exchange realities."

"You talk as if reality were something you could slip on and off like a balaclava. I don't think it's that simple. Take you, for example."

"I'd rather not. Not on Christmas Eve, thank you."

"Your assumed persona of so many decades. It still doesn't work for you, does it? At heart you're a central European, not an aging soldier of fortune in the Central American forests."

"I admit I would rather be back in Austria, especially tonight. Rather we had won the war, for that matter, and that I were collecting an honorable pension as a retired warrior for my country. What is so revealing about that? What has that to do with the slip and tumble of changing realities?"

"Come off it. What's so honorable about being a warrior? You talk about it as if it were a profession set on Earth to save humanity rather than destroy it. Is that something to get passionate over? Destruction?"

"Another brandy?"

"Please. Well?"

"You really do insist on jousting tonight?"

"Yes."

"All right. Remember that first night, Miss O'Brien. You were looking at my statues on the mantel?"

"Yes, and I couldn't disagree more with your interpretation of the stone Venus."

"Your prerogative. But I'm thinking of the jaguar now. You know what that symbolizes?"

"Probably something to do with war."

"Very good, Miss O'Brien. In point of fact, it was the symbol of the Maya warrior elite. Their palace guard. We live in a world of symbols, Miss O'Brien. Symbols to communicate, to motivate. The runic slashes of lightning we wore on our black Staffel uniforms are only part of a long tradition of warrior elites. We are related to the jaguar just as we are to the Spartan youths who fought battles without any quarter given or desired. There in a nutshell, or rather in the form of that onyx jaguar, is my passion. My reason. The warrior is one of the oldest of professions."

"And we all know what the oldest is."

"One of the most noble, as well."

"Bullshit. You talk as if you and your comrades symbolically fought at Thermopylae. It would be closer to the truth that your great forebears were scribes in Egypt, recording how many slaves died per day building the Great Pyramid. By your own admission you're just a salesman and transporter. Where's the nobility in that? Where's the passion?"

"—"

"How about another brandy? Lovely stuff. Where was I? Yes, passion. That's the ticket. Where's the passion in your life at all? The only bit I see of it is Frau Wotruba, whom you abandoned."

"And what of you, Miss O'Brien? You talk grandly enough about it, but have you ever had what they call a grand passion? You seem to be quite alone in the world now."

"Oh, yes, I have. When I was seventeen. It was real love, and it hurt like the very devil. But you're changing the subject. Just a drop more, thank you very much. I had a point to make. Wear my hat right and it won't show. Christ, I do believe I'm getting tipsy."

"We could continue this tomorrow, if you wish."

"You haven't slipped me a Mickey Finn, I presume? Which would be rather poor alliterative taste, to be sure. Slip a Mick a Mickey."

"I assure you, Miss O'Brien—"

"Do please stop calling me Miss O'Brien. It makes me feel like a schoolmarm."

"—"

"Deep down you're just like all the rest. Want to get into a lass's knickers at all costs. Get her oiled, have your way. Sign of masculinity and all that. Even when everything else is failing, that must function. The dynamo. Funny image. I conjure that up from you fellows. Old Nazis together. I hear Churchill's pronunciation: Nahzzee. All you boys in black uniforms. Comparing girth and entrance requirements. Why wasn't that on your SS chart? Sorry. I do get a bit vulgar after I've knocked a few back. We really should continue this tomorrow. By Jesus, it's almost one o'clock. It's Christmas Day! I asked him out once, you know. This grand love of mine when I was seventeen. Wasn't going to sit around waiting for it to happen to me. Take life by the lapels. That sort of thing. Much too advanced for my age, even then. He accepted, he did. And I spent the rest of the night fending off digital advances under my knickers. Ruined it completely with my invitation. To the flickers, not my knickers. But he didn't know. He was just a big dumb tit-puller whose dad owned the local dairy. God, what rosy cheeks he had. Christ, I'm tired."

"—"

"You sit watching me like a cat. A fat tomcat waiting for the bird to fall asleep. Fall off her perch. Feathers in your mouth, puffing in the window-drawn breeze. Yellow feathers drifting like sea horses in the ocean . . ."

"You're drunk."

"Tipsy. A woman also glistens, never sweats. Any gentleman could tell you that."

"You can find the way to your room?"

"Which means you're disgusted with me. You won't join me. Just this once?"

"Good night, then. Any longer and I fear we will overstep the magic line."

"Wouldn't want that. Damned fine drink you pour, though. That's what I can't figure."

"—"

"What I can't figure is how a person so dry as toast as you could have such fine old brandy. Now there's a passion worth having, the drink. Or at the very least knowledge about the passion. God, how sad, Lancelot. I just discovered your secret. You do know about it, don't you? All about it. The passion and the hunger and those things that make you feel good in the night. But there's not a thing you can do to actually feel it, is there? I mean, you're cut off from it somehow. All you men were then. Cut off and out. Such a pity. A waste. To know about it and not be able to experience it. That's why you collect people, prisoners. So you can watch life; experience by watching."

"Is there anything more, then?"

"Too close to home? I have found it, haven't I? You're all empty, aren't you? Empty and hungry, but never to be fed. Never to be sated. God, how sad."

"Until the morning, then."

"So, so sad."

On Sundays, Mother and Father would walk together in the park. Lying in my bedroom alcove I would hear them up early, bustling about the flat, dressing, making coffee, warming yesterday's Semmeln in the oven, for the bakeries were closed on Sundays. Birdsong came from the open window; a bright light illuminated the paisley patterns on the curtain across my alcove. Spring. But I longed for winter. I turned the snow bubble on the bedside table upside down, then righted it. A white flurry descended upon the miniaturized Stephansdom inside. Mother called, but I pretended to be asleep. Finally, Mother tapped on the wall next to my bed; she would not draw aside the curtain without first knocking.

"Sleepyhead. Breakfast is on."

I told her I was not feeling well.

She entered the alcove, put her cool hand smelling of lavender water and rolls over my forehead, looked into my eyes.

"Maybe you'd better stay in bed today, huh?"

I nodded.

"Some rest. Some reading. You'll feel better by tonight?"

Another nod. We never talked about it. We were secret conspirators in my battle with Father. He didn't believe in privacy, in curtains across alcoves, in letting young boys spend all their free time reading novels. Healthy young men, to his mind, were out of doors walking in the woods or playing soccer with other healthy young boys. Fourteen-year-old boys who, like me, enjoyed books, being alone and privacy—well, such boys were suspect to Father. One never knows what tricks one might get up to behind closed curtains.

"Pot roast tonight," Mother reminded. "Your father will want you at the table."

I assured her I would be better by evening. I just needed a little time in bed.

I heard Father's gruff voice after Mother left the alcove: protesting tones. Her soothing ones. Footsteps drew near, then receded. I felt a trickle of sweat under my left arm. Finally, the front door opened, then closed with a heavy finality. Alone at last, for they had taken my little sister with them, too. Alone. The delicious freedom of it. It is always that which we don't have that we value the most. For one forever in the midst of family, to be apart and separate is salvation. Being alone held no fear of loneliness for me.

I waited several minutes until I was sure that Mother and Father had forgotten nothing, were not returning, then I let my hand trail down to my middle slowly. I luxuriated in this—in the expectation of touch. My love organ was responding to the thought of touch, twitching toward my snaking hand.

You see, Father was right. No telling what one would get up to with enough privacy. Masturbation was not something I felt guilty about. It was something that felt good, something that I might have enjoyed doing with a girl instead but was far too embarrassed and shy to attempt. Even if I had known a promising girl. Which I didn't. So I enjoyed my own touch instead. No use denying myself pleasure just because of the lack of a partner, I reasoned. I know how my father felt on this score, and that is why I waited for Sundays when I might be alone: unafraid of interruption, discovery, calumny.

So I lingered over the snail-creep of fingers over my belly, my penis jerking spasmodically in anticipation. There was a knock at the door. I lay perfectly still. My parents would have used their key. This was a visitor. A visitor who need not know I was home. Another knock followed by a voice: "Hello, hello. Your father asked me to check in on you. Wake up."

It was Frau Wotruba, our recently widowed neighbor. So the old man had foiled my plans after all.

"Schatz? Are you there or do I call the municipal fire department?"

I called out that I was here, to wait a moment. I threw a bathrobe on, hoping it would hide any lingering signs of my excitement, and went to the door. She smiled mischievously when I opened it.

"Up to your old tricks again, I see." She rumpled my hair.

I turned a violent red. How could she know? I stammered a protest: I was sick, I had been asleep.

"We know better, though, don't we?" She winked at me and a blast like pressurized steam went straight down my stomach to my groin. *"What is it this time? Shatterhand or Winnetou? Lord knows you wouldn't play sick just to brush up on your Latin text."*

The crimson at my cheeks began to fade.

"Well, which is it?"

"You know me too well, Purgi." She forbade me, when alone, to call her Frau Wotruba. She'd much rather I use her Christian name, Walpurga: Purgi to her friends.

"'Frau Wotruba' makes me feel so old. Like I should have stockings rolled around my knees and wear housecoats and my hair in a kerchief. And I'm not that far gone, am I?"

Indeed she was not, dressed today in a simple muslin dress that clung to her every curve and showed off the beginning of the plunge between her breasts. She looked hardly old enough to be called a frau, if you didn't know she had been married and widowed already. And if you did, one look into her eyes would let you know she was not a staid old widow. Humor also showed there, and warmth, and a great deal of playfulness. I loved Purgi's eyes. I loved looking into them.

"Sorry to bother you, Schatz. Your papa requested it. Demanded it would be closer to the truth. But you look fine. A little reading isn't going to kill you. I need my beauty rest, too."

"Were you out late last night, Purgi?"

Suddenly, I did not want her to go. I wanted to hear about her social life. I sometimes saw a beau of hers drive up in the sleekest of roadsters with its top down, pull to the curb, and gracefully leap over the door of the car instead of opening it. He was a tall blond man who wore tennis whites most of the year and walked as if he had India rubber balls in his arches. Though I pretended to shun such role models, I secretly wanted to look just like him. I wanted to leap over car doors, but we had no car. My only door was the paisley curtain separating my alcove from the rest of the apartment.

"Dancing."

She said the word with enough verve and pep to conjure up the entire evening for me: Moonlight in the Volksgarten outdoor dance arena. Her escort swirling her around the podium to the new jazz tunes from America. Some ornate newfangled cocktails on the candlelit tables when they sit a dance out, sweating and laughing, squeezing hands under the table. A kiss on the neck, perhaps more in the dimly lit garden as they sway to the music.

"Is he a good dancer, your friend?"

"Marvelous!" She laughed her high exquisite laugh. "But what do you know about my friend?"

"Is he the one in the roadster?"

"Arnulf? No, Arnulf and I . . . have gone our separate ways."

Her face turned so tragic at the mention of him that I was deeply sorry to have brought him up.

"Do you dance?" she asked.

I mumbled something about taking waltz lessons at Dobmaier's.

"No, silly. I mean jitterbug, Charleston. Fun dances."

I had never heard of them.

"Of course," I told her.

She grabbed my hand. "Come on, then. I've got some new records. Let's dance."

I made no protest as she dragged me, still in my pajamas and robe, to her apartment down the hall. This was night and day as compared to ours. Mother loved heavy somber furniture, Turkish carpets, and tasteful prints on the wall. But Purgi's place was something out of a new world—all chrome and glass and lightness. Some mad swirls of color on canvas on the walls. Clothes strewn here and there. Everything in disarray. I thought I saw a pair of knickers by a rattan couch and blushed once again.

"What'll it be? Glenn Miller? Oh, let's do Glenn Miller!"

"Sure." It was as if I were giving her a present.

There came a lovely and pure line of trumpet—high and tight, followed by drums such as I had never heard before, and Purgi began swaying to the music like a willow in the breeze. Watching her ecstasy at the music, I was suddenly filled with the same feeling she was exhibiting. But in me it was translated to sexual excitement, and I tried hard to hide it with my hands in front of me. She reached out to take hold of me and dance, but I had to hide the bulge and acted as if suddenly I did not want to dance, as if the music did not please me.

She stopped swaying. "Shall we listen to some Benny Goodman then?"

"I'd better go back," I said. "Mother and Father—"

"Oh, they won't be back home for hours. Not to worry."

And she grabbed my hands, brushing my erection as she did so. It stood out like a conductor's baton.

She giggled. "So that's what's wrong. Don't be embarrassed. It's healthy. With the right person."

And she led me to the center of her living room floor and taught me the magical steps of swing. Then after what seemed hours and hours of this glorious free motion, she took me to her huge round bed and taught me how to dance without feet. . . .

———

"But that's not the way it happened!"

"It's the way it should have happened."

"I won't have you mucking about with my life, Miss O'Brien. When we started this, it was only a matter of a little editing here and there. I don't want a collaborator. It's my life!"

"Saying it's so makes it so."

"No haiku today, please, Miss O'Brien."

"I mean if you say a thing often enough, it will be so. It becomes a reality."

"But you can't play fast and loose with the historical record like that. I was never an onanist. Portraying me as such highly perturbs me. Even your decadent D. H. Lawrence knew enough to condemn the practice: the cancer of the twentieth century, he called it. Moreover, I did not even see Frau Wotruba at age fourteen. All my experiences with her were confined to an earlier age. And having Goodman and Miller on the gramophone. They don't fit that period at all."

"I'm not interested in the small historical truths any more than you Nazis were. You rearranged history to fit your needs. Don't carp at me about historical accuracy. I repeat—we are talking about what should have been, not what was. And you can rewrite your own history. You can free yourself of the burden of it by writing it the way you want to make it."

"But it already is the way I want it."

"A child pawed over by a bitch in heat? I doubt it. I doubt that's really the way you want it."

"It's always the same with you. Sex, sex. You dwell on it."

"If I do, it's only because I know that a society sick in its sex is a sick society. And I don't mean simply one without so-called free or gymnastic sex. I mean one deeply injured in its heart and soul as well as its cock and cunt. Yes, Herr ____. I use those hard-edged words. Those good old Anglo-Saxon words for a good old Anglo-Saxon concept. Don't you feel it? Something's gone wrong with the world, very wrong. It was something desperate just at the turn of the last century. As if the planet Earth passed through the dusty tail of a comet of perversity. It's no accident that

Freud should have grown out of that time, for the distillation of centuries of woman hatred came to a head then. The Madonna-whore nexus had been fought for millennia in the hearts and minds of men who did not understand love, and the whore finally won out. It's as if anyone who lived through that time was infected by a great sexual blockage, and central Europe was the center of the malignancy. The bottled-up rage of those millennia finally came spilling over in a froth of sadism and cruelty that was made official by a political conceit: your Nazism."

"Facile."

"But nonetheless true. Perhaps it is so obvious because it is true. And it is hardly me who dwells on sex. Every scene you write implies it. Your life seems to be one extended botched job of sexuality. From Frau Wotruba to . . . what was her name? The little prostitute? Oh yes, Miranda. You write of the lack of synchronicity between men and women. About how, when a woman finally is ready to give her love, then the man no longer wants it. And that is so telling. You're not talking of love there. You're talking about opening up. The unfurling of the petals in the sex act. And it is hardly a woman's fault if men require no sensitivity in that act."

"Sentiment is not what I was writing about. You distort my words."

"No worse than how you distort the concept of love. Was what you felt for Miranda love?"

"Compassion perhaps. It was quite often almost passionless."

"You say that as if to defend your actions. As if compassion is not one of love's perimeters."

"She was a child."

"But you did love her?"

"What do you mean by love? It's a colossal ambiguity, love is."

"You know what the feeling is. Or what the lack of it is. Why are you so afraid of saying it? Didn't you love her?"

"This is exactly what I mean. This sort of hectoring. I won't have it anymore. Not about my manuscript. Not about my private life."

"You must have loved her, then. Go ahead. It's an easy word to say. Like falling off a log. There is absolutely no need to bottle it up. Not in front of me."

"__"

"I'm not your enemy, you know. You say we started this editing of your manuscript out of solely professional need. I would clean up your misspellings, your word choice. Not so. If you remember, it was at the time of the first postcard. I wanted an assurance. Belief in you, that I might trust your word. Of course that was before I knew you developed the postcard trick to help in the smooth operation of the Final Solution. But I hoped for a window to your soul. Not an editing job. That's why we started this. And I got my window, my view. In ways, I feel I know you intimately. In others, I don't know you at all. But there is understanding. There's no need to fear me. I am not the snake in your garden that you make me out to be. The young girl, Miranda. You did love her, didn't you?"

"Yes. I loved her. I thought she loved me, too."

"She hurt you somehow. She betrayed you?"

"That is the hurt one expects from a woman. Yes. She betrayed me. I installed her in a quite lovely apartment. High up on Asuncion Hill, all the red-tiled roofs of the city sprawled out below. At night, it was like looking at a field of stars with all the lights of the city below us. Very nice. Even a couple of my little works of art on the walls. We were happy there, until he came. . . ."

"__"

"She said it was her brother and I believed her. I wanted very much to believe her. An old man's folly. But I was still virile in those days. I believed I could satisfy her needs. Old man's vanity, as well."

"And he wasn't her brother?"

"I will be frank with you, Miss O'Brien. She liked to make love in the dark. It was her breasts, you see. They were so small. She was ashamed. And there was also a downy patch of hair around her nipples. I loved her little breasts. I told her so many times. Just as I loved her hips so narrow, so prominent. Her tiny rumps. My little boy, I sometimes called her in jest. She hated that, but it was only joking. Yet in bed—lights out. That was her rule. I finally discovered why.

"It was not long after he came. She had urged me to find work for him. I did, at a factory producing tires, owned by an acquaintance. After a couple of weeks, this man told me the boy was no good. He would do no work. But Miranda pleaded. The owner owed me a favor for certain reasons, so the boy kept his job. She was appropriately grateful. That night, the night I am speaking of, she was warmer to me than she had been in weeks. When I close my eyes tightly now just before sleep, I can sometimes still feel her tiny body wrapped next to mine. She was like a cat: Miranda could always find a comfortable place next to me or on my lap. She folded up like a warm breath of air. Those tiny breasts. She would rub them against me as she grew more and more excited. I am not trying to shock you, Miss O'Brien. Merely to explain. And this night when I reached out to fondle her breasts, she whimpered. It was not delight registering in her voice, but pain. I asked her what the matter was, but she only kissed me harder and pulled me on top of her. I was suspicious, however, and reached to turn on the light. She screamed at me not to, but too late. The bedside light had a red shade, but still I could make out the welts across her chest and belly. I turned her over. Across those perfect tight rumps were more signs of abuse. I demanded of her who had done such a thing, but she only began crying and would say nothing. I thundered at her, threatening and cajoling all at once. I knew it was the lad she called her brother. I screamed my suspicions at her, that I would have him killed for this. She spoke then, her face full of fear. It was not his fault, she pleaded. She had driven him to it.

"Absurd, I countered. But then she told me she liked it. Wouldn't I give it a try, too?

"I was sickened, Miss O'Brien. Shocked and sickened. My Miranda! I had at one time even considered marrying the girl. Whether she said this as a truth or merely to save the skin of her 'brother,' I did not know. Either way, it was revolting. I got up immediately, dressed, and left that apartment for good. She held on to my leg halfway down the hall, naked, striped with welts, pulled along the floor like a slattern.

"I never saw her again. Later, I learned from my friends that she had never stopped working, if you know what I mean. She saw customers in the very flat I had rented for us. Did unspeakable things in the bed we shared. It was one of those customers who had left the marks. And the irony was that the boy really was her brother. Totally ignorant of his sister's doings. Totally innocent. What a joke on me."

"How did you find this out if you never saw her again?"

"I have persuasive friends."

"You had the pair of them disappeared, didn't you?"

"—"

"Didn't you!"

"I was advised that this would be the safest course. She might have compromised me."

"And yet you loved her."

"She betrayed me."

"But if you love a person. To have her killed? No sadness? No remorse?"

"A man must be hard."

"Nothing reaches you, does it? Not love, not death. Do you have any feelings at all, Herr ____? Any nerve endings left?"

"Don't touch me like that, Miss O'Brien. It's not right."

"No nerve endings at all?"

"Please stop it. It's—"

"How long has it been? You know you want me. I read how you had to stop yourself from having me after you'd doped me. Is that feeling gone, too? Along with the rest?"

"No, Miss O'Brien. Leave the blouse."

"They aren't small like a boy's. They're a woman's breasts. See? Won't you touch them? Taste them? You've wanted to often enough. You can make love to me here and now. No need to watch me, spy on me. We can lie together and make love in the here and now. Touch and embrace like humans. You want that, don't you?"

"—"

"Help me with these, won't you? Here. Hold me like this. Harder. Yes. That's good. I told you before, I won't break. Yes."

"No! Get away from me. You're just like all the rest! A whore at heart. Don't touch me with your filth. Away!"

I took a shower, as long and hot as I could stand. Now I sit at my trestle table gazing out at the brittle blue sky. The first clear days of January are upon us and it is a surprise to me. As though I have awoken from a long sleep. The events of this afternoon have done that for me.

I feel as if something were spoiled, as if a world has been destroyed, in fact. Cordoba is right. We are locked in mortal combat, Miss O'Brien and myself. First she attempts to rewrite my life, then to ensnare me in her sex.

They are all the same. Thank God I awoke from the dream in time to sense the blatancy of her seduction. That she would make love to me in some blind hope of attaining her freedom thereby. That hideous scene played out on the bed I so lovingly built for her, that I decorated with flounces from the trimmings of Miranda's very dresses. I can hardly bring myself to write this scene, but I must:

I watch as she undoes her blouse and brassiere, letting loose her large pendulous breasts. The areolas are as big as silver dollars. She kicks off her boots and pulls off her khakis and stands in her blue panties for a moment, then pulls them down and is completely naked, holding out her arms to me.

"Here," she says.

And I dumbly come to her.

"Hold me like this," she says, putting my arms around her bare back, squashing her breasts between us.

"Harder," she insists. "Yes, that's good. I told you before, I won't break."

She leads me to the bed, actually pushing me down, and then lays on top of me. She begins wriggling on top of me.

"Yes," she whispers into my ear. A sudden darting of her

tongue there sends an electric shock through my body. It is not a pleasant sensation. I suddenly see what she is up to. Her left hand is trailing down my shirt to the pocket where I always keep the hypodermic syringe for emergencies. She is sneaking her fingers there with her tongue in my ear and her pubis grinding away against my waist.

"No!" I suddenly yell, pushing her off. "Get away from me!"

I draw out the syringe and hold it menacingly.

"A whore at heart!"

I spit the words out at her, but still she holds my hand, pulling at me, thrusting her disgustingly naked pubis at me. There are stains on my pants from her juices. It is more than I can tolerate. I strike out at her, open-handed, slapping her cheek. This brings her back to reality, and by the look in her eyes I see I have made my point. She knows who is in control. Her little game won't work on me.

"Don't touch me with your filth."

I get off the bed. She has finally shown some modesty and uses her hands to cover her nakedness. It is a gesture that takes me back over almost fifty years to a sunny day on the eastern borders of the Reich. I am on an inspection trip with Eichmann. We are following in the wake of the *Einsatzgruppen*, seeing how well they do their work. It is outside some shanty village in Estonia, and the Jews have finally been rounded up. The bulldozers worked during the preceding night digging deep channels like moats outside the village. The Jews are led to these ditches, are told to disrobe, and are taken in groups of twenty to be eliminated, thrown in the ditches, lime thrown over their bodies for sanitary measure, and then the next group of twenty is sent for. Birds are singing; it is early spring. Plum trees are in bloom. A plane flies high overhead. It is one of ours out on a routine reconnaissance mission. Its drone amid the bird-song is reassuring, pleasant. The staccato burst of machine guns periodically interrupts this lovely scene. I do not follow the Jews to the place of execution. I feel it is enough that I have examined the preparations. One does not want to know or see too much. But back to the gesture: Miss O'Brien's modesty. It is the same with these Jew women. They are going to certain death, yet they hold protective hands over breasts and pubes. I see one young girl with only the beginnings of breasts and the soft down of pubic hair, and she clutches these parts as if they will fall off. Or, perish the thought, as if the sight of them will incite our troops to rape. I could assure her, that is the last thought on any of our minds. The job is hard enough without adding that to the mix. We are soldiers doing our duty, not barbarians.

I watch this young girl being led away. She has noticed my attention and tries to keep her eyes on the ground. Her buttocks are high and tiny. I imagine she keeps her hands protecting her nakedness even as the bullets I hear instants later tear into her body, splintering her fingers; as they rip the lower hand off the wrist and penetrate her abdomen, throwing her against the mud bank of the ditch, the dirt turned to mud by the blood of those who have gone before.

"Away!" I yell at Miss O'Brien as I move forth from the bed. Her eyes look down to her feet; they do not follow me. At the door, I look back. She is still on the bed, still covering her nakedness with her hands, still averting her eyes from mine.

She reminds me of that young girl in Estonia so many years ago.

"You're still going to feed me, then?"

"Of course. What did you think?"

"I don't know. I'm the pariah now, aren't I? Jezebel, et cetera. I'm sure your fertile imagination can come up with the appropriate appellation."

"Nothing of the sort. We're both to blame. This sort of thing happens."

"Stockholm syndrome again. Is that what you think? Or that I'm like one of the Jewish women at your camp, ready to bargain sex for freedom. Or even for just two more weeks of life? Got you wondering, doesn't it?"

"I should think this would be a fruitless conversation. The red hen's laying quite well again."

"Speaking of getting laid. Hello, Sigmund. Let's do a word association test. Verbal Rorschach. Come on. Quit looking so glum. It was only a little cuddle then, wasn't it? The world isn't going to end because of it. I doubt you'll even get pregnant. And I'm being very proper today, see. No carnal designs, yet."

"Miss O'Brien, you'll pardon me for saying so, but I find this problem with your entire generation. You are so frivolous about everything. You take nothing seriously, not even the mystery of sex. Indeed, there are no mysteries you do respect."

"That's because the people of your generation destroyed mystery forever by kitschifying it. You made us realists and cynics because you were such ever-loving idealists and romantics. And look at the results of your ideas. We're frivolous because your brand of seriousness about destroyed the world."

"All right. I see there is no point to this."

"No. You're going to listen for once."

"Get away from the door, Miss O'Brien."

"Not until you listen. You are forever opening the can of worms and then throwing your hands up at the sight of them, running off to hide like an old woman. When you should be hooking those worms up to a good hook and using them for bait to catch new ideas. You look at me as a threat. True. But not to your Nazi identity. No. Not that literal. I am a threat to your human identity. I see through you, and that is my great crime. I'll blow your cover, put a mirror to your face and body and show you the hole where your heart should be. That's my real crime, isn't it? That's why you're holding me here."

"Really, Miss O'Brien. If you don't step aside—"

"And what's the sentence for a mirror these days, Herr _____? Fifty to life? You talk of frivolous sex. How you honor the mystery of it. What a fucking laugh. With your SS stud farms and leaders who couldn't get it up. Who loved dogs more than humans. That's the German way, isn't it now? Gas the human vermin and let the hounds eat at the table. But you've gone one up on them, haven't you? You got rid of your dogs. Now you run humans in their cages. How many like me have there been before? How many human mirrors who you couldn't look in the eyes? So, yes, I was acting out of desperation yesterday. Especially after learning about your postcard trick and then finding out what happened to your little Miranda. I was frightened. I still am. I wanted to reach you, to make you feel for once. Make you know passion at least before it's too late."

"Too late for what, Miss O'Brien?"

"For me, asshole! For my life!"

"I must insist, Miss O'Brien."

"Fuck you and your insisting."

"All right. You ask for truth. I shall supply you with a most straightforward one. I no longer have faith in you."

"That's a rich one! You no longer have faith in me. You fucking kill me, you arrogant asshole."

"That may be true. But there it is. Mutual faith and trust is integral to any amelioration of the present circumstances."

"So why don't you trust me? Because I touched you with my cunt?"

"Don't be disgusting."

"Words again, Herr Sturmbannführer. The words bother you. More than the actions. Should we make our own speech rules like you people did? My *dye-dee* instead of *cunt*. Would that please you?"

"___"

"Should I play like the Jews did, then? Roll over and die? Strip and get a Zyklon shower?"

"There you go again about the Holocaust. It's the great liberal curse. So easy for the weak-kneed to gnash their teeth over. To point the accusing finger at Germany. But the Jews themselves were also to blame for what happened. Zionists worked hand in hand with us. Other Jews sold out their own people. Bartered and traded bodies. You're so concerned with the truthfulness of words, then why don't we hear of those Jews?"

"You mean Kastner in Budapest? Not that red herring again, please. One isolated incident. And besides, he was trying to save some of the Hungarian Jews rather than have them all deported by your boss."

"___"

"Well, don't disappoint me, Herr ____. You must have some snappy retort to that one."

"No, none. I'm just thinking."

"About what?"

"About why you know so much of our history. Zyklon-

B, the gas used at Auschwitz. The Hungarian Jew, Kastner. *Sprachregeln*."

"Maybe you don't know it, but there was a trial. Jerusalem in the early sixties?"

"Yes. I know about that only too well. You've already told me about your interest in that trial, as a matter of fact. But I also know that you were an adolescent at the time. A young girl growing up in the west of Ireland. That television was hardly the commodity there and then that it is today in, say, New York. Yes, there are many things I am thinking about, Miss O'Brien."

"You're crazy. A fucking paranoid. You think I'm a Mossad plant because I know bits and pieces of Third Reich history? You might as well round up half the civilized world if that's the criteria. You're public fucking knowledge, or hadn't you realized? You and guys like you are a goddamn cottage industry for writers and researchers. I mean, Hollywood's waiting to cast your part in its next miniseries."

"Is that why you're here, then?"

"I give up. It's like talking to a turtle."

"You'll excuse me then, Miss O'Brien. I have things to attend to. Your eggs are getting cold."

"You know what I just had, Herr ____?"

"____?"

"A shiver. Like the goose walking over my grave. You frighten me, you know that? You scare me shitless, as a matter of fact, and send cold right down to my marrow."

"I'm sorry I have such an unpleasant effect on you."

"That makes two of us. I'm not a plant, you know. You've got to believe that. And about yesterday. It wasn't just a bid for freedom. I'm in your life in many ways. There's a shared intimacy here. You cared for me at one point. I mean literally, physically, when I was ill. That creates a bond. You feel that, don't you?"

"We'll see."

"Did you hear me? Are you listening at all?"

"I must be going now."

PART V

I am listening to Barber's "Adagio for Strings." Though I find most music later than the twentieth century to be decadent, there are exceptions. This is a painfully melancholy piece. It wrenches one's very soul. It matches the day: all gray and gloom with thunder to the east. And it also matches my mood.

But to return to my memoirs. Writing them will, I hope, act as a palliative to Miss O'Brien and her eternal bickering.

Late in 1942, I was transferred to a new posting, one that I did not care for, but one I worked hard at, nonetheless. Relations had grown increasingly strained between Eichmann and me: He accused me of undermining his power base in Vienna. As if doing my job as diligently as possible were an affront to this man. I won commendations from Berlin and Oranienburg for my efforts. Eichmann took these to be a sign of my competition for his position. So he had me transferred to Mauthausen KZ, or concentration camp, in the late fall of 1942, something of a comedown from my duties at IVA, 4b, but I did not grouse.

Mauthausen was the largest concentration camp in Austria, or the Danube-East District as we referred to it in the Reich. Opened in 1938, the camp was capable of holding thirty thousand undesirables and was a hotbed of activity with a quirky mix of political and criminal prisoners. Very few Jews were sent here: most of them were being resettled farther to the east.

I remember quite well the day I traveled to my new posting. No farewell party from Eichmann, merely a second-class ticket for the morning train. Once on the train, I forgot my bitterness at my demotion and was transfixed, after we had steamed out of the precincts of Vienna, by the unrolling autumn landscape out my window—I had personally upgraded my ticket to first class and so had the compartment to myself. The charming late-fall light of almost amber hue suffused the day with a deep peaceful somnolence. When we arrived at Melk, I decided to detrain. It had been many years since I last visited the town and the lovely monastery built by Prandtauer—though monastery hardly describes this elegant castlelike edifice perched precariously on an escarpment over the river Danube. I had decided I would make this an outing and damn Eichmann for the ponce that he was.

After surveying the fine library in the monastery, I strolled in the courtyard and then had a pleasant late lunch at an unpresuming *Weingarten* in the vicinity, the pine bough over the door announcing itself to me from a block away. Now as I write of it, I remember exactly what I had that day: Sulz, or headcheese, and a plate of sliced wurst and onions doused in vinegar, which I rather greedily mopped up with black bread—this latter a rather sorry wartime affair with an admixture tasting not unlike sawdust. All this accompanied by a tart white wine from the Wachau. One glass only.

The afternoon train then took me on to the railhead at the village of Mauthausen some thirty miles away. A car from the kommandator of the camp was there to meet me. I had, in fact, kept the sergeant waiting and he showed obvious impatience at my tardiness.

As chance would have it, I arrived at the railhead just as a load of new prisoners was arriving from the north. The sergeant indicated that I might want to stay and see the fun. But I was not amused at the sorry lot of ruffians who detrained there. They were transfers from Dachau, politicals mostly, or Reds as they were known in the KZ system for the red triangle they wore to identify them. There was also a sprinkling of Greens among them—these were prisoners of the criminal class. The boots of the waiting Schutzstaffel troops were more lenient with the Greens than the Reds, it seemed, but there was little need for violence. These men were old pros: no undue force needed to be applied to set them on the double to the camp. They knew from long and hard experience—many of the Reds having been in the KZ system since 1933—that their one chance of survival was to be unobtrusive and cooperative.

We followed close in back of these trotting prisoners up the hill to the imposing structure of the camp itself. When I describe the structure as imposing, I am not merely using some literary convention. The whole seemed to be constructed of granite blocks, rough-hewn and quarried from the nearby hillside. Indeed, it was such quarries that provided the work for the entire camp. Two tall watchtowers flanked the huge entrance; the men continued trotting on the double into the first courtyard, the receiving area. They finally came to a halt at the base of a block of administrative offices made of the same granite blocks. This was surmounted by a balustrade along the top. From here, the camp commander, a certain Sturmbannführer Ziereis, berated the new arrivals for being such subhumans as to end their days in a KZ—he promised them they would never see the free world again if he had anything to do with it. They should forget all the propaganda about reforming them to function again in the outside world; it was his job to keep them from plaguing the world with their contaminating souls. This he pledged to do even if hell froze over. If they looked sharp, they might survive without punishment. They could go on living, if this was to be called a life.

He absolutely froze the men with the cold ruthlessness of his speech. It was delivered in such a severe and yet unimpassioned manner that it sent chills up and down even my spine. He only noticed me then—I had been sent to take over the role of administrative officer in the camp and would, therefore, be, if not an assistant, perhaps a competitor for authority. He sized me up, I thought, and decided I was unworthy of attention.

The men still stood at a semblance of attention and Ziereis paraded back and forth on the balustrade dressed in riding boots and jodhpurs, a small-caliber rifle in his hands. Their lives and deaths were his concern and decision. His alone. God played no part at Mauthausen, he said.

By now, the sun was setting and a chill wind came into the compound off the river along with the sound of tramping feet: the first shift was back from the quarries, each of the near skeletons in formation carrying a heavy stone. Their nightly task after laboring all day long hauling and breaking up rocks was to bring back building materials to the camp for its continual expansion. The sergeant and I in the staff car were between these workers and the new arrivals. The eyes of the former never flitted my way, either because they were too tired to be curious or because my black uniform warned them against such looks. It was said that, in some camps, prisoners would lose their lives merely for looking at a Staffel man.

Ziereis continued hectoring the new arrivals, regardless of the exhausted men who wanted to enter the camp. He warned them against all foul vices, conspiracy to escape being foremost among these. No one escapes, he told them. No one. Death was the only way out of Mauthausen.

I suddenly believed him. Up to this point, I had had little direct contact with the camps. There had been the odd visit now and again, escorting some foreign delegation or the infernal Red Cross to this or that exemplary KZ to ensure that the degenerates incarcerated there were being treated with kid gloves. But never had I actually witnessed the reality of camp life before this afternoon. It was not that the sights and sounds filled me with abhorrence; rather, I was sickened that a portion of society should necessitate such a system. I feared for the souls of those men running such camps.

Finally, finishing his harangue, Ziereis had his adjutant, one Lieutenant Bachmayer, come down among the rabble and "look for disagreeable types." I had no idea what this meant; obviously it was some kind of camp code word, for the workers outside the gate stirred restlessly. The sergeant at my side whispered: "Now you'll see something."

At Bachmayer's side was his enormous Schäferhund, which he called Lord. Bachmayer walked among the men for a moment, then finally stopped in front of one: a cringing little Red who did not look as though he would have given anyone any trouble. Bachmayer pulled this unresisting man out of the line and pushed him toward my car, toward the entrance. The man stumbled a few unwilling feet and then turned back. On the balustrade,

Ziereis took aim with his rifle and shot. The bullet landed at the man's feet. It was obvious that he was intended to keep going toward the entrance. He hesitated; another shot rang out, this time striking his foot. He cried out in pain, but understood. He began limping toward the giant entrance gate. Lord was on him before he reached it, and there right in front of my eyes, the hound tore him to shreds. No man intervened. No man even blanched at the sight.

I knew then that I had entered another realm from the outside world.

———

"You don't bring your writings to me anymore."

"The way things stand, Miss O'Brien, I think that would be senseless."

"How do things stand?"

"No feigned insouciance, please."

"Really. I'm not acting. I want to know where we are. Where I am."

"Something broke between us. You must sense that, as well. A certain mutual respect and trust. One cannot simply regain that overnight."

"Which means?"

"For one thing, that I keep to myself. My memoirs are mine."

"Why bother writing them, if you don't want anyone to read them?"

"There you have it, Miss O'Brien. The apposite pronoun. Anyone. The unknown reader, that is who I write for. Not the known. I am not writing polemics here, but the simple story of one man's life. To make sure there is a record of the time from our side. I have no wish to hide from the past. I feel no shame in it."

"—"

"You are maddening!"

"Why? What did I do now?"

"Even in your silences you criticize and find fault."

"Don't blame me for your own misgivings."

"You are like a pestilence that has gotten inside me, always questioning, questioning. Never allowing the spontaneous action."

"It's called being human. And it's not spontaneity we're talking about here, but irresponsibility."

"And who made you the arbiter of such things, Miss O'Brien? Where are your credentials in life?"

"But I don't set out to tell big truths as you do. I have no vocation for the position of savior. Those who do, however, need always to be judged by the strictest standards. You bring it on by the very task you set yourself."

"Poppycock."

"Strong words, Herr ____."

"Don't mock me."

"—"

"It's time for your exercise."

"I don't feel like it today."

"You need fresh air. Do as I say."

———

It is true: the bond between Miss O'Brien and myself has been well and fully broken. I feel a sort of disgust when I see her now, moping about the dog run outside, picking at a bit of grass to chew on, just like a cow.

Strange, but I actually long for those early days when

we were just getting to know each other, when I cared for her during her sickness, bathing her soiled body and sheets as I would a baby's. But it seems she has forgotten all that. She only wants to dominate now, like all women I have ever known. Dominate and then betray: It is their formula.

There she sits now, chewing on her plucked stem of long grass; she looks up at my window and waves. She knows I will be watching. It is as if I have become the prisoner, she the jailer. I feel trapped in my own home.

Back to the memoirs.

Such was my introduction to Mauthausen KZ, where I was to spend the rest of the war years; indeed, the rest of my Schutzstaffel career. It was a shocker, I can assure you, especially following so hard upon my reposeful visit to Melk earlier in the day. (A subcamp of Mauthausen later opened within sight of the monastery at Melk—there seemed to be no place removed from the war.) But perhaps the most shocking thing about this introduction and the new life it presaged was how quickly I adapted to it. Already by the second day I had learned to look away from things disagreeable, to occupy my mind with more urgent organizational matters in the face of so much personal misfortune.

Early on, I also secured myself against the treacherous reefs of sentimentality. After all, these men were in the camp for crimes against society. We were doing society as a whole, and even these individuals, a favor by segregating them from the healthy part of the body politic. They had brought incarceration on themselves. Such had to be my mental stance, otherwise insanity awaited me. Ask any warder and he will respond the same way: Never open the doors to empathy. One must be hard to survive in such a situation.

And what was the situation? Specifically, the camp was built around a central field, the *Appelplatz*, or roll-call area. If one faced west, toward the main entrance, the barracks and workshops were to the right, and on the left wing were the laundry, showers, kitchen, bunker, hospital, and crematorium. In back of this wing were some more Staffel barracks, and toward the entrance were the offices of the administration, mine among them. There were also outbuildings: civilian barracks to the northwest and the Russian tent camp to the southwest. The whole was surrounded by immense granite rock walls, giving it the aspect of a medieval fortress.

Just outside the main gates was the way down to the quarries, either by single-gauge railway, upon which only the stones quarried were lucky enough to ride, or the 186 steps down into them. The entirety covered some four square miles, most of which was taken up by the camp itself, but one-third of which was composed of the quarries that provided the economic basis for the entire enterprise.

Additionally, housing for the higher Staffel officers such as myself was located outside the camp, along pleasantly wooded slopes overlooking the Danube. One positive aspect to this posting: I was away from the villa in Hohe Warte, away from the loneliness of being with Uschi. I had, by now, grown to hate her cheery voice on the phone as she arranged golf meetings and bridge afternoons.

Into this physical configuration then, lump the myriad caste of prisoners we had: political, criminal, religious, asocials, homosexuals. As administrative officer, it was my responsibility to see that all ran smoothly: that there was room for the prisoners sent to us, that there was food to feed them, that work details were managed efficiently. The infinite minutiae of my job were quite unbelievable. And such responsibility thrust on me, who only had a captain's rating at the time!

Of course the personalities at camp were also part of the situation report. I have shown both Ziereis and his second in command, Bachmayer, in a situation that largely reveals their character. There was, in addition, a whole range of lesser functionaries, from quartermaster to medical doctors, even down to the cooks and crematorium engineers. They all had to be dealt with, arranged, and smoothed when their feathers became ruffled for one reason or another. One would have thought we were running an opera company, so temperamental were the egos involved. Stories I have of those days, some grisly, some insane, some merely mediocre. But one thing I want to make clear from the outset: We were running a concentration camp, not a death camp. The alleged death camps—Auschwitz, Sobibor, Treblinka, and the like—were far to the east in the former Polish territory. Mauthausen had nothing to do with these, despite propaganda I have read claiming over two hundred thousand died there. I even read, in one supposedly scholarly review of Mauthausen, that Auschwitz used the threat of transfer to the quarries at Mauthausen to keep its prisoners in line. Poppycock!

Ours was a job of housing, feeding, and clothing hundreds of thousands of men and, later in the war, women who were dangerous to the Reich. Other societies simply eliminate their undesirables; we put ours to work in the quarries. The symbolism is good here, I think. Those who would tear down the Reich were instead forced to dig new building blocks for it out of the earth. From such quarries at camp sites throughout Europe came the granite not only for buildings, but also for cobbled streets and roads, even the dust for bricks. A most constructive occupation for such asocial pariahs. Thus, with the prisoners quite literally working for the Reich, it would hardly have been in our best interests to simply kill them off as has been alleged since the end of the war.

Of course there was a crematorium at Mauthausen. We were a small city and people died there as they die everywhere, and we had no other means of disposing of the bodies than by cremating them. Also, and despite repeated warnings, there were those who would attempt to escape. It was wartime; escape attempts were dealt with swiftly and harshly. Thus there were also a number of "unnatural deaths." But we did not just unload incoming prisoners and send them to supposed gassing showers and certain death as the media portrays. Such hogwash will not do. I want to set the record straight on that account.

During my nearly three years at Mauthausen, I kept copious diaries, which I took with me when I eventually fled Europe in 1947. They are with me still, but I am of two minds whether to include them in this record or not. Actually, they are a book in themselves, recording the turbulent days in a wealth of detail and emotion. Emotion, for they were my one outlet in all those years. I had no real friends as such at the camp. Uschi stopped paying dutiful monthly visits after the first year, and as administrative officer, I posed more of a threat than a promise of friendship to the rest of the staff, who were all busily engaged in making themselves rich off the spoils of the system. There were rake-offs and scams at every level: from kapos or trustees who extorted any and all favors from other prisoners for easy treatment to the quartermaster and doctor who sold part of the camp's provisions on the black market and even up to the commandant himself, who had a special contract with local builders for cheap laborers.

I, the newcomer, was suspected by all those with something to hide, until in the fall of 1944 when I, too, succumbed to such rewards. It is my great shame: the contract I signed with one Herr Wenzel to supply laborers for his brick factory. It made me a rich man, enables me even now to live comfortably, but Wenzel turned out to be greedier than even I suspected: His bricks were made so cheaply and shoddily that they would crumble under too great a stress. A *Volksschule* constructed with his bricks did exactly that in January 1945, killing fifteen children and maiming many more.

I confess to feeling I was a party to that crime. The ones I stand convicted of at Nuremberg are paltry by comparison. Though ignorant of Wenzel's shoddy manufacturing standards, I still hold myself as responsible as he was. Whether rational or irrational to do so, I will carry that burden to my grave.

Otherwise, I performed my duties at Mauthausen with supreme efficiency and dedication. I have nothing to be ashamed of on that score.

Herewith, a sampling of my diaries to give the flavor of the times:

> *6 December 1942—First Advent Sunday. How I do love this season, though I wonder if the joy will be there for me this year. Seems a miserly thing to indulge my individual pleasure in the Yuletide when all about me there is suffering and death. But our valiant soldiers at the front might forgive this one indulgence; otherwise it is work, work. I constructed a tiny wreath for my worktable, gathering pine boughs surreptitiously lest the others here at administration find out what I have been up to. I employed one kapo—a Polish brute who I believe was a child murderer, though he is sweet as treacle to me, happy*

for his chance to curry favor. At any rate, this man I employed to gather holly from some difficult-to-reach bushes in the quarry—what is an advent wreath without holly? In the event, it was a mistake, for he soon proved his brutishness by forcing a couple of the younger French prisoners to form a human chain, dangling over the edge to reach the plant. Sergeant Mayer, one of the quarry guards, later rather glee-fully reported the incident to me, ignorant of the fact that it was I who had commissioned the kapo in the first place. One of the young men fell to his death against the rocks far below. Mayer found this part most amusing, for the French youth still held the sprig of holly tightly in his grip when they reached him. The kapo overseer took it from the dead man's hands and added it to that already gathered. This, of course, took some joy out of my wreath, but I burned the first Advent candle today nonetheless.

3 February 1943—In blizzard conditions. The camp functions are at an absolute standstill. With the pipes frozen solid, water is nowhere to be found. Prisoners lick bits of ice they have chipped out of the water beakers. The condition these people are reduced to in such a short time after arrival! Quite shocking. One knows why the Führer wants to segregate them from the rest of the gene pool. Forty-eight died today in the quarry, frozen to death at their work. Had they shown a bit more diligence in their work, their body heat alone would have saved them. But they are malingerers.

Yesterday, Berlin announced the end of the fight-ing for Stalingrad. The announcer on the state radio had a quaver in his voice as he reported the "sacri-

*fices of the army, bulwark of a historical European
mission, were not in vain." Three days of official
mourning throughout the Reich. They say 150,000
of our boys were killed trying to take the city.*

*21 March 1943—Some say it is spring; winter
lingers on, however. And this is a winter I will not
be sad to see the last of. Five thousand have died in
the camp during the last two months, many of them
from the cold. A merciful death, perhaps. Yet I continue to do my best for them and the Reich. I have
yet to feel a part of things here. Ziereis has his family; he ignores me whenever possible. Bachmayer is
a lout and I should never choose to mix with such a
person other than professionally. He is also a drunk
and a whore chaser, out most every night satisfying
his base desires. The camp is buzzing with his inexcusable behavior upon returning this morning after
an all-night spree. The men were just leaving the
main gate for the quarry and Bachmayer—blurry-
eyed and hungover and just getting back from his
debauches—unholstered his machine pistol and
began shooting indiscriminately into the crowds. Ten
killed, thirty-two more wounded before his comrades
could take his pistol from him. Yet Ziereis does nothing about it; no disciplinary action at all. I have half
a mind to report him to Berlin. With reason, too.
Not only is Bachmayer a beast, a sadist who has no
business wielding power over human beings, but also
his absolutely indiscriminate beatings and killings
undermine any real leverage we may have over the
prisoners. We Staffel here are outnumbered perhaps
twenty to one. We have weapons on our side, certainly, but we depend on the innate belief in author-*

ity on the part of the prisoners, as well. They do not step out of line for fear of punishment; the lash is commonly used here. Punishment is thus a deterrent for them. Its threat keeps them in line. Destroy the prisoners' belief that if they behave properly they will survive, and there will be the devil to pay. We shall have an uprising here. Irresponsible actions such as Bachmayer's erode the prisoner-warder bond: the unspoken pact that good behavior will be rewarded, bad punished. I must make Ziereis understand this.

1 June 1943—Uschi stays on in the Hohe Warte villa. She has missed the last two monthly visits. I must confess to relief on that part. I feel well rid of her. Mother writes that her new flat is glorious. She and Maria thank me a thousand times again. So they should. Typhus outbreak in camp and production is down at the quarries. In spite of what I do, I cannot seem to get this place shipshape. Whenever I approach a point of control, we are flooded with new shipments of prisoners. This despite a twelve-hour working day—I am at my desk before the six o'clock shift reaches the quarries. Just let the prisoners grouse and grumble about their ten-hour days in my hearing!

A rather unsettling occurrence last week: The last of the Viennese Jews were shipped out via our camp, en route to eastern resettlement. I have initiated a little trick that is now also used at Auschwitz to soothe the fears of the new arrivals: I have organized a camp orchestra of three violins, a tuba, and an accordion. These meet incoming trains with sprightly marches. They also provide Sunday afternoon entertainment in the Appelplatz, in the intervals of boxing matches between prisoners. Well, I used the Vienna train to try out my little orchestra on, just to see if it works. The music did, in fact, appear to reduce anxiety, stimulating even a smile here and there from the rabble detraining as a familiar tune was heard. But in the midst of this came the most frightful sight: In one boxcar, guards discovered three bodies. Two men were riddled with bullets—obviously in an attempt to escape. The third body was that of a woman. Well, barely recognizable as that sex, I can tell you. Her head was battered into an unrecognizable pulp; her left breast all but torn from her body. Raped repeatedly and savagely by her own kind, she was then beaten to death with almost cannibalistic fury. Our doctor tells me that the unfortunate woman had apparently recently been a mother and was still lactating. Abominable people!

8 September 1943—The Italian surrender, which apparently happened several days ago behind closed doors, was made public today. It is perhaps no more than we deserved, this stab in the back, for being so stupid as to go into the business of war with such people in the first place. Radio Berlin tells us that Mussolini is too great a person for a nation like that; I cannot credit his greatness. He prevaricated at the outset of the war, causing no little confusion and setback to our early plans in Poland. This I know firsthand, for I was directly involved in Operation Himmler; I knew what his last-minute cowardice meant for our well-laid plans. The lives it cost.

4 January 1944—A most distinguished "guest" arrived at camp yesterday. It was a Tuesday and I

was making my usual rounds of the laundry in the morning. This inspection tour takes me uncomfortably close to the crematoria and interrogation cellars. I would rather not be reminded of what transpires in those cellars. The political officers have a hard row to hoe: They must be ruthless in service to the state. Like me, they receive little credit for their efforts. At any rate, as I was saying, I was busy with my inspection of the laundry, making sure the prisoners were not wasting precious soap, when I heard Ziereis on his megaphone addressing a new arrival of prisoners from his perch over the administrative offices. I finished my inspection tour and was passing back to the administrative wing when I gave the new arrivals a glance. As motley looking a crew as we had yet received. Mostly Reds, political prisoners, by the look of them. That anemic, intellectual pose. They would surely not hold up under the labors of the quarry. Give us some more thieves and forgerers, I thought then. At least they can handle the physical abuse of breaking rock and hauling it up the 186 steps. One of the prisoners looked familiar. A strange sensation for me to recognize one of these misfits, but nevertheless an experience I had prepared myself for. I approached the prisoner and saw that my eyes had not tricked me: Though much wasted and diminished in grandeur, here before me was the famous Advokat Haberloch, the lawyer and professor who had been a boyhood idol of mine, who had once offered me a position as his aide.

Haberloch did not see me, but I smiled to myself as I passed. So they finally got him, I thought. Arrested for his homosexuality. I scanned his uni-

*form for the telltale pink triangle and was quite
surprised to see the red one instead.*

*12 January 1944—I am told Haberloch is here
for crimes against the state: seems he was actually
trying to investigate our KZ system! The arrogant
man. Searching for scandal, as is his wont. Ziereis
let slip that the fellow had actually come close to
uncovering various contracts between the camps and
private industry.*

*17 February 1944—Haberloch is dead. He fell
to his death in the quarry. Such a strange man he
was. And another chapter of my life closed.*

*18 May 1944—Monte Cassino has finally
fallen. And who should raise the ragtag flag of
victory but some blackguardly Polish division. The
ironies of war that those from the guilty country of
Poland should now act the role of liberator. Quite
disgusting.*

*We are feeling the influx of prisoners originally
resettled in the east. As the Russians push farther
and farther west, we will be experiencing more
and more such overcrowding and dislocations. How
strange: I read of the great events of the day in Das
Schwarze Corps and hear of them on Radio Berlin,
and yet with all this information, here I sit, a miserable scrivener unable to affect the course of these
events. I work ceaselessly but receive no commendations, let alone respect for what I do.*

*7 June 1944—So they have come, the new bar-
barians. They landed yesterday at Normandy, and
two days earlier took Rome. The classic pincer movement is on. It is only a matter of time now. Despair-*

*ing thoughts. I shall no longer follow the war news.
To that effect, I have taken down the ordnance maps
in my bungalow, all so carefully pennoned with
armies and their movements. No, the war no longer
interests me.*

*13 June 1944—The first of the secret weapon
rockets fell on London today. Perhaps we, with German know-how, can stem the tide after all.*

*I do not think I ever want to see another trans-
port in my life. When this is all over, I shall find
some place very quiet in which to retire, much to
myself, and simply give over to relaxation and
inner peace. Perhaps even compose my memoirs.
But someplace free of the stench of this place with
its load of noxious smoke released nonstop from the
crematorium chimneys. The influx from the east, as
our lines there fall, is insupportable. Trainload after
trainload of every imaginable sort of scum is being
dropped on our doorstep. Increasingly, Mauthausen
is becoming the dustbin of the Reich. No figures can
be accurate any longer, but I estimate we have now
upward of forty thousand prisoners, at least half of
whom live in tents and other temporary shelter. The
satellite camps have grown at Gusen and Ebensee,
but even so, our camp system simply cannot take in
such numbers. Something must give. Lucky that we
are now in the summer months, but when winter
hits, and if the fronts are no better than last year,
well, then we shall have trouble on a major scale.
Ziereis is phlegmatic as usual about it: "Things will
sort themselves out," he says. "They always have a
way of sorting themselves out." Of course, for Ziereis,*

if the hunting is good in the fall and the trout fat in the spring, then life is satisfactory. A man of limited needs and means.

21 July 1944—News has reached us of the attempt on the Führer's life yesterday. Colonel Count von Stauffenberg, chief plotter, is in custody. One wonders how deeply the rot has set in, how many more darlings of the military are involved in this cheap assassination attempt. And one can only wonder what the ramifications will be vis-à-vis the Allies. Now they see us bickering among ourselves, the push will be even stronger on their part. They will be able to catch the scent of blood. They see us weak and vulnerable now. The rot of the old aristocracy, of the professional army man, is responsible for this. It is something that we in the Schutzstaffel have long suspected—one need only look to the Blomberg-Fritsch affair of 1938 for early proof of decadence in the highest levels of the Wehrmacht: One man marries a known prostitute, the other is caught out as a homosexual. So now these "noble" military men have shown their true colors and the Allies, especially the British, are gloating. Listening to the BBC last night—for it comes in better than Radio Berlin now—we heard their commentator with his awful supercilious voice explaining the significance of the affair. According to him, even if Hitler had been eliminated—which thank providence he wasn't—it proved how beaten the Germans were. A strange thought went through my mind: How well my English is coming along. After listening so much to the radio, the language feels almost natural in my ears now. And I experienced a prescience, a sort of reverse déjà vu, that I should be using it quite a lot in the future. But what is this to portend? That Germany will indeed become an occupied territory of the British? Or worse, that the Americans with their democracy and jazz will be the new imperial power in Europe? Is it to be that these people will despoil our culture and our very language?

25 August 1944—Paris has fallen. The writing is surely on the wall for all to see.

9 September 1944—V-2s falling on London. Aptly named: Vergeltungswaffe (reprisal weapon). Are we to believe the Führer, after all, about the miracle weapons that will pull this off for us at the eleventh hour? One can only hope. Meanwhile, it is only prudent to prepare for the worst. Shall see about making that trip to Switzerland in the very near future, just to ensure that my finances are all in order there.

2 February 1945—The escape has been put down now. It started in Block 20 with the Russian and French prisoners of war. That should teach us to show leniency to any of them. Some four hundred of them escaped in the night, but the dogs were sent out for them and the local populace alerted. All but seven were recaptured. All know the punishment for attempted escape: One hears the execution squads at work even now, the steady crack of rifle fire from behind the Appelplatz. Let this teach the scum.

12 February 1945—Upward of sixty thousand prisoners in camp now, and the Red Army is on the move. Time to begin making plans on an individual scale. . . .

———

"Please stop doing this."

"This what, Miss O'Brien? Let's not go into it right now, please. Just eat your food or I shall have to find some other means to deliver it."

"This mutual antagonism. Both becoming each other's scapegoats and caricatures. You are not the incarnation of evil because of your career in the Reich. I am not the snake in your garden for trying to seduce you. I am neither Eve nor Mary Magdalene. I am me. Another human!"

"Yes, quite."

"Don't 'quite' me. Treat me like a human."

"Act like one."

———

I confess to losing my temper. I almost struck the woman, she pushes me that far. This situation becomes less tolerable daily. Yet I see no way to resolve it. We are afflicted with each other, but I cannot in good conscience simply give the Irish over to Cordoba and his military friends. I am a victim of my own moral scruples. She knows this about me and plays on it. And then she has the gall to say that she is not the snake in my garden! Errant flummery!

So I gave her the latest bundle of papers I have been writing. What harm can it do, after all?

Back to the war years.

In February 1945, word of the Red Army advance on Budapest spread quickly. Once the Danube was secured, there would be no stopping the Soviet advance. The situation now was truly hopeless. One cannot imagine the utter chaos of those final days. Here is a case where no amount of book learning could educate one as to the turmoil, fear, and despondency we Germans and Austrians went through at the time.

The days went by in a blur, and suddenly it was spring again, and I had news from Eichmann himself, just returned from the east on his way to Berlin. Vienna was about to fall to the Russians. He paid a surprise visit to Mauthausen late one afternoon, pulling into the compound in his black Mercedes, its sides heavily caked in mud. He looked pale and weak. His eyes were terribly bloodshot and large bags hung morosely under them. This was from lack of sleep, I thought at first, but then I got close enough to him to smell the alcohol on his breath. He had been a heavy drinker in the days I worked for him in Vienna. Now he seemed determined to outdo even that sorry reputation. He and the commandant secreted themselves in the latter's office, but not before Eichmann exchanged a few words with me:

"I see they've got you hard at it, then?"

I said that I did my job as a humble soldier is expected to.

"Still playing the martyr, are you? Don't imagine it goes down much better here than in Vienna or Berlin."

I felt my ears go red with this scathing remark. Others of the staff were within earshot and smiled at this put-down. I'd had to deal with such calumny in Vienna but had never become accustomed to it. I made no reply to this attack, and Eichmann must have felt that he had overstepped the boundaries of decency, for he came right up to me, breathing the sweet smell of cognac on me, and said: "Things are very bad in the east. The Russians are coming. We all must do our duty to the very last. I want no one to walk out of Mauthausen. Is that understood? There is only one way they will leave—through the smokestack. *Verstehst?*"

I saluted him in tacit understanding but made no comment. I noticed he was not overeager himself to remain in Austria to see to the final special treatments. "Urgent" business in Berlin beckoned him. I could only too well imagine the nature of this urgent business, and I doubted he would ever reach Berlin. Subsequent reports proved me correct, for Eichmann disappeared two days later, on April 11, 1945, on an inspection tour of the Theresienstadt camp to the north. I suppose he had been planning such a disappearing act even at Mauthausen while he was telling me sanctimoniously how I should do my duty to the very end. So there was, even at the onset of *Götterdämmerung*, no love lost between us. How strange it is that when the entire world is falling down around one, one still has time for these petty private feuds. Indeed, small controllable matters take on a new importance in the midst of such global chaos.

For my part, I effected my own disappearance on April 13. I had intended to wait at least until Hitler's birthday on the twentieth—there seemed something appropriate about such a gesture—but the Russian advance on Vienna disallowed this formality. The city fell to the Russians that very day, the thirteenth. We at Mauthausen also had news that the Americans had taken both Belsen and Buchenwald KZ. A Staffel courier, himself seeking refuge, told us the horror stories of some of the instant justice meted out to camp guards at those installations. I listened to the youth's story, for he was a mere sixteen-year-old fresh from *gymnasium* in Heidelberg. I betrayed no emotion, even when Ziereis sucked his teeth in distress. I had more important affairs in mind than dwelling on the days of destruction. Mother and Maria were in Vienna without protection. They had refused an earlier suggestion from me that they should get out of the city, go to the west of Austria, to Salzburg or Tirol. There the American or British armies were sure to be the "liberating" ones; the matter was most uncertain for Vienna. Or had been, at any rate. Now I knew the Russians had taken the city and one knew what that meant for the women. Uschi, of course, had taken herself off to the Salzkammergut to her family's summer house in Altaussee two months earlier.

I was forced then, as the young courier's story droned on and on, to make a desperate choice: duty to my Führer and fatherland, or duty to my only blood kin. I had pledged loyalty to Adolf Hitler unto death and it was not an oath I took lightly. Yet I was filled with terror thinking of my poor mother and rather simple sister alone in Vienna. They had stayed on—it was Mother's decision—to protect the new flat I had secured for them. And lovely it was, overlooking Stephansplatz. The booming of the bells rang through its rooms at matins. Mother would not leave this flat and her belongings to be looted by the Russians or her neighbors. A strong woman, my mother, strong and stubborn.

By the time the courier had finished his story of how guards had been hung by their former captives while the American soldiers stood by applauding, I had made my decision. I excused myself after lunch to visit the quarries. But of course I had no intention of going there, and once outside the gate, I pulled the car into a copse of trees, fished out a small suitcase from under the passenger seat, and changed into the Wehrmacht corporal's uniform I had concealed there for just such an eventuality. First, however, I fitted my money belt snugly around my middle. The car I left in the woods; I should like to have driven it part of the distance but could not risk it. Alone and on foot, I would be conspicuous enough: All the world seemed to be pouring out of the east into the west, and here I was, a soldier traveling east. No, I should have to make the journey on foot and in stages. Perhaps I might even be able to hide away in a train, if there were any traveling amid such utter chaos.

So I kept to the quiet back roads to the north of the Danube where the villagers paid little attention to my passing. Indeed, they averted their eyes as if they no longer wanted to be witness to the army's existence. Stopping occasionally for food or drink, I was paid common courtesy but no more. It was as if, dressed in the uniform of the Wehrmacht, I was carrying the plague. What would the reaction have been had I been decked out in my black Staffel finery? Wondering this, I was once again thankful for the precautions I had taken vis-à-vis that uniform.

Despite this leper syndrome, I could not risk going it in total mufti. If captured—and I had to reckon on that possibility—my captors would only suspect the worst by finding one of my age and health out of uniform. They would reason this was because I had something to hide. My Schutzstaffel past would be their first guess. One examination under my left arm would give them proof of their suspicions: my tattooed service number was there. This was one thing that could not be changed by clothing. Thus, better to admit to Wehrmacht than to risk all, even though I had no intention of being captured. And as events proved, God was with me.

I completed the arduous trip to Vienna in two days, arriving April 15. The city was in absolute turmoil with roving bands of Soviet soldiers rounding up all men of draft age, in or out of uniform, to be sent to provincial prisoner of war camps. For the most part, the Soviet command attempted to keep some semblance of order by day, but at night, Vienna, my home and the capital of culture, turned into a jungle.

I approached the center of the city warily, hiding in

bombed-out buildings on the outskirts of Brigittenau until nightfall. Then I walked the darkened streets toward the First District, little recognizing the neighborhoods where I had once played as a child. Six years of warfare had wrought terrible suffering on the city: Where there was no bomb damage, there was neglect and crumbling façades. Children, as frightened and hungry looking as any of the ragtag ghetto children I had dealt with earlier in the war, huddled in one alleyway ready to pounce on any dropped crumb from a passing serviceman; ready to beg a piece of bread or a negotiable cigarette. I knew these children well from a hundred transit camps, from dozens of big-city ghettos Eichmann and I had cleared. Yet, now they were my own; they were Viennese children, but behaving like little animals. This sight disgusted me. Was this the brave new generation we had fought and sacrificed so much for? One could not tell them apart from a Jewish or Polish child under far worse conditions. I had, however, no time to consider this rather distressing observation, but merely gave the band the same evil scowl I had reserved for their brothers in Warsaw or Budapest, then pressed on into the heart of the city.

As I neared the Ringstrasse, the frequency of Russian patrols increased. I was forced to take immediate shelter wherever possible whenever one of their American-supplied Jeeps suddenly turned a corner. On one occasion, I had to hurl myself into a refuse container in front of a bombed-out building to hide. Peering up over the edge of the container, I was shocked to discover that the destroyed building had been my former *Realschule* before we moved from Hubertusgasse. I was in my old neighborhood, but took no sentimental pleasure in it.

The First District was as dark and deserted—but for the

Russian patrols—as the outer ones had been. I entered it off the Ring by the Borse and then picked my way through the garment district and thus to the old Jewish quarter behind the Hoher Markt. By the look of the jagged skyline to my right, I could see that an entire block of buildings had been destroyed on that square. I kept to the backstreets past the old Ruprechtskirche and then down by the long-closed and partially destroyed synagogue and finally out onto Rotenturmstrasse. No street women were out: Not even they were brave enough to take on the Russians by invitation. One could only imagine what barbarities such men were capable of with seasoned women of the night, let alone with innocent Germanic wives, mothers, and sisters. Such forebodings drove me on toward Stephansplatz, dodging in and out of the main thoroughfare on my way to the cathedral. It was a shock, I can tell you, to see that noble edifice a bombed-out shell. The merciless Allied bombing had seen to that, along with the State Opera, though I was not to see that wreck at the time. Of course, Allied propaganda after the war blamed the retreating Nazi artillery for leveling the church, a sorry excuse. More victors' hagiography and demonology dressed up as history. All around the Stephansplatz was a rubble: The finest square in the finest city of Europe, and it looked like a filthy construction site.

Here there was a standing guard of Russians smoking and laughing. The victors. God save the world over which they were victorious, I thought. Here were peasant boys with slanting eyes and thick fingers fresh off the steppes of Asia. The new lords. I heard a muffled scream from one of the apartment buildings still intact on the square. The guards heard it, too. They cocked their heads toward the building and then laughed together as men do at a dirty barracks joke. The scream came from the very apartment building where my mother and sister lived. It was all I could do to wait for these soldiers to pass by. Ten minutes crawled by—an eternity in the still, cool night—until three Russians clumped out of the apartment building, adjusting their tunics as they came onto the street, and then the entire squad went in search of other game.

I entered the main door of the building. It was unlocked, even after ten at night, the usual locking-up hour. The portier's bottom-floor apartment was firmly shut and curtained. Usually, she, Frau Bechman, was the nosiest of women, checking the comings and goings of any visitors from the little office adjoining her apartment. Negligent in her duties now, Frau Bechman hid behind her curtains. I could see the outline of her bunned hair as she sat in her easy chair. Symbolic: Vienna had become a frightened city of shadow dwellers.

The elevator was out of order. The hall light switch glowed pink in the gloom. I pushed it, but no overhead light appeared. Climbing the stairs, I listened carefully for any sound of more Russians, but there was absolute quiet behind the closed apartment doors.

On the third landing, I lit a match to make sure I was at the right door. There were gouges and nicks in the door to Mother's apartment, as if it had been battered by rifle butts and heavy boots. I tapped twice lightly, but there was no response from within. Another three taps, louder this time. Then came the shuffling of feet on the other side of the door, and the laborious unbolting of useless locks. No question asked of who the late-night visitor was. Before I could reassure Mother that it was her son, not a Russian mongrel come to terrorize her, the door was thrown open revealing a banshee, a harridan skipping madly in the doorway holding a candle under her blackened face, her hair sticking straight up as if electrified. I jumped back from this apparition, and just as quickly, the specter threw her arms around my neck, sobbing uncontrollably.

Mother pulled me into the dimness of her apartment, checking the hall to ensure no one had seen me. She said not one word as she led me down the darkened hallway to the kitchen and the *Diener*, or servant's room, attached to it. From this room emanated the only light in the flat; its window gave onto an air shaft that could not be seen from the street or courtyard. Servant's room, it was called, though Mother never employed one. Said they poisoned the air, and besides we had been too close to being in service ourselves at one point. Inside, huddled in a cherrywood wardrobe, was Maria, in the same frightful getup as Mother. They had blackened their faces with coal soot, put lard in their hair to make it stick up, and wore ancient housecoats covered on top with bagged-out sweaters. I asked no questions as Mother pulled this frightened animal from her hiding place, stroking her face and telling her it was all right, just her brother, her brother. Come home to protect them. Maria kept her arms tightly wrapped around her chest, as if holding in a precious breath. It was only then, confronted by the very real plight of my blood relatives, that I fully comprehended the enormity of our defeat. We of the Reich had not only lost the war; we had lost our souls in the bargain.

They had been raped the first night the Russians entered Vienna. Five soldiers took their turns at both of them here in the lovely flat they had stayed to protect from vandalism. Mother vowed it would not happen again the next night, hence the disguise.

"And I can tell you, son, we have had some very frightened Ruskies opening that door."

She laughed: a dry cackling sound like fall leaves blown over asphalt. Maria still stared at me, not recognizing or not comprehending, I was not sure which.

"They run back down those stairs as fast as their moth-eaten boots can carry them. Teach them to try their tricks on an upright Austrian woman. Scream like women, they do."

So it had been the Russian soldiers who had screamed earlier, I thought. Of course that scream would not have come from Mother; not from strong-as-a-rock Mother. She had not even cried when Father died and we were left without a provider. The violence done to her had not affected her. She took it as an affront, a bit of uncivilized behavior like smoking in the house or taking a glass too many of wine. And she would discipline the brute for it. But Maria, made of weaker stuff, was shattered by the rapes. Never a full woman, a secure human being, the experience had thrown her into the fearful posture of a forest creature fearing the shadow of an owl. She would not unfold her arms; my gesture at a commiserating hug sent her hyperventilating to Mother's bosom. Her fear was infectious; I began hearing footfalls in the stairwell where there were none to be heard, and I suddenly recognized the futility of my homecoming gesture. After all, what could I hope to do for Mother and Maria that they were not already able to do for themselves? My presence here was more of a threat than a protection for them. I gave Mother some of the money from my hidden belt. Swiss francs rather than the now-worthless reichsmarks. I tried to fill them in on the military situation, but they, civilians, naturally had more information than I. Mother wondered about my uniform, and I explained to her that I would be much sought after by the victors. They would, in fact, probably call me a war criminal. I told them they were not to believe such fantasies. I had merely been a loyal soldier doing my duty. But scapegoats would now be needed. I would surely be one of those selected for that role. But I did not intend to make their witch hunt easy. Of course, I did not tell either Mother or Maria my plans. I am not sure these were fully formulated in my own mind then, but had they been, I would not have—for their own sakes—confided such information to my family.

We talked late into the night, Mother and I, while Maria curled up in the single leather chair in the room, sleeping fitfully, awaking now and again with a whimper, a plea to be left alone. It was piteous. Mother winced once at these somnolent pleadings; otherwise, she showed no sign of anguish, no chink in her armor.

It was she who, toward four in the morning, proposed that I should be off again. If caught in Vienna, I would stand no chance at all, for everyone knew the Russians were animals. They had well and truly proven that in the past few days in Vienna. Better for me, she said, to head west, into the Alps. Hide there, and if captured, at least it would be by the Americans or British. The French were also a possibility, but choosing between them and the Russians as captors was a no-win situation, for the French also had old grudges to settle with the Reich.

Oddly enough, this was exactly what I had been intending to do; I had come to take care of Mother and she ended by taking care of me one last time. Our discussion that night was not in the least political; Mother was not sending me away to be the vanguard of renewal, but to save my skin. For years, I had been thinking only of the highest good. It was not an easy task for her to convince me that I should consider myself for once. She persisted: I should take myself off immediately. The more she considered my position, the more frightened she became for me. There was no time to lose. She would never forget my bravery in coming to them, but now . . . She could not go on. She embraced me. It was one of the few times I remember her ever doing so. Maria, still curled in the chair, sucked loudly on her thumb.

I promised Mother that I would send for her when I got settled. She laughed that she would hardly want to uproot and move halfway around the world. She had been born in Vienna; she would die here. No one had mentioned such distances: her prescience at work again.

"But Maria is a different matter. She'll need someone now. When I'm gone . . ."

I laughed, chiding Mother that she would in all likelihood live longer than either of her children.

"Well, someone will have to look after her. You can see that."

Maria seemed to be getting great relief, nay enjoyment, out of her thumb. Her sucking sounds resounded obscenely in the room.

Well, the upshot of it was that I promised Mother to protect the girl, to ensure that she was looked after when Mother was gone. It was a tearful farewell when finally it came. The night was still upon us as Mother hugged me at her apartment door. The second embrace in so short a time! I felt the soot from her face rub off on mine. Maria slept on, oblivious to my coming and going. I did not turn around, for there were tears in my eyes, and I did not want Mother to see. Thus, my final image of my mother is in black face and dressed in fantastical garb to ward off sexual assault. I wonder how many sons have such a final memory of their mothers?

———

What an odd occurrence. Today, after finishing my writing, I could only remain sitting at my trestle table, so moved was I by this final memory of Mother. I do not believe I knew before the depths of my feelings for that woman who gave me life. For so many years, she, or her memory, has been merely a caricature. The bossy imperial figure of our tiny household; the ur-matriarch if you will, with a touch of vaudeville. But today, writing of that final visit, I finally realized how much I love her, how much I owe her.

And thinking this thought, gazing unfocused at the ravine out back, I suddenly became aware of Miss O'Brien in the compound below my window. How long had she been there? I really had no idea. Then I realized I had not been aware of her presence because she fitted so well into my vision at the moment; she matched exactly my memories.

Upon first meeting the Irish, I commented how much she reminded me of Frau Wotruba. I was wrong. Today, I know truly who she reminds me of. My God!

———

Several days have passed. We are speaking a little more to each other and have called a truce about my memoirs. Or, rather, I have, regularly allowing her once again into my intimate thoughts. She is still reading my latest batch and penning a lengthy response, it would seem.

Since my last startling revelation, I have begun to look at Miss O'Brien in a different light. Perhaps all her prodding and insisting have some purpose. Perhaps I have been too quick to reject. As she says, I may be dismissing her comments because they hit too close to the bone. Her counsel may be valid. It is something to think about.

Yet this is a most bizarre volte-face for me, I think at times. Simply because one afternoon I gave in to sentimentality vis-à-vis my mother; simply because I saw for an instant in the way Miss O'Brien held her head, the way she moved with a purposeful bustle as my mother always did in the kitchen (Father liked to say that she attacked the sauerkraut rather than cooked it—his one bon mot, I believe, in all their years together); simply because of these gross physical similarities I have begun to go soft on the Irish again. To even, in fact, wonder at the morality of holding her here like this against her will.

I cannot afford the luxury of such softness, I tell myself.

But on the other hand, why not? I ask myself. *What, after all, have I to lose? How many more years do I have, anyway? I have money and some connections; I could resettle elsewhere. Invent a new persona for myself. Perhaps even return to Vienna with a new identity. Play the part of some Jew from America returning home for his final days. What a lark that would be!*

So let the Irish go, that soft part of me whispers. *There is no real harm she could do you. Even if she breaks her promise and tells the authorities about you.* And of course she would. It is too good a story not to.

The thought of spending my final days in Vienna has infected me like a benign virus. I am full of expectancy and hope suddenly. Grateful that the Irish has stolen her way into my life to create this possibility.

So all is forgiven, it seems. All her foolish antics when first installed here, even her ludicrous attempts at seduction. After all, would I have done less if the situation were reversed? Would Mother have?

Mother was a fighter, too. How comical was her coal-dust makeup, how brave her stand against the thieving Russians in the final days in Vienna.

The similarities between the two women are not only startling, they frighten me, as well.

Of course I have not apprised the Irish of any of these thoughts. I need to process them further, see if there is any reality to these daydreams. It would take a good deal of planning. It is fortunate that I already have a fallback identity in hand. Indeed, an American passport for which I paid dearly a number of years ago when the Klaus Barbie stink was making news. It is a kind of insurance for me. And once back in Europe, I would need to change my appearance somehow. Perhaps a beard would be enough. Perhaps surgery. But the timing would have to be perfect if I was to lose myself at precisely the time O'Brien was released.

How fun it all is! And who would think of looking for me in Vienna? It would be the perfect hiding place.

———

"You look exhausted."

"I've been working most of the night. I wanted to finish this."

"Have you read the latest bit, then?"

"Ages ago. This is for you."

"A long critique."

"You'll read it?"

"Of course. I always do."

"Even if it's painful?"

"Please, Miss O'Brien. No lectures on the obligations of a reader. I always read your 'stuff' as you call it, even when I cannot make heads or tails of it."

"I don't think there will be that problem with this."

"Why the long face? I said I'd read it. You need some rest."

"I don't think I can write anymore. This may be my final testament."

"Nonsense, Miss O'Brien. Eat your breakfast and then nap some. It's a beautiful day today. You'll want to take some sun."

———

. . . And then they closed the door. The indignity of it. Imagine, a cattle car used for humans. I shall remember that grating of door on rusty runner, the final hollow fwoomp *as the door shut, until my dying day. We were thrown into immediate darkness despite this being in broad daylight. (For no longer were the transports routed in the middle of the night. All of Vienna knew what was transpiring by this time. Neighbors, acquaintances, everyone knew of someone missing by the early spring of '42. No need to be secretive about the roundups by then. All in the national interest, don't you know.)*

I had looked around before the doors shut; there was no one in the car whom I knew. Some I had no desire to know. But nearby there was a family, and I made my way in the darkness to where I remembered them being. I wanted to be near good people. There was no telling how long this trip to resettlement would take. The vaguest destinations were given us when the Gestapo came to round us up. Resettlement in the east, they said. Well, that could be anywhere from Poland to Russia. No matter. I intended to make the most of it. I excused myself as I edged by other faceless people. Once, I stepped on someone's foot, said a blind apology, and got a rough slap on my rump as reply. My husband used to tell me about such chaps on the trams: frotteurs, *they're called. The French have a word for every sort of perversion, it seems. This kind liked to brush against women on public conveyances. They had to be on the lookout for those, my husband would tell me. Well, they would have a fine old time of it on this cattle car!*

I pushed on through the bodies, and my eyes were slowly adjusting to the dark. Soon, I saw the little family I had earmarked as my protectors. As I approached, the train suddenly lurched forward and I tumbled straight into the husband's arms. A rather embarrassing introduction, I can tell you. But the kindly man understood. This miserable condition made us comradely at once. I joked that I was looking for my seat in the first class compartment, and those around us laughed loudly. A little humor goes a long way in such adverse situations. We introduced ourselves: all formalities of "Sie" were dispensed with, and soon Frau Gigi— the wife went by her pet name—and I were chatting on as if we'd known each other since grammar school. Which would have been rather difficult, as she was considerably younger than I, but there you are. Amazing what humans can do once the artifices are torn away. It turned out they were neighbors of mine in Brigittenau, but then the district is so large, how is one to know even those who share the same street? Their two children said scarcely a word, but one could see the enormous glistening whites of their eyes in the darkness. I admit I was frightened also, but their need was so much greater than mine that I put up a brave front. The dithering chatterbox from Brigittenau. To buoy the man, I even played the flirter and sly insinuator with him, though he was so hollow chested that not even a woman from a sexual Sahara could find him alluring. One can never understand the choices women make, for Frau Gigi was a full-bosomed, wide-hipped sort of woman who one knew instinctively would have a healthy sexual appetite. He was, however, a kind man, and that counts for much. Alternatively, I was the good frau, consoler and swapper of cleaning tips and recipes with Frau Gigi, then the irreverent oft-married aunt to the two children. I am accustomed to playing many such roles. All women are. We are rainbow chameleons in a colorless world, mynah birds in the concrete wilderness. My husband used to joke with me, lying abed on a Sunday morning after all-night lovemaking: He would call me his schizoid angel. Frumpy housewife during the week, wild sexual Amazon on Saturday nights. Joseph wore a coat of many colors, too, *I would reply. (My husband's name was not Joseph. It's the other one, I mean.)* You'd be better off going around in red velveteen pants yourself, *I'd say to him.* We all hide our true natures, *I'd say.* Each of us playing the appropriate role for the appropriate occasion. But who set up the guidelines? Who said what was appropriate?

That's why I loved him so, we could talk like that, as equals. We made love as equals, too. Side by side. He used to look into my eyes as he climaxed. He never closed them, never shut me out. He was always aware of that other human he was touching even as he became lost in the sensations of touch. I remember his eyes at those times: almost pleading. And surprised! It's the sort of surprise I imagine to feel at death. So this is what it is like? This slipping away. This jerk of the body as before sleep.

Someone on the boxcar emitted a noxious sound; some men laughed at it. I realized I had not heard a word Frau Gigi had been saying for the past several minutes.

One could not tell when daylight ended and night began, so dark was it in the cattle car. After what seemed hours of huddling together on the floor, taking turns holding the children, the husband suggested we adults sleep in shifts. He allowed me and his wife the first sleep. By this time, we were all terribly thirsty, for they had shared some of the wurst they had brought along. But no one had thought to bring water with them. Also, I had a terrific need now to use the facilities; there were none.

We shall soon be stopping, *the husband assured us.* That is one thing we can trust the Germans for: efficiency. He laughed. They will have this thing organized.

I curled around the little boy, and in his sleep, he snuggled closer to me, sighing in a primal sort of relief at the feel of another human being next to him. I slept but did not dream. The boy twitched in his sleep and cried out. I put my hand to his brow and smoothed back his hair. It was damp with sweat, though the car itself had grown quite cold with the night. He was feverish, and I felt an instinctual fear for him.

I speak of instinct, yet I no longer know if I should be allowed that vanity. In truth, I do not know instinct any more than I know what love is, or when love is. Was it my instinct that brought me to my husband? Was it instinct that told me he was dead long before the news arrived or that spoke to me of the new life inside of me before the doctor confirmed it? And was it instinct or despair that made me trade that new life? Or simply another vanity?

I had no conception of time or distance. The rattling of the boxcar made it seem we were going quite slowly, as if through shunting yards. Several times we stopped for hours on end, it seemed. Hope would rise then that we would be allowed to use the facilities, or that food and water would be supplied. I checked the boy's fever periodically, and the back of his neck. Both were clammy to the touch, and he whimpered once when I touched him behind his ear. There was a swelling there.

The train started up again, then stopped. People around me stirred in their sleep. For all any of us knew, it had only just gone dark. One loses sense of time when deprived of light. But the other senses grew more acute: the smell of fetid bodies and dirty socks grew more unbearable as people settled down to sleep; somewhere in the car someone had obviously relieved himself. The stink of excrement grew increasingly palpable, making one's own bowels loosen in disgust. Hearing, too, became refined. Someone only two or three crumpled bodies away was drinking. That is certain. It made me all the thirstier and not just for my sake alone, but for the boy's as well. He needed liquid to cool him. As I was thinking this, the boy gave a little shudder, a shiver, a spasm as if cold.

I took off my winter coat and wrapped it around the poor little thing. I clung to him even tighter now, as if clinging to life. We slept that way for some hours.

I was walking along the Danube Canal, my young husband at my side. White bodies, some sprawled like commas in the sun and others sitting hunched in question marks, punctuated the banks of either side of the water. Summer. Heavy, torpid heat. Those who could afford it were in the mountains. We held hands as we walked. I could feel the callus ridge above the palm of his right hand; not separate ones at the base of the fingers as one would get from usual manual labor, but one large callus stretching from index to little finger. The tram conductor's knob, the men at the transport bureau called it. From operating the metal lever for speed and direction. The dutiful hausfrau, I knitted him warm wool mittens for the winter; mittens not for his hands but for the metal steering knob. All tram wives did so for their husbands. So many woolly tram mittens knitted over the years! He squeezed my hand and nodded at a barge coming down the canal. A dog on deck was barking at the birds flying by. It was a little dog, sturdily built, and as it barked it lunged forward on its stubby front legs. It made no movement forward for all this exertion. It kept barking and lunging forward, but stayed in place as if it were on a lead. Why should that dog make me suddenly sad? A feeling of extreme melancholy washed over me, as heavy and thick as the humid air. I knew in that instant that our lovemaking last night had created life in me.

I squeezed my husband's hand in return, but he was no longer there; a young boy had taken his place and on his hand there was no tram conductor's knob. The dog barked on the passing barge; a pair of women's bloomers hung like pennons from a clothesline on the deck. The dog barked once more, lunged, and this time he did not stay in place but went skidding over the edge of the vessel into the canal. The little boy on my hand laughed as the dog paddled its way to shore. My breasts suddenly ached; they were full of milk and the little boy had not been a baby first and so had not nursed on me. And in my breast was an ache for the man with the tram conductor's knob who was gone forever.

I awoke and knew two things simultaneously: We were no longer moving, and it was morning. There was a faint glow coming from outside; several lines of light shone between the boards of the boxcar's walls. Birds were chirping nearby; their lives continued as usual, indifferent to what happened to us inside the boxcar. Others began stirring now, as well. There were grumblings about hunger and thirst, about the desperate need to relieve oneself. We still kept to our small groups; no one attempted to organize us as one body. A man of very dark and oriental appearance began pounding on the door, demanding fresh air. His shouts and pounding on the door woke the boy up. He asked me if we had arrived yet. I told him soon. The man at the door grew increasingly frantic, for no one outside had answered his calls. The echoing silence angered him; it frightened me. One man nearby tried to restrain him, but it did no good. Soon the man had enlisted others and stood on the shoulders of a fat bearded man and pounded with his fists at what looked to be a slatted transom above the sliding doors. He succeeded finally in breaking the closed slats; fresh air flooded the car and a beam of light, narrow and filled with suspended motes, shone into the car straight into the upturned face of the young boy at my side. Then a burst of shots tore the silence; the men at the door, both the fat man and the dark one who had been on his shoulders, were thrown back like marionettes and lay crumpled atop several other screaming people. Blood was everywhere. The two men were dead. Quite dead. A new smell filled our cattle car.

We stayed at the siding all day. The men's bodies were pulled to one corner. Sunlight now streamed in through the splintered bullet holes in the door as well as through the transom. I managed to avert my eyes from the bodies for a time, but some perversity made me finally look at the crumpled and bloody mess. The boy did not register what was happening; to him we were all a dream from which he tried valiantly to awake. He murmured and rolled about. I asked Frau Gigi if he had been sick before getting on the train. She did not remember: The night had taken its toll on her, and the shooting had completely broken her resolve. She, like all the others on the train, was only now fully awake to the enormity of our fate. A thought went through my mind: As with the men's bodies, a perverse curiosity made me face this thought. Unruly behavior deserved some punishment, perhaps, but guards could only fire blindly into a car loaded with men, women, and children if they firmly believed there were animals inside. Quite literally, we had been relegated to the position of cattle headed to market. Worse. For cattle would be supplied water. Otherwise they would lose value. We were less than cattle in the eyes of the Nazis. And if that were the case, why should they bother to "resettle" us on the land they had promised? Why not simply eliminate the nuisance? That was exactly what Hitler had been urging for years in his public speeches: destroy, eliminate the Jewish malignancy. Why not take his word at face value? That was the thought that perversity made me confront.

And Frau Gigi could not remember if her boy had been sick days or minutes. Her husband stared blankly at the holes in the door. The ragged rays of light flooding through these holes mocked us by their joy and lightness. The birds began singing again. The boy shivered under my heavy coat as sweat poured from his forehead. Neighbors nearby—one of whom I knew had water— looked at his frail body guiltily, but offered no help. The death of the two men at the door had torn humanity from them, for they all were staring at the same dark thought I was. The time for self-delusion was past. Yet we were still breathing, weren't we? We still had life. And that was the most precious thing at the moment: each of us in his own private compartment delineated by skin. Each against the other. Only others die. Any possibility for unity was gone by now. I cradled the boy in my arms and rocked him to sleep.

All that day we remained at the siding. By midday, it was stifling inside. It was nearly spring. The sun was still weak, but it pounded on the flat roof of our boxcar. The stench inside was unbearable. Not only the old and infirm, but also the younger by now had relieved themselves in a corner. The urine drained along the floorboards. Excrement steamed in a ghastly pile. We had now fulfilled the Nazi prophecy: We had become little better, possibly worse, than cattle. A fight broke out between two men over a bit of wurst one had been hiding. No one attempted to stop it; the stronger of the two simply took the wurst from the weaker, beating his head against the floorboards until the man lay still. By the time the victim had regained consciousness, his food had been devoured. He whimpered for hours afterward. At one point, we heard men in jackboots march by the gravel siding outside; they spoke, laughed. We could not understand what they said, but it was in German. We had no idea where we were; we could have been hundreds of kilometers from Vienna or only hundreds of meters.

Frau Gigi, her husband, and the young daughter drew into themselves, leaving me in possession of their young boy. I did not even know his name. Would my own baby, left behind yesterday, grow as old as this boy? Would he understand the risk I had taken for him? The reason? The faith in life rather than in death that had prompted my decision? Would the orphanage give him away to the authorities? There was no way to trace his birth registry; he looked the perfect Aryan, the spitting image of his father.

They had come with the news on a Friday. I had just done the shopping and was unpacking the basket. The tram official and his wife from across the hall were suddenly at the door. Their *son and daughter peeked out of their flat at us, giggled, and then ducked their heads in again. The man worked with my husband; his wife was an acquaintance, no friend. I had sat with their children at times when they went out to the light opera. I saw by their faces that something was terribly wrong. I heard the man's words, smelled wine on his breath, registered the stain of an egg yolk on his blue tram conductor's uniform. The woman folded her hands in front of her. One finger played with the wedding ring, turning it around and around on her finger. A radio sounded from down the hall: the call signal of the first channel on the state radio, then music by Strauss. All these things I took in, but not the content of what the man said. Though I knew the import: that my husband was dead. The baby in my stomach kicked violently as if to refute the notion. Twelve hours later, I was delivered of a baby boy. I named him after his dead father. Three months later, I answered a Gestapo summons. My baby is with the nuns of the Cistercian abbey.*

We sleep; we wake. An old lady passes gas in her sleep; a young man stares at me. The sun no longer streams in the holes; it is now on the other side of the car and the light is failing. Another day. We have survived. And now comes the long night. I think of my baby and in so doing, notice how my breasts ache for him. I feel him at my nipple feeding, suckling. Warm waves pass over my belly at the thought. The young boy I cradle wakes for a moment, his eyes wide and frightened. I soothe him with words. With a touch. He sleeps again. A man by the door says loudly that they will surely come tonight. There will be food and water. God has spoken to him, he says. Others tell him to shut up, to keep his mouth closed, to go fornicate with his god.

It is inevitable now, I know it. I only wait for darkness to carry out fate. Only the boy matters now; it is as if he is my baby. I stand for a time; my legs have fallen asleep. The boy whimpers when I release him, but I must have circulation. The man next to me tries to crowd into the space I have allowed, but I kick at him and retrieve it. He looks at me with hatred in his eyes.

More time. An enemy now. But so finite. The counting of it makes it unfriendly. Being aware of it makes it the foe. It is limited, therefore suspect. Cursing from others nearby. Snores. A pounding at the door from the inside. A man and woman copulate in the back of the car. She tries to stop him at first, then gives way to the feeling, her moans clearly audible. There is electricity in the car for the instant of her climax, then stillness. More snores. I sit again and instantly wet my pants. I can no longer hold it; the wet warmth is all over my legs. The standing has done it.

Total darkness at last. Coolness descends. A fresh breeze that partially restores. My tongue has begun to swell. The dryness in my throat extends to my stomach. The man with his god by the door begins to pray in Hebrew. A thump of flesh against flesh; a groan. Then more silence. More minutes; more hours. The woman and man perform their pleasure again, her cries almost desperate as he moves on her like an animal. The boy's breathing comes slowly, painfully it seems. I wait until I can wait no longer, until the copulating couple have finished, until those around me are no longer stirring. Then I wait a few more minutes. Quietly, I unbutton my bodice. There is already moisture at my pulsing nipples. I bring the boy's lips to them, rub them against the nipple to agitate, to make them erect, to make the milk flow. A drop on his lips. His tongue swipes it automatically. I put his mouth to my nipple and slowly, spasmodically his lips respond. They are chapped and dry and tickle my flesh at first. They make smacking sounds, then go hard and suck against me. The milk flows. I feel my life pour into him. A warmth and exultancy spread over my middle, a gentle tingling sensation. My baby will live.

But as quickly as this feeling comes over me, so sharply is it ripped away. The boy is dragged from my lap by the man next to me who pushes me back and takes the boy's place. I try to resist, to scream out, but his hand is on my mouth. He is sucking the life out of me and smothering me with his hand. I feel more hands on me, on my body, ripping my blouse away. Another's lips at my right breast: two of them chew and suck on me at once. Others hold my hands down; someone tears my skirt, my panties. I am mounted like an animal. Useless to resist. Someone beats me about the face after I bite a hand. I no longer squirm. Mouth replaces mouth; penis follows penis. But my passivity enrages them as much as my earlier struggles excited them. Fists pound at me; there is wetness in my mouth, teeth come loose; I try not to choke on them. My hair is ripped out. A kick at my body. I sense no more. I sense no more. I am back walking along the Danube Canal and my husband's calloused hand is in mine. The dog barks on a passing barge. My baby lives inside me. . . .

Early in the morning, the transport continues to the concentration camp of Mauthausen. At first light, it is pulled up to the platform. The camp orchestra is on hand to welcome the new arrivals. The "Kaiser Waltz" is the day's selection. Music in the air, the order is given to open the doors. Stunned, weakened near-humans stumble out of the boxcars. Kapos and guards check the transports to make sure no malingerers are hiding. Three bodies are found in one of the cars: a short dark fellow and a stout bearded one, both shot to death. And a female of indeterminate years, apparently gang-raped and bludgeoned to death so that her features are unrecognizable. The camp second in command receives the news with fatalistic chagrin. After all, what can one expect from such people. Men on the left, he shouts, women and children on the right. . . .

"This is one of your most vile fictions."

"I do not believe in fiction."

"Have you no sense of humanity, Miss O'Brien? No decency at all?"

"It's a report, not a creation. It happened, over and over and over."

"I want you to stop giving me these . . . these pornographic snippets."

"It's history and prophecy. Can't you see that? It's life that's sometimes pornographic. I only report it. You did these things in the Reich. It goes on today in cells around the world. It is called interrogation and information gathering and counterterrorism. But it is all pornography at heart. And you are the pornographer, not I."

"I trusted you with all this information. And what do you do? You twist it. Pervert it. Then throw it in my face. Why do you harp on that woman? You're fixated, that's what you are. It's become an obsession with you."

"Yours. Your obsession. Only you don't recognize it."

"Errant flummery. You demean the memory of Frau Wotruba by such fictional re-creations."

"Do I? How can you be so sure it wasn't Frau Wotruba you discovered on that train at Mauthausen? You make no mention of the poor woman's identity in your diary entry."

"It couldn't have been her. Don't you see? She was sent away long before I went to Mauthausen."

"I give up. No. You're right. It wasn't Frau Wotruba. But it was a woman, for Christ's sake. It could have been her. That's the bloody point! I used her persona to get through to you, to touch you with the enormity of what you and others allowed to happen, facilitated even. We are all Frau Wotruba. The world is Frau Wotruba. Can't you see that?"

"__"

"Is there no way to reach you? Can't you understand your own writings? Haberloch, there's another perfect instance. . . ."

"The man was a meddler, a nuisance. I don't condone what happened to him, certainly."

"Yet, in another time, you might have pushed him into the quarry yourself."

"Nonsense."

"You admitted to dealing in slave labor. It's what made you rich. Advokat Haberloch was investigating such corruption."

"Again, Miss O'Brien, you have your dates confused. Haberloch was long dead by the time I myself became involved in such shameful schemes."

"But if he hadn't been? If it had been you he had been investigating? What then, Herr ____? We're all Frau Wotruba. The world is the victim."

———

I admit to being moved by Miss O'Brien's arguments. A chink of light shone through. I begin to understand what she is saying, but I could not let her see that. We parted once again as enemies locked in deadly combat; I am still shaken by her last story.

What did happen to Frau Wotruba? Perhaps I should have saved her.

I feel my entire body churning, seething, bubbling. God, how that woman has shaken me up! But I do not hate her for it anymore. No. I begin to feel the deepest sort of affection for her, not romantic in the least. Deeper than that. Like a blood tie.

I feel suddenly that I want to live up to her challenge. To write the true story, to get through all artifice.

This is such a story. One that I had not intended for these pages, the thought of it being too much for me to bear. Too much pain.

It is 1947 and I am just about to leave Europe forever. I have been hiding out for two years in various places—the last fifteen months spent on a chicken farm in the Harz Mountains, the hireling of one Frau Magda, who knows nothing of my past but who has taken it into her head that we will soon be married.

I have secured help through some of the other men in the corps who formed a network to help those of us wanted by the Allies. The show trials in Nuremberg are still in progress; I have changed my looks with a mustache and longish hair dyed jet black.

Through our network, I have secured passage on a freighter leaving Naples in three weeks. Frau Magda knows nothing of this. I have also secured my assets in a safe hiding place, even the few lovely canvases I will take with me into exile. Uschi long ago renounced me and changed her name. From contacts in Vienna, I hear only the scantiest reports of Mother and Maria. It is not thought safe for me to visit.

Then, one day, through these selfsame contacts, I learn that Mother has died and Maria has been packed off to a home. It is my last link with my former life, and one that I am both saddened and relieved has been broken. If Maria is in a home, then there is no need for me to return. The time is so close now: I sail in a week. But I am drawn to Vienna; I know I cannot leave Europe without returning one more time. Perhaps Maria needs me? There is the promise I made Mother. It is no good. I must risk all and return one last time.

I simply steal away from Frau Magda's bed in the middle of the night; a rooster crows at my departure.

It is a dangerous trip for me on public transport, for my picture has been in the papers along with other wanted war criminals, but finally I arrive in my native city only to discover it quartered up like pieces of strudel to accommodate the four victors. I show my forged papers three times simply to reach the First District: first to the British, then to the French, and finally the Americans. The fresh carefree chewing-gum faces of the Americans pollute all of Europe. One cannot turn around anymore but there is one of them, a Hershey bar in hand, ready to call you by your Christian name, slap you on the back, and let bygones be bygones. There is something profoundly obscene in such insouciance. Give me the French any day, those who hold a grudge unto death and show it in their faces. Or even the Russians—damned ignorant and mean. Distrustful as the peasants they are beneath those wool uniforms. But the Americans! Such a surface life as they demonstrate is frightening; they are the type to shrug with a winning smile as they blow up the world.

Stephansplatz is still a disgrace; the cathedral has begun to be rebuilt, but there is so much that needs to be done and so few resources. It is broad daylight as I enter our apartment building this last time. Frau Bechman still hides in her portier's lodge; it is just as well, for I have no desire to explain my presence. There are few enough who would recognize me now. Most believe me dead or to have defected to the Russians to work in their secret service. I have spread several versions of my fate abroad.

Up the stairs, I see that the nicks and gouges are still in the door to our flat. I reach over the sill and find the key to our flat, concealed after all this time in the secret place I showed Mother at the join of wood and plaster. I insert it in the lock; the click of tumblers opens the last door in my room of illusions. This is a trip taken for the rawest of sentimental reasons, I soon discover. I have not come to check on Maria, but to fetch some memento, some sign of my former life. Something to take with me into exile.

I lock the door in back of me. The flat is much as I left it two years before. Not even the smells have altered: a mixture of talc and coal dust. In another week, the flat will be in the hands of a receiver; all traces of my family will be erased. In another week, I will be sailing for Central America, my identity changed for that of another. It will be as if I had never existed. I want desperately to latch onto some physical manifestation of my real life; something to remind me not only of Mother and Father, but also of my life as it was spent in Europe.

Mother's room is filled with her collectibles. She never gave up her passion for the secondhand shops, not even when I was at the height of my career and had settled a healthy allowance on her. There was the old marble-topped dressing table she had been so elated to find—only five reichsmarks from a dealer in the Second District. An eiderdown quilt covers yellowing linen on her simple metal-framed bed. On the wall are reproductions of von Alt and Waldmüller. A steamer trunk sits in a corner, covered with stickers from some of the great hotels of Europe and the Far East: the Savoy in London, the Gritti in Venice, Raffles in Singapore, the Plaza in New York. Another bargain from her searches in the Second District, once belonging to a famous mezzo-soprano at the State Opera. Mother prized this trunk as if it were her ticket of admission into an exotic world. If there is anything in the flat that will be of consoling service to me in the coming years of exile, I know that it will be found in this trunk. The lock was sprung years ago while we still lived on Hubertusgasse. Father's impatience at getting cuff studs out while Mother searched high and low for the key to the lock. It had been on one of their theater outings, and his ravishing of her trunk had put a sore damper on things. Inside the trunk are photos of weddings and graduations, mostly mine, as well as documents: birth, marriage, death, and promotional certificates, all of which I ignore. Such two-dimensional representations of life will not see me through the future. Besides, I cannot risk carrying with me any such proofs of my real identity. Beneath the papers and photos are boxes containing the odd bit of jewelry—an amethyst broach in the shape of a butterfly I had once purchased for Mother; Father's gold watch chain (what had ever become of the watch?); a set of garnet earrings that Mother had last worn on her fateful trip to the Volksoper the night Frau Wotruba and I had indulged ourselves; nowhere in sight are the pearl-studded cuff links Father had been in search of when he broke open the lock of the trunk.

Perhaps I will take the cuff links if I can find them. They have a symbolic if not intrinsic value to me. Other boxes contain scraps of Maria's and my schoolwork: rulers and pencil stubs we had discarded, a pencil sharpener in the form of a lion I had used my first year at school. None of this speaks to me, however. I continue my search, and at the very bottom of the trunk, I come upon one item I know will be worth taking.

Carefully wrapped in a Wednesday edition of the *Kurier* from 1936 is my glass ball with the miniature of

St. Stephan's in it. I tip it upside down and the tiny world is shrouded in a veil of snow once again. There is snow outside too, now. A real Austrian snowfall swirling about outside Mother's window. The globe in my hand mirrors this real world. It feels alive. I can smell the freshly washed, line-hung linen of childhood beds when this glass ball was continually on my bedside table. I tip it again and smile at the swirl of white confetti in the liquid. Yes. This will be my memento, my talisman of a European life.

The front door clicks. I freeze in place with the glass of snow in my hands. The second turn and clink of the tumblers opens the door. Caution has, by this time, become my main motivator. Trapped in the rear bedroom, I can hardly brazen out a confrontation with the estate agents or police or any other people who might be letting themselves in the flat. I close the lid of the trunk and am under the bed in a flash, snuggling with the dust balls and odd stocking and camisole that still linger under there. And none too soon, either, for footsteps sound down the hallway, headed straight for this bedroom. A woman's voice, the solemn grunting tones of a man in assent. The bedroom door is thrown open: four legs present themselves for my inspection, from the knees down. It is my only field of vision from my position under the bed. The woman's are encased in black fishnet stockings carried on impossibly high-heeled shoes open at the toe. They are the sort tarts might wear at midday. The man's legs are covered in khaki of that particularly repugnant shade sported by the US Army. These pants are tucked into black combat boots imperfectly polished. Both pairs of shoes carry clumps of dirtying snow on them. It melts onto the parquet as they stand.

"*Komm, Schatz. Sei nicht unruhig. Wir haben ein Gaudí. Sicher . . . Du . . .*"

The voice sounds strangely familiar. No. It can't be, I

reason. She is safely ensconced in the asylum in Purkersdorf. More likely that Frau Bechman is making money on the side. A sort of interregnum until the formal disposal of the flat. She has obviously sold the key of the flat to street women. This is only logical with housing so tight in the city. Love as an industry has to continue. Still it rankles me that the portier has done so.

"Whose place is this, little girl?"

The man's voice is thick and drawling. A caricature of voices one hears in the undubbed Hollywood movies. Something melancholy about this, deep and sad as treacle.

A high heel is kicked off on her passage toward the bed; there is a second kicked off and then an explosion above me as the girl throws herself onto Mother's bed.

"*Komm, du. Ich will dich. Aber jetzt!*"

A black-stockinged leg dangles over the bed lasciviously, ticking back and forth like a metronome. The combat boots approach the bed, then hesitate.

"This okay, baby?"

"*Ja. Schön.* Okay. *Mama's Bett. Schön.* Okay. *Mama ist tot.* Dead. *Verstehst? Jetzt, fick mich!*"

The words pierce like a stiletto in my ear: Mother's bed! Then the click and swoosh of an unfastened belt and the khakis dropping, exposing legs as black as onyx.

A gasp from Maria atop the bed: "*Schön . . .*"

The rip of soft fabric and then a groan of springs as he mounts her. Her groans are raspier than those of the spring. . . .

So there it is, my first confession. My sister fucking (yes, the ugly Anglo-Saxon word) a Negro soldier with me cowering under the bed all the while. My ultimate humiliation. We had fought the war for racial purification, and then this.

I hid under the bed until they both left, then departed, not giving a second thought to Maria. She could take care of herself, apparently.

I was shipped across Switzerland into Italy and to Rome where the Holy Fathers hid me at the Abbey of ____ until it was time to make my way to Naples and board a ship. I departed the shores of Europe on a rainy March day in 1947. I did not look back as the old freighter pulled out of the harbor.

———

I awoke earlier than usual today, filled with a kind of Scrooge-like glee that it is not too late. It is never too late. It is, to continue the metaphor, as if I have laid Marley's ghost to rest, have begun to deal with my own past truly for the first time. To see it for what it was.

My God! What a vista opens before me! What an endless horizon of past, present, and future.

That painful ugly story of my sister, Maria, is partly responsible. But it is the Irish who forced me to it, who prodded and poked at the truth.

I have finally come to a decision about Miss O'Brien. I see it quite clearly now: She must be set free. But I admit to a bit of teasing pleasure: taking her breakfast this morning, I gave no inkling of my decision. Rather, I was as cold as Scrooge was with Bob Cratchit when the poor clerk came in late the day after Christmas. I made little response to her pleas for an outing, her tirade that she is losing her mind with inactivity and indifference. I smiled inwardly, but only grunted in reply: "We shall see."

Oh, Miss O'Brien. Shall we ever see. I can just imagine the look on her face when I tell her this afternoon after her yard time.

Cordoba is coming to dinner tonight; perhaps we shall all three have it together.

The day draws on, and I have been busy in the kitchen. A simple meal for tonight, and my mind is not really focused on it. Rather, it is on Vienna. These are not sentimental daydreams of my youth, however, but fantasies of what life will be like for me there now. I will take a simple flat somewhere in the Inner City, near the sound of church bells. Lunch at the local beisl, concerts or theater at night. No more wild animal calls from the ravine to disturb my sleep.

So much to do, so many plans to make. I feel alive again after decades of cold storage. Well, hardly cold, but in limbo nonetheless.

I sit at my trestle table again and I cannot wait to tell the Irish, to see the look of disbelief on her face. She is out in the compound now, sitting on a boulder. No pad and pencil for her today. She simply gazes into the heavy blue sky overhead.

A "V" of seagulls fly over the compound. "*Kaaa*," they call at O'Brien as if she is food. She does not flinch at their harsh cries. Her gaze takes in the compound itself now, then seconds later she flinches. Perhaps she sees something in the compound. It is time I clear the long grass again, a task I do not look forward to. But then, perhaps there is no need what with the decision I've made. A shiver from Miss O'Brien, but she cannot be cold, for now she very nonchalantly unbuttons her shirt and takes it off. I have complained of this behavior; it is unseemly. But she says she enjoys sunning herself and that I needn't watch if the sight sickens me. I go back to the kitchen to check on the fish marinating.

After ten minutes in the kitchen, I decide to go down and let Miss O'Brien in. I can no longer wait. I am positively glowing with anticipation. I call through the door at her naked back. She rises, her shirt a ball held in front of her breasts so that I cannot really complain of immodesty. She brushes past me: I notice a mole below her left shoulder blade. The skin of her back is freckled with all her recent sunning. She stops midway between the outside door and her room and turns to me.

"Have you given any further thought to letting me go?"

How incredible, I think. *It is as if she reads my mind.* But I want this moment to last, to defer the pleasure of my announcement that bit longer. I assume the Scrooge-to-Cratchit tone of voice.

"A degree of thought. Yes."

"Any decision?"

I treasure this moment, twist it in my hand like a diamond cutter in search of facets. "It's very difficult. How can I be sure you won't tell the authorities? I would like to trust you, Miss O'Brien."

She clutches the crumpled shirt to her chest as if it is a baby about to suckle. I recall her own story of Frau Wotruba in the train; suddenly she reminds me of that woman again, not of Mother at all.

"You're never going to let me go, are you?"

I let the question go unanswered a teasing moment and am about to reply in the affirmative when she quite calmly takes the shirt away from her pendulous bosoms and begins unfolding it.

The peacefulness of the action catches me completely by surprise, for out of the tangle of shirt she draws a small green band that coils around her arm like a bracelet, its thicker end held firmly between her thumb and forefinger. The snake's tongue flicks out at me, deep and obscenely red. She comes toward me with the hideous reptile, aiming it like a gun. I am completely speechless, terrified at the sight of it, for it is the deadly poisonous variety.

She continues to approach with the snake about her arm, bare breasted like some Minoan princess.

"I think I'll be leaving now. Back into your room very slowly, Herr ____. Slowly and quietly and without letting your hands go to your pockets. Otherwise, I'll be forced to throw my friend here into your face."

But I am too frightened to move. The snake's presence has struck me to the very marrow. I feel my knees weaken.

"Now!"

The harsh edge to her voice makes me move, unwillingly, toward her room. She makes me enter first and then follows, the snake eyeing me all the while. I am struck with the most horrid fear: All my worst dreams are coming true.

"Now you will give me the key to the Land Rover and any money you might have. Also, that little popgun of yours."

"It's . . . upstairs." My mouth and throat are dry. I can barely form words. This is obscene. I want to shout out, to tell her how unnecessary all this is. *I am going to free you anyway.*

"Where?"

I tell her. She is insane. No telling what she will do.

"And where's your needle?"

I lie and tell her it is upstairs with the gun. A stupid lie.

"You wouldn't dare come near me without some weapon."

She wriggles the snake in my face and I jump back, tripping and tumbling on my back onto the bed. She runs at me, straddles me with the snake inches from my face.

"Where is it, pig?"

Water spurts from every pore and out my eyes. I am all but blinded by my fear of the snake. I motion my hand toward my hip pocket.

"Get it out, slowly. Unless you want to kiss Melinda here."

The snake unwinds itself from her wrist and trails its tail over my chest. I can smell strong animal must, whether from the snake or Miss O'Brien or me, I cannot tell.

She rises a bit, and I move my hand slowly into my pants pockets and withdraw the syringe.

"Drop it on the bed," she orders. "Just drop it."

The snake whips its tail about madly.

"Melinda is impatient."

I do as I am told. She gets off me, picking up the syringe.

"And now the keys," she says.

I do not bother to bluff her about these; they are in my right hip pocket. I pull them out and put them on the bed, as well.

She orders me off the bed and to take off my clothes. I protest; this is humiliating. She gives a reason: She does not want me following her immediately. I am less likely to do so in the buff. It sounds almost reasonable. I do as I am told, removing even my socks and underwear. I stand naked in front of her, my hands trying to cover my genitals. It is a helpless, miserable feeling. She looks at me as if appraising a cut of meat.

She then gathers the keys and clothes in her left hand, the snake still in her right. I do not make an attempt to catch her off guard. The snake unmans me.

"Very nice." She smiles coyly. "You look a ripe picture, you do. Be seeing you."

She backs toward the door and I stand bathing in my own sweat, just wanting her to be gone, not caring about the consequences. Just wanting her and the snake to be gone. She throws the clothing outside the door, backs out herself, and then slams the door in back of her. I hear the bolts sliding shut. My whole body slumps in relief. Safe at last. A prisoner in my own house, but safe.

Then my eye catches movement at the door. It can't be. I look again in the gloom—only the bedside light is on. I scream. It's as if the snake zeroes in on the sound. It glides toward me, its tongue flicking over the rush matting. I hear the fuzzy sound of its movement on the mat. I am paralyzed with fear, but do manage to climb on top of the bed. The snake comes to a stop at the foot of the bed, its head darting this way and that. My heart races in my chest; my sternum feels as if it will burst open with the pounding. I cannot catch my breath. It is as if I am being gassed, gassed and asphyxiated. I scream once again. I appeal to I know not what agencies for deliverance. At one point, my bowels loosen. I soil the bed. I look for something to throw at the snake; there are only the pillows within reach, and the bedside light, but I dare not risk losing my only source of light. I am so terrified that I step in my own excrement on the bed; it oozes into the spaces between my toes.

I plead to her, to Miss O'Brien. She must still be outside the door. She could not leave; this would be too sweet for her to miss, getting her own back at me. She is the sort of vindictive whore who must listen to her victim's agonies. I offer all sorts of assurances to her on the other side of the door, tell her of my plans to let her go, offer to share the wealth I have tucked away in my Swiss account, debase myself in all manner of ways, even to apologizing for what I did in the Hitler days. If only she will take away the snake. The animal remains at the foot of the bed, coiled as if to spring or sleep, I am not sure which. But my naked helpless state keeps me from leaving the relative security of the bed.

Minutes go by; I think they must be hours. My heart will not slow down; my breath becomes harsher and more strained. I feel light-headed and fear that I will faint. A vertigo overcomes me, such that I am sure I shall fall to certain death on the floor next to that horrid snake. I scream one last time, that God might save me.

The door bursts open; it is Cordoba, gun in hand. He takes in the situation at a glance, aims at the snake, then looks again at me and begins to laugh so uncontrollably at my predicament that it takes him three shots to dispatch the snake.

———

My deus ex machina was prompted by Cordoba's desire to come early for our card evening and perhaps cadge an extra drink or two. I learn this once I calm down, which takes me over an hour and two brandies. I finally relate to Cordoba what has happened, how O'Brien has effected her escape.

"I'll get on the phone to the capital. We'll set roadblocks."

"You'll do nothing of the sort." By now, I have dressed, we are sitting upstairs in the leather armchairs by the fireplace, and I once again have control of the situation.

"But she'll get away."

"She already has. You think I want the generals to know

the bird has flown? They are most vindictive people. Worse enemies than the Irish."

"Then what are you going to do? She'll set the Israelis on you."

I sip my third brandy. "Perhaps." For I have my backup plan in full operation by now. "I may just drift into the night once again."

"At your age!"

Cordoba is not one for sucking up. One of his more endearing qualities.

"Yes, at my age."

Suddenly, I remember my memoirs. If she has stolen them . . . I rush into the kitchen where I have taken to storing them after the daily writing. The lump in my throat subsides when I find the papers still in place behind sacks of rice in the top cupboard. Thank providence for that, at least. Miss O'Brien must have been in too great a hurry to bother searching for them.

I return to the living room, papers in hand, and Cordoba nods, raising his eyebrows.

"Get rid of that damned thing," he says, but I ignore him and instead make preparations to leave my home of over fifty years.

This is accomplished rather smoothly, in point of fact. As I reported earlier, I already have a new passport, and I always keep enough hard cash in dollars about the place to be able to survive several months. Long enough to get to my funds in Switzerland. I pack only a small valise. Large enough for two changes of clothes. After all, I won't need my tropical wear where I am going. A few mementoes: the jaguar and my Kreuzberg Venus. The snow globe of Stephansdom I leave for Cordoba. I shall have the real thing soon enough. I also fetch the Mauthausen diaries as well as this sheaf of papers.

"Burn them," Cordoba insists again. "Haven't they caused you enough trouble already?"

But I shake my head, stuffing the papers in under my shirts. I am strangely calm. I even take time to transcribe the awful scene with the snake, so to purge it. Meanwhile, Cordoba paces the room, throwing back gin. But I am peaceful, sure of myself as my hand traces the pen over fresh pages. It is as if the scene writes itself, and I am quickly done.

My way is mapped out now. I did not lock the door of the house as we left. It is not a fungible property; it can rot in the jungle for all I care.

Writing these final pages, in Cordoba's taxi on the way to the airport at the capital, I think of Miss O'Brien. If only she had waited just those few more minutes, I would have set her free without the need for violence. The eternal female, Miss O'Brien was out of synch with me to the very last, proving my theory of the eternal imbalance between man and woman.

But would I actually have set her free? Wasn't I, even as Miss O'Brien produced her snake, already having doubts? Already seeing her resemblance to Frau Wotruba once again rather than to my mother?

Perhaps I should get rid of these memoirs as Cordoba advises. But what could be the harm in taking them along? Once I have altered my appearance and taken up my new life in Europe, I will be safe.

Europe. The word is an elixir to me, bracing me as Cordoba's taxi jolts over potholes in the barbaric tarmac.

Know this, gentle reader. If you have read the pages of this text, one of two things has transpired: either I have determined, nearing the end of my days, to publish or the Irish, that vexatious female, has somehow managed to track me down.

But the latter option is quite impossible. She will never be able to find me.

Bouncing along in the dark, I've noticed twin beams in the side mirror. They are approaching rapidly. My heart is racing. Nonsense. It cannot be her.

Will I never be free of O'Brien?

ACKNOWLEDGMENTS

First, a note of gratitude to both Otto Penzler, founder of MysteriousPress.com, and to his able associate publisher, Rob Hart, for taking on this novel. A big thanks also to freelance editor Heather Boak, who embraced the spirit of this book in every sentence and helped to make it a much stronger novel.

The folks at Open Road Media have, as always, been professional and savvy in their editing and production. Thanks particularly to Lauren Chomiuk, senior production editor; Laurie McGee, copyeditor extraordinaire; and proofreader Anna Stevenson for their work on *The Edit*.

And lastly, but in no way perfunctorily, a tip of a loving hat to my family—you make it all worthwhile.

ABOUT THE AUTHOR

J. Sydney Jones (b. 1948) is an American author of fiction and nonfiction. Born in the United States, he studied abroad in Vienna in 1968 and later returned to Austria to live there for nearly two decades. In the late 1970s, he began writing travel books, many of which concern Central Europe, and published his first thriller, *Time Of The Wolf*, in 1990. In 2009, he published *The Empty Mirror*, a mystery set in late-nineteenth-century Vienna that would become the first book in his Viennese Mystery series, of which the most recent installment is *The Keeper of Hands* (2013). Jones lives with his wife and son in California.

J. SYDNEY JONES

FROM MYSTERIOUSPRESS.COM
AND OPEN ROAD MEDIA

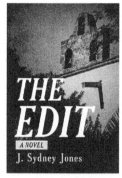
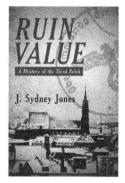

MYSTERIOUSPRESS.COM

MYSTERIOUSPRESS.COM

Otto Penzler, owner of the Mysterious Bookshop in Manhattan, founded the Mysterious Press in 1975. Penzler quickly became known for his outstanding selection of mystery, crime, and suspense books, both from his imprint and in his store. The imprint was devoted to printing the best books in these genres, using fine paper and top dust-jacket artists, as well as offering many limited, signed editions.

Now the Mysterious Press has gone digital, publishing ebooks through **MysteriousPress.com**.

MysteriousPress.com offers readers essential noir and suspense fiction, hard-boiled crime novels, and the latest thrillers from both debut authors and mystery masters. Discover classics and new voices, all from one legendary source.

FIND OUT MORE AT
WWW.MYSTERIOUSPRESS.COM

FOLLOW US:
@emysteries and Facebook.com/MysteriousPressCom

MysteriousPress.com is one of a select group of publishing partners of Open Road Integrated Media, Inc.

THE MYSTERIOUS BOOKSHOP, founded in 1979, is located in Manhattan's Tribeca neighborhood. It is the oldest and largest mystery-specialty bookstore in America.

The shop stocks the finest selection of new mystery hardcovers, paperbacks, and periodicals. It also features a superb collection of signed modern first editions, rare and collectable works, and Sherlock Holmes titles. The bookshop issues a free monthly newsletter highlighting its book clubs, new releases, events, and recently acquired books.

58 Warren Street
Info@mysteriousbookshop.com
(212) 587-1011
Monday through Saturday
11:00 a.m. to 7:00 p.m.

FIND OUT MORE AT:

www.mysteriousbookshop.com

FOLLOW US:

@TheMysterious and Facebook.com/MysteriousBookshop

OPEN ROAD

INTEGRATED MEDIA

Find a full list of our authors and
titles at www.openroadmedia.com

FOLLOW US
@OpenRoadMedia

CPSIA information can be obtained
at www.ICGtesting.com
Printed in the USA
BVOW08s2043141116
467321BV00006B/3/P